Praise

"This tremendously gifted author has done it again. *Sea Cruise* is in a class by itself, with so much going on that keeps the reader completely involved, especially with all the zigs and even larger zags that take place in the Harding family. Richardson spins engrossing crime tales with ease as a result of his experience as a federal prosecutor. *Sea Cruise* is going to be another award winner for Doug Richardson, for sure."

David Richter
Federal Bureau of Investigation, Ret.

"Featuring protagonists in their seventies, a colorful Sri Lankan money launderer who puts her own distinctive stamp on crime, and a group of wonderfully colorful villains, *Sea Cruise* continues the Victor Harding Adventures series' riveting journeys to exotic dramatic destinations. Intelligent, refreshing, sometimes intensely scary, Sea Cruise keeps you thrilled and fascinated."

Kokila Mallikarjuna
International Marketing Executive

"Richardson puts a unique and refreshing face on crime thrillers Like all his books, *Sea Cruise* comes at you from multiple angles, with an engaging plot. It's a novel twist on international crime with plenty of action and suspense."

Pamela Heuszel
Literary Leadership, LLC

SEA CRUISE

A VICTOR HARDING ADVENTURE

Douglas Richardson

Copyright © 2025 Douglas Richardson

All rights reserved.

No portion of this book may be reproduced in any form without written permission from the publisher or author except as permitted by U.S. copyright law, or except in the case of brief quotations in critical articles and review.

Published 2025 by Late Start Press

Paperback ISBN 979-8-218-60315-1
Library of Congress Control Number: 2025902893

This novel is a work of fiction. All characters, names, events, organizations and dialogue in this novel are either products of the author's imagination or are used fictitiously.

DEDICATION

For all the real-life villains, living and dead, who populated my career as a prosecutor and provided the raw material for the Victor Harding Adventures.

Chapter One

Hijacked

"Drone."

"No way."

"Si, Ernesto, just above the horizon. Look there. Two o'clock. Drone, for sure."

"*You're right.* God damn! Who be flyin' a drone out here? We over fifty miles offshore, man. Can't be the Mexican Coast Guard or the fuckin' Cubans. Neither of them patrol out this far."

Ernesto Muñoz was standing in the open hatch of the bizarre narco-sub, hoping to vent some of the dreadful stench emanating from the cramped crew space, a miasma of diesel fumes, human sweat, and overfilled porta-potty stink. Now Muñoz slid down into the tiny wheelhouse and pulled the hatch closed behind him.

Painted a mottled blue-green and pointed at both ends like a giant perfecto cigar, the narco-sub rode low in the water, its domed deck washed by waves. Muñoz prayed the drone would mistake his sixty-foot craft for a whale and just bear off and fly away.

As its little diesel engine pushed it along at nine knots, the narcosub somewhat resembled a submarine preparing to submerge. But this was not a true submarine. A "semi-submersible," this boat ran on the surface, showing a minimal amount of freeboard and leaving a nearly undetectable radar signature. Instead of a "sail"—a conning tower—projecting proudly up from the deck like on a true submarine, it had what looked like a small square dog house perched near the stern, encircled by a row of narrow portholes. A strange metal pipe protruded from the deck behind the dog house, made a semicircular loop in the air, and then ran straight back off the sub. This served as the narco-sub's exhaust system.

The boat Muñoz was piloting was a typical second-generation narcotics runner, a large but otherwise run-of-the-mill drug sub, at fifty-nine feet a little longer than most. Such semi-submersibles had become the drug cartels' container ships for the modern cocaine and heroin trade. This one was carrying five tons of cocaine bricks with a street value of about $125 million once the coke was run up through the supply chain of grabbers, transporters, cutters and dealers across the U.S.

At the end of this trip, the boat Muñoz was driving would become a "disposable," meaning this was a one-way trip to a secluded bayou near Grand Isle, Louisiana, somewhere west of New Orleans. There the narco-sub would be scuttled after offloading its cargo, its construction cost—probably less than fifty thousand dollars, given the low cost of South American labor—a small cost of doing business in the lucrative Pan-American drug trade. Each of the sub's support crew of Colombian farmers, all eager to escape grinding poverty in their homeland, would become $10,000 richer. All would vanish into the bayous, joining the swelling ranks of America's undocumented immigrants.

The newer narco-subs being built for the Venezuelan *Cartel de los Soles* by Checo Paredes' boatyard on tiny Isla Gazela were going to be different. Like Muñoz's boat, which was fiberglass with a big steel hatch on the front deck for loading and offloading cargo, many narco-subs were still built the old-fashioned way by local shipwrights, including those at Paredes' tidy little yard hidden in a mangrove swamp on a little island off the Venezuelan coast. His boatbuilders had grown skilled with fiberglass layup—but some of the new boats from other yards hidden along the coast now were aluminum or steel, and a few were true submarines, built to submerge fully, if only to shallow depths.

The Paredes boatyard's newest fully-submersible sub, now nearing completion and soon to be ready for sea trials, had a steel deck perched on a fiberglass hull, and there had been a lot of trouble with its fabrication. Paredes' shipwrights were proving to be poor welders, and preliminary immersion tests in a slip at Isla Gazela suggested the new sub was a creaker and leaker. Muñoz had heard all about the problems and was perfectly happy to be driving the older, slower, but more reliable boat.

The new generation of narco-subs would be "keepers," meant for repeated voyages, including an astonishing one-hundred-foot steel craft already making trans-oceanic runs to Spain from Cartagena carrying over ten tons of cocaine per voyage. The hundred-footer was not a Paredes boat, but Checo Paredes wished it was—this was the face of the future: big boats, unlimited trips, new markets, bigger profits. As Alberto Mafin's front man, Paredes knew how his standing would rise in the cartel if his new boats could increase the enterprise's profit margins.

A few of the new Caribbean narco-subs had abandoned the double-ended cigar shape and adopted a configuration borrowed from ocean-racing speedboats. Instead of the pokey, smelly diesel inboard engines transplanted from sailboats, these sported two or three massive outboard motors that could drive the boat comfortably at thirty knots. This new breed got there fast—if they got there. These rakish boats used a lot of fuel, needed mid-ocean refueling from "wet nurses," and left large white wakes easily detectable from airplanes and patrol helicopters aloft.

The Colombian, Venezuelan, Mexican and U.S. drug interdiction agencies were reporting good results grabbing these expensive high-powered giants, and several of the cartels had switched back to doing things the old way—slow and steady and nearly invisible. Some of the cartels had pretty much given up transporting drugs on planes—U.S. coastal radar defenses now saw to that—but more and more of the older semi-submersibles, including the one Ernesto Muñoz now was piloting, were being returned to service.

Now Muñoz again poked his head out from the doghouse, and looked out over the glassy sea, scanning the skies, watching the drone draw closer. *Big bird*, he now saw, maybe five feet across. Cost someone a ton of bucks, for sure. Muñoz felt his flesh crawl: *This can't be good. Oh, Dios mio, tell me we're not being hit again.*

Muñoz called down urgently to his navigator. "Javier! Gimme the AR-15! And the binoculars! *Pronto.*"

A pair of skinny arms thrust the requested items up through the doghouse hatch. Muñoz threw the strap of the binoculars over his head, panned across the horizon. These were very expensive, very powerful gyro-stabilized binoculars, and now Muñoz had a clear, rock-steady image of the drone planted solidly in the middle of his field of vision.

He did not like what he saw. Four rotors flashing in the sunlight. Ugly black body, antennas all over the top. Hemispherical camera pod hanging beneath the rotors. No armament, though.

"I see you, muchacho," Muñoz whispered.

And muchacho saw him. The drone transmitted its own razor-sharp image down to a large receiver on the bridge of the scruffy green fishing trawler motoring just over the horizon from the narco-sub. The picture the drone was transmitting looked like a large whale cruising the surface, heading northwest, past the western coast of Cuba. But this whale was leaving a wide, V-shaped wake, and whales don't leave wakes. And whales don't have dog houses with hatches and portholes.

"Got 'em!" said Olifante. "And it looks like one of Mafin's big guys. Sitting duck. *Les' go get 'em!!"*

Hugo the helmsman pushed the throttles forward and the sound of the trawler's twin diesel engines deepened and boomed. But rather than gaining speed, the green trawler groaned and strained, squatting at the stern as it took up the slack on a thick black tow line leading back to a long rusty barge riding high forty yards behind the trawler. The barge had a hefty black crane, formerly used for loading light shore cargo, bolted to its aft deck. Today a large yellow disk dangled from the end of its boom—a powerful electromagnet.

The tow line now lifted from the water and snapped taut with a sharp crack that Olifante could hear over the roar of the diesels. The tow line sported an unusual accessory: a heavy deep-sea fishing net draped across its full length, making the connection strung between trawler and barge look like a giant tennis net. The trawler and its tow now accelerated as they headed for the drug sub.

"Can you see 'em?" shouted Olifante to Hugo.

"Not yet, boss, but I can see our drone up there, and from the picture it's sending us, it has to be right on top of them. I'm jus' gonna head for the drone."

Ernesto Muñoz had no radar, had no way of knowing what was coming his way or how far away it was. But he was damned sure that *something* was coming his way, and the drone was serving as its guide dog. *If I can down the drone, I can still get away,* he thought. His sub was slow, but it was really hard to see from the surface, and most marine radar sets weren't capable of picking up the narco-sub's nearly invisible radar signature.

Muñoz braced a knee in the hatchway opening, trying to steady himself for a good shot with the AR-15. He inhaled deeply, held his breath and squeezed off a long burst of automatic fire.

Clear miss.

Undamaged, the drone continued to hover a hundred feet over the sub, revolving slowly. Then it began to dance, swinging almost gaily from side to side in a gentle arc, as if the drone pilot was playing with them. Muñoz realized it would be a waste of ammunition to try to knock it down. Now the drone orbited in a slow lap around the narco-sub, running high-resolution video from all angles, sending a splendid array of perspectives back to its mother ship.

"Finest kind!" shouted Olifante as he looked at the video feed. "Looka that, Hugo! They sent out the big guy! Single diesel, slow as molasses. Hugo, you see them now?"

"Yup," said the wiry helmsman with his lopsided, snaggle-toothed grin. "Just barely, but I got 'im. No more'n two miles."

Olifante squeezed the all-ship intercom. "All crew! Arm up and get your vests and helmets on. These guys sure as hell gonna be armed, and I do not want any of you to get shot up as we approach. They're gonna take one look at that net on our tow line and know we're on a fishing trip. There's gonna be bullets, folks.

"Okay, here's what's gonna happen. Howie's gonna pull tight across their bow and stop engines. Our barge's drift will keep the net pulled tight behind us, and that sub's gonna plow right into that net. Their momentum is gonna pull us right into them, our trawler up against their port side, our barge on their starboard. Piece of cake, *neh?*

"Kimo, you and Luca gonna step out on deck and take out anyone standing in their doghouse hatch. Shoot flesh, guys, don't go punchin' a lot of bullet holes in the sub. We don't want to go sinkin' a hundred mil worth of product. Squeeze your chest mike if you understand what I'm sayin'."

Four loud radio clicks echoed from the ceiling speaker in the bridge.

"*Hokay.* Next comes the hard part. Birdman, you and Javier gonna pop out our forward hatch and jump on that sub. Their boat has this big forward loading hatch, and you gotta stand right behind its aft end. You guys drop your chain mail mat right under your feet, because sure as shit those clowns gonna be firing up at you, right through the deck. The hull's only fiberglass, guys, so get your mat down quick if you want to keep your feet from getting shot off.

"Now, when LeRoy swings the boom of the crane over from the barge, you guys gotta make sure it's positioned right over the loading hatch when he drops the magnet. The hatch is steel, and you should hear a big clank when LeRoy drops it on the deck. The crane's gonna hold the sub on the surface while we poke our guns down through their stern hatch.

"When we got a drop on 'em, Kimo, you shout at their crew to throw their weapons out the rear hatch if they want to stay alive. They will—they're farmers, not soldiers. Give 'em about a minute. If they don't surrender, you're gonna drop down that hatch and sweep the place.

"Larry, for sure they're going to open the seacocks to try to sink that sucker, so your job is to get those valves closed fast. Best bet is that there's two, maybe three of 'em—engine cooling water for sure. Then maybe a sink drain and a drain for the head. The seacocks will likely be clustered right at the side of the transmission, probably out in the open, but maybe under the engine cover. Our net and our magnet can keep that sub from sinking, but we don't want it taking on a lot of water, hear me? Wet coke is useless coke, and the *Cartel de los Soles* guys tend to wrap their bundles real loose, so they'd soak up water like sponges."

The interception went exactly as planned. The trawler and the barge approached the sub from straight ahead. When they were about thirty yards ahead of it, Hugo spun the helm sharply to starboard to throw the net-covered tow line across the sub's path.

Still running at seven knots, the sub plowed into the fish net and was jerked to an immediate stop, the sub's forward momentum pulling the trawler and the barge tightly in along its sides.

The only deviation from plan was that Ernesto Muñoz elected to play hero, spraying the trawler's pilot house with a long burst of AR-15 fire. Behind Olifante, the pilot house door swung open and the trawler's First Mate, Long John, moved to the railing, bending from the waist to avoid Muñoz's bullets. He was carrying a small pillow and a gigantic rifle with a sniper scope fastened to its top.

Long John propped the pillow on the pilot house railing, calmly rested the rifle on the pillow, stooped to peer through the scope, fiddled briefly with the telescopic sight, and gently squeezed the trigger. Ernesto Muñoz's face disappeared in a sheet of gore as he was flung backward in the hatch. His feet caught on the hatch combing, and now his body dangled over the rear deck with his arms flung over his head. A red stain began to spread on the water behind the sub.

Kimo Erkunnin and Larry Diamond now leapt from the front deck of the trawler on to the deck of the narco-sub, and Kimo ran back to the doghouse and reached down to jerk Muñoz's feet free, sending his body tumbling into the sea.

A chorus of voices screamed from below. "No shoot! No shoot! No shoot! Got no guns! Got no guns!" Kimo leaned into the hatch and took stock. He straightened and then slid himself feet-first into the hatch. "S'okay, Larry," he called up. "Three down here, squattin' and cryin.' C'mon on down."

Moments later there was a shout behind him from Larry. "Water comin' in! Water comin' in! Can't find the fucking seacocks!"

Olifante raced down the stairs from the trawler's pilothouse, sprinted across the deck and made a long leap onto the deck of the drug sub. He slid gracefully down through the doghouse hatch. Once below, Olifante stopped, peered deep into the sub's dark interior, and listened for the sound of inrushing water. He felt a twinge of panic. The seacocks were not where he'd been told they'd be.

The sides of the hull were lined with what looked like floor-to-ceiling bookshelves, each stacked with several layers of tidy packages – bricks of cocaine wrapped in shiny white plastic. The floor was stacked with several more layers of white bricks. Olifante could not see the floor, could not tell where the open valves were. Water now bubbled up from the bilge and began to lap around his ankles.

Olifante reached behind his back and pulled a Sig-Sauer pistol from his waistband. He grabbed the nearest cringing crew member by the hair and shoved the pistol under his chin. "How many seacocks?" he screamed. "Where? Where?"

"Jes' uno, jes' one!" wailed the terrified man. "Only one zeekosh! Under rudder shaft, back nex' stuffing box!"

Olifante flopped on to his belly, slid past the diesel engine, which was now idling quietly, and reached back behind the transmission. Under the propeller shaft his hand found the large marine seacock with its flat stainless-steel handle. The thick black hose leading from the seacock had been severed completely, and water was gushing in so fast that Olifante could barely grasp the slippery handle.

He finally was able to twist the handle on the seacock a quarter turn, and the sound of rushing water stopped abruptly.

For a moment there was only silence. Then there was a deafening *clang!* from the front of the sub. LeRoy obviously had dropped his electromagnet onto the steel forward hatch.

And that was it: one drug sub, signed, sealed and delivered. To hijackers. To the Venezuelan *Cartel de los Soles'* enemies and to the cartel's Bolivian business rivals, the *Cartel de Santa Cruz*. Olifante shouted in triumph.

The narco-sub's crew members, terrified and sobbing and dressed in filthy rags, were only too happy to help offload the coke into the barge. They kept their faces averted from the hijackers, well aware of the dangers of being able to identify their attackers. Many hands made light work, and the entire cargo was transferred and stored neatly in the barge in just over two hours. The hijackers left fifty bricks behind: too wet, now spoiled and useless.

As his own crew made its way back to the trawler, Olifante again grabbed the man he'd threatened before with his Sig. The man trembled with terror.

"Juan? Pedro? Pablo?"

"Gilbert."

"Well, Gilbert, tell me this. Did that guy we shot get a radio call off before we boarded you?"

"Si. No. *Yes*. Don' kill me. I jes' hire guy."

"I'll take that as a yes, Gilbert. Who did he call?"

"Base. HQ. Mafin base. We be *los Soles* guys, Mafin guys, too. This boat his show."

"I see. How far away are they?"

"Mebbe two hunnert, two hunnert fiffee."

"Clicks or miles?"

"Clicks."

"What will they come with?"

"Fiffee-foot Cig'rette, I'm bet. Three Suzuki outboards. Go seventy, seventy-five. Gotta machine gun they can stick on. Badass."

"Okay, Gilbert, here's what going to happen. You and your guys are going to get into those life jackets over there, okay? Then you three are going to jump in the water."

Gilbert looked confused.

"I'm going to disable your diesel. We are going to set a little grease fire down below. Then we're going to padlock your hatches shut so you can't get back in, can't put the fire out. We'll see how long your narco-sub will stay afloat. Maybe it will still be floating when your buddies arrive in their Cigarette, maybe not. Maybe you guys will still be alive, maybe not. Maybe some sharks will have finished their din-din, maybe not. But we know you're not the bad guys, the *Cartel de Santa Cruz,* they're the bad guys, right?"

"Bad guys, *si,*" said Gilbert.

As the trawler spun away from the smoldering narco-sub and began its fourteen-hundred-mile tow to East Texas, Olifante called out to Long John, who was still holding his sniper rifle, and pointed to the three figures floating near the narco-sub's stern. "Take one of 'em out, John, just to send Mafin a message. But hey, don't shoot Gilbert. He's my *man.*"

Chapter Two

WELCOME TO CAPE VERDE

Grinning broadly, the dark-skinned gnome stood outside the customs exit at Cape Verde's new Cesaria Evora International Airport holding a hand-lettered sign: *Hello, Hardings!*

This was Alva Batek, the Sri Lankan mother of my sister-in-law, Delia Chamberlain, the famous goldsmith and former high fashion model.

Alva's appearance was as unsettling as Delia's was exotic. Wearing a short khaki skirt, hiking boots, and a flowing, elaborately embroidered blue Balinese print blouse, she reminded me of some kind of a diminutive doll, delicate and feminine, but not demure. Alva radiated an intense, intelligent and faintly alarming energy. Her chocolate complexion contrasted sharply with a blinding white smile both coy and disarming.

I was quite astonished by her eyes, which were a bright metallic gray, like they'd been forged out of titanium and buffed to a bright finish, proclaiming "here there be steel." Overall, despite the differences in our stature and our age, I immediately felt vulnerable in Alva Batek's presence.

I had been forewarned. When Delia had exclaimed, "You two would really hit it off!" I thought she was simply suggesting that Alva and I were a lot alike. That is, that we were similarly heavily defended, hypercompetitive, smarter than the average bear, and, while placing a high value on personal integrity, on occasion willing to play fast and loose with the law.

"The difference between you two," Delia had added, "is that Alva gets a charge out of being provocative and outrageous, whereas you, Victor, are merely aloof and condescending. Either way," Delia had laughed, "a lot of people would tend to describe you as assholes."

I had expected Alva to greet us alone, but standing next to her was a slim gentleman, medium height, impeccably attired in sharply-creased gray slacks, spit-shined black oxfords, a starched white shirt buttoned at the neck and a dark green loden hunting jacket with silver buttons, the kind German and Swiss burghers wear. *Strange attire in the heat and humidity of the Cape Verde islands,* I thought.

This man—this *gentleman,* I should say—perhaps in his early fifties with carefully-barbered salt-and-pepper hair and carefully manicured nails, wore horn-rimmed glasses and a calm, thin smile. His arms were crossed loosely across his chest, a posture that communicated neither offense nor defense, merely spectator status. His head was cocked slightly, as if waiting to see how this reunion between a long-estranged mother and daughter might play out, as if waiting for who would make the first move.

What happened next was that Alva and Delia approached each other, paused long enough to size each other up and undertake a visual weapons check, and then moved to embrace—first tentatively, then strangely fiercely. It was a long hug, but as I saw it, it seemed more tense than intimate. Finally, Delia pulled back, took Alva by the shoulders, and looked her in the eye.

"It's been so long, I don't even know what to call you. Mother? Mom? Alva?"

"Well, if we were speaking Sinhalese to honor our Sri Lankan roots, it really should be Amma or Abbe, but it's been so long since either of us played the Sri Lankan card that I think we should just go with Alva. Yes, let's just do Alva. And Delia?"

Delia, usually the model of brash confidence, tensed, no doubt expecting sarcasm.

"My God, you are still the most beautiful woman I have ever seen."

"I don't know what to say to that, Alva."

"You don't have to say anything to that, Delia. It was just an observation. Perhaps a greeting, perhaps just my guarded way of saying how glad I am to see you in person after all these years."

My brother Colin and I looked at each other, trying to figure out how to play our cards. Now Alva turned to me. "You must be Victor. You look exactly like your letters."

Evidently, without warning or the courtesy of a direct challenge, I had been thrust into a battle of wits. I forced what I hoped was a jocular smile: "You mean dry, gray, and wrinkled…but with neat handwriting?"

Alva smiled back. "No, I mean attractive, but…*self-contained.* Curious, but cautious. Good posture. A crooked smile but straight teeth."

My God, I thought, *this is exhausting. Are the next two weeks going to be like this?*

Now Alva turned to Colin, switching on an even broader, wider smile. "Colin, I'm so glad Delia convinced you and Cara to come. I hope you two will provide some relief from all Victor's seriousness."

"I'm a country club golf pro, Alva. I can banter endlessly and never get out of breath. I just have no idea what we're talking about here."

Alva clapped Colin on the shoulder, threw back her head and gave a deep laugh.

Delia reached out and took her mother's hand. "Before we hand out the mallets and climb on our polo ponies, would you care to introduce your friend?"

"*Aiee!* Forgive me! How I have forgotten my manners! Family, this is Herr Hannes Schlossberg. Formally, he is the Swiss Consul to Cape Verde, the highest-ranking representative of Switzerland in the islands. They have no ambassador or embassy here, so he is the top Swiss dog.

"His law office is also the Consulate. Hannes also wears many other hats. He is my *consigliere*—my lawyer, my Swiss banker, my political advisor, my enabler, my shield and protector. My *ally*. He makes all good things happen for me in Cape Verde and keeps the bad things at bay. Hannes knows all about my criminal history in the U.S., and he's cool. None of you has to watch what you say around him.

"Hannes, although I know you know who all these people are, may I introduce my daughter, Delia Chamberlain, my daughter-in-law Christine Harding, and the brothers Harding, Victor and Colin—often called Collie. And of course, Collie's new bride, Cara Spaaks-Harding."

Hannes bowed slightly from the waist and gave each of us a double-handed handshake. His voice was soft, his accent stereotypically German, with hard 'T's,' strongly sibilant 'S's', and 'V's' that he pronounced like 'F's'.

"I do know who all of you are, but I am very pleased to meet all of you in person—to put faces to all those astonishing stories of your Wisconsin dramas. Please, please, if there is anything I can do to be of service to any of you—*anything at all*—officially or otherwise, I hope you will not hesitate to call on me. I have our transport van waiting outside in the no-parking zone with the engine running. Please, let us get your luggage and be off to Alva's aerie."

It was late afternoon when we pulled up to the top of a craggy cliff into what looked like a broad macadam parking lot. There was a long open shed tucked into its back corner sheltering a Mitsubishi pickup truck and an ancient rusting Toyota Land Cruiser. Other than that, there was…*nothing*. No house, no walls, no garden, no fountains. It certainly did not look like the splendor Delia had told me to expect.

"Everyone vacate," Alva chirped, clambering out of the Swiss Consulate's Mercedes van and walking briskly toward what looked like the edge of a cliff, leaving us to collect our luggage and hustle to catch up. As she approached the cliff's edge, Alva began to disappear, seeming to sink straight down into the smooth black asphalt. "Be sure to grab the handrail as you go down," she called. "Stairs are super-steep."

There was a glass-enclosed landing half way down the stairwell, and Alva was holding the door open. I was first in line.

"Welcome to paradise," she smiled. "Heaven for aesthetes and haven for crooks, money launderers and senior citizens."

I continued down to the main floor and gasped in surprise. The entire south face of the huge living room was open, providing a dazzling panoramic view down the length of the entire Cape Verde archipelago. Directly in front of me was a broad terrace with a long infinity-edge pool that appeared to flow over the horizon, flanked by a Japanese mineral bath, an *onsen,* this one in the form of a large wooden hot tub.

To my left, a sheet of water flowed almost silently down the wall and into the infinity pool. A long serpentine couch separated the living area from the spectacular gourmet kitchen and marble-topped island along the back wall.

Alva was beaming. "Well, mister world-famous architect, pretty spiffy, eh? I can close the whole place up with a wall of concealed glass panels if a storm blows in, but I seldom have to do that. Usually, I leave it open and live mostly outside on the terrace. Sometimes in winter, storms blow in from the Sahara, but the days are mostly sunny and pleasant around here. I haven't turned either the heat or the air conditioning on since I bought the place."

I spun in a slow circle, savoring the understated Japanese vibe of the décor—grass cloth panels with rows of dancing calligraphs, watercolors of mountain nature scenes, alcoves in the walls with stunning flower arrangements, tatami mats on the polished cement floor. The whole effect was almost impossibly elegant, speaking volumes without pushing to make a statement.

"Breathtaking," I said. "Did you build this place?"

"No, but it's what I would have built if I had built it. It was constructed about fifteen years ago by a 'creative' international financier. A lot like my late husband, I'm told, big time scam artist, except this guy was an Arab, not a Sri Lankan like Lloyd. Apparently he had annoyed some powerful Israelis, and he did not escape the tender mercies of the Mossad. He was found at the bottom of the cliff. The Cape Verdean police shrugged, called it a suicide and drove away."

Now Alva called out to the rest of the family. "The sleeping rooms, sauna and exercise room are in the level below. C'mon everybody, let's head down and get you settled. All the rooms have double queens in them, except the smaller room at the end, which only has one. Victor, we'll put you there. Cara, you and Collie take the room at the foot of the stairs, the one with the samurai swords on the wall. My room, the one with the giant Japanese four-poster is right across the hall from you. I'm a light sleeper, so please keep the conversation down in the hallway. Christine and Delia, you take the next room down the hall on the right. It's got a bigger bathroom.

"When you've unpacked, come up to the terrace for drinks and conversation, and I'll introduce you to Artur, my chef, and Gracia, my everything else. You are in for a feast tonight, Cape Verde Style, and for every night you're here. Artur cooks, which is a huge understatement, Gracia bakes and does desserts. Dear family, you are about to have your minds utterly blown."

Early that evening, Alva and I stood at the edge of the veranda, sangria tumblers in hand, now both feeling loose and well-lubricated. Alva began dipping her toe in the pool. Pretending to admire the view, I stepped back and ventured a long appraising look at Alva Batek.

I was well aware that Alva was no spring chicken—my guess was mid-60's—but from outward appearances her age was hard to determine. No gray in her coal black hair, no jowls or double chin, no deep lines on her dark mahogany-colored face or forehead wrinkles apart from some smiling crows' feet around her eyes. Alva obviously took good care of herself and was aging gracefully. I found myself intrigued, attracted.

Apparently, my appraisal wasn't subtle, and Alva realized she was being checked out. She turned toward me and fixed me in her gaze. Her smile was warm, but inscrutable.

"So, Victor, am I what you expected?" she said.

It sounded like she was calling for candor, so I stepped up.

"Shall I be frank?"

"Victor, you will find that I am an *extremely* candid person. I speak candidly myself, and I ask for absolute candor from others. If you're not capable of being straight with me, you can get right back on that fucking airplane."

"Well, okay then. I didn't really know what to expect, Alva. Delia warned me that her perspective is hardly objective, that she's toting a lifetime of baggage when it comes to you. Nonetheless, I got the sense that she really was hoping you and I would click. She urged me to keep an open mind, come to my own conclusions."

"So, give me the highlight reel."

I took a deep breath. "First of all, Delia says you're the smartest person I'm ever going to meet in my life."

Alva laughed out loud. "How curious! She said exactly the same thing about you."

"Well, that's good. Means we can put aside the IQ tests and false modesty and go directly to displays of brilliance."

"Done," said Alva.

"Delia also said that first and foremost you are a survivor, a very successful survivor, but still, highly-defended and generally rather suspicious of other people's motives. She said that also makes you a person who absolutely hates surprises."

"Sounds like she's describing herself. A survivor describing a survivor. But I admit that what she says is basically true."

"Above all, Delia also said you're a highly sensitive person who craves warmth but doesn't always know how to get it."

Alva's eyes opened wide. *"She said that?* Wow, that's surprising. That's a much fairer judgment than I would have expected. Delia's an angry person, Victor, and she's particularly angry with me."

I didn't like where this conversation was headed.

"Alva, I did not come to Cape Verde to referee some mother-daughter guilt-slinging competition. All I wanted to do was to get my sorry ass out of Green Lake, Wisconsin, have some relaxing time on an exotic island with my family for a couple of weeks, maybe make an interesting new friend."

"Message received," Alva said. "Let's lighten up. How about a refill on the sangria?"

Now she paused. "I do have one question. You know, to set the stage for this visit."

Alva's toe described another gentle circle on the surface of the pool.

"*Am I being played?*"

"Hunh?"

"Please don't get me wrong. I'm glad all of you came for a visit, and I'm particularly glad you came, Victor. But as she touted your charms, I couldn't tell whether Delia was pitching sugar-plum fairies between you and me or simply seeking my help with some criminal venture—present or future."

I struggled to find the right words, to convey my feelings without misrepresenting my motivation or putting my foot in my mouth.

"Look, romance or business, either one—*or both*—I'm certainly interested. But here's the rub. At least as far as I'm concerned, there several different interests at play, and whichever one I bring up first, well, you might assume that's the only reason I wanted to come to Cape Verde."

I smiled sheepishly.

"On one hand, I'm a lonely old fart in his seventies whose siblings both just got happily married. I admit I'm envious. So yeah, I want to see if our meeting here in your realm amounts to anything.

"On the other hand, it's no secret that I'm fascinated by your criminal aptitude, your money laundering expertise. Would I be interested in joining forces in some way? *You bet.* And I don't think this is some kind of devious…*entrapment*…because you've already made it clear you are curious about my past criminal activity and, ah…*current interests.*"

I shrugged. "So that's my concern, Alva. When it comes to romance versus business, whichever one I suggest first, well, you're going to assume that's the *real* reason I'm here and think that any other motive is just incidental or just a diversion. Or worse still, you might think I'm being deceptive."

Alva nodded. "Good point. That's exactly what I'd think."

Chapter Three

A Rough Day in the Boatyard

To all outward appearances, the *Cartel de los Soles'* narco-sub building facility on Isla Gazela—as opposed to its sprawling inland cocaine manufacturing operation—was nothing more than a quiet little marina and boatyard. Nothing suspicious, nothing that would attract attention of a spotter plane or a coast guard cutter motoring along the heavily-forested coast. Someone had evidently put serious money into this place, making it look fresh and inviting without being ostentatious.

The marina's most prominent feature was a long, corrugated iron shed, freshly painted in teal, sporting wide white sliding doors. The shed fronted a newly-paved parking lot dotted with several dark-colored SUVs nuzzled up to a combined office and accommodations building, simple and neat, with a red metal roof.

Down at the shore, the marina had a long cement fueling pier and three finger docks with new planking and modern lighting and slips of various lengths. Out in the harbor, a series of white moorings tethered perhaps twenty open motorboats, fisherman style, some wood, some fiberglass. A single graceful fifty-foot sportfisherman with a tall tuna tower and outriggers, floated high at the end of a T-dock.

Curiously high, in fact. The boat's bright red waterline sat perhaps eighteen inches above the surface of the water. This was because this was no longer a fishing boat. The entire interior of the boat had been gutted, and the elegant-looking craft was now actually little more than an empty shell lined with tier upon tier of lightweight plywood shelves. Stolen months before from

Jamaica, it was now being converted into a drug-runner. The boat had made the high-speed passage down to Isla Gazela with the engines running for hours at maximum RPM with no one checking the oil, and that oversight would prove costly. Both of the boat's powerful turbo-diesels had overheated, and both finally gave up the ghost, pouring out huge stinking plumes of smoke well short of Isla Gazela. The crippled sportfisherman had been towed in by its own little inflatable tender over ten miles of rough sea. Now, out of action indefinitely, it awaited the complete engine rebuilds that no one on the boatyard's staff was qualified to perform.

Across from the useless sportfisherman, a construction-style crane, quite unlike the lifts most boatyards use to hoist boats in and out of the water, sat on the quay in front of the long shed. The crane had four enormous tires and a single extendable long neck, like a giraffe. It was white, with a dark green operator's cab perched over the front wheels. At the moment, its boom was angled out over the water, two slings looping down around a long, brown indistinct shape in the water.

This new narco-sub, the first fully-submersible steel-deck fiberglass-hull boat Checo Paredes' yard had attempted, would not soon make its maiden voyage.

Checo was running cash flow figures in the office when the boatyard's emergency klaxon jerked him away from his laptop. He knew that a rhythmic *beep-beep-beep* meant they were being raided or were under attack. This was different: *beep-boop-beep-boop-beep-boop* meant there was an emergency at the waterfront. He sprinted down toward the docks.

The scene at the launching slip looked like a distressed ant colony. Perhaps a dozen men now surrounded the crane, obviously panicked, running around randomly, screaming and yelling in several languages. The overloaded crane belched dark blooms of diesel smoke as it struggled to hoist a stubby cigar-shaped craft out of the water. The cigar, now pitched steeply downward at the bow, was starting to slide out of the slings, its nose buried in the water, its rudder and propeller rising out of the muddy slip at its stern. Now the crane suddenly tipped up onto its front two wheels, teetering on the verge of tumbling over into the lagoon. The operator desperately loosened the slings, letting the sub splash back into the water, and the crane crashed back down on all four tires again. Now the operator tried another, slower lift, and this time he managed to get the sub clear of the surface, where it swung back and forth in slow arcs.

Like many narco-subs, the new boat had a small square enclosure perched on the top of its hull, a four-by-six-foot doghouse near the stern with windows running around its periphery. A desperate workman was banging on the top of the doghouse with a huge monkey wrench, trying to fracture the hinges in order to get the hatch open, as several of the other workmen stood by, crying and gesturing wildly.

Now a wiry dark-skinned man with Indian features ran toward the precariously swinging boat, carrying a short-barreled shotgun. He pumped four rapid rounds into the boat's fiberglass bottom, just above where the propeller shaft exited the hull, opening a small hole. A thin stream of water started to flow from the sub's bottom. The man with the shotgun screamed, *"No es suficiente! No es suficiente! RPG! RPG!"*

A second man, this fair-skinned, dark-haired, and tall, vanished into an outbuilding and reappeared moments later with a dull red shoulder-held grenade launcher. This was Checo Paredes, and from perhaps twenty feet away, he fired a grenade into the bottom of the hull. It exploded in a roiling white cloud of smoke and fiberglass debris just in front of the rudder.

The bottom of the boat disintegrated, and a huge gusher of water poured out from inside the hull. A limp human form slid out of the hole and plopped down into the slip, then a second one. The bodies were wearing brown shorts and dirty tee-shirts, and they floated face down until they were fished out with gaffs and laid, now face up, pale as mackerels and dead as doornails, on the dock.

Relieved of much of the weight of the water in the sub's hull, the crane, now solidly planted back on all four wheels, lifted the remnants of the craft out of the water and, with a loud crash, dropped the wreck on the quay, where it lay balanced precariously over the edge. The man with the monkey wrench continued to bang at the hatch cover, finally smashing the hinges and throwing the hatch aside. He screamed, "Esta vivo!" and dragged a lanky figure, an emergency pony-bottle of oxygen still clenched in his teeth, out of the battered hull and down on to the dock. The rescuer dropped to his knees next to the limp but living figure of his compadre, embracing him, crying, "Dios Mio!" over and over.

Apparently, the weight of these two men had been all that was keeping the sub from sliding out of the slings and tipping back into the water. Now, relieved of that weight, the sub tottered briefly and then slid back gracefully into the water, where it promptly sank to the bottom of the slip.

―――――

An hour later, Alberto Mafin and Checo Paredes sat across from each other at the conference table in Mafin's office. Checo had showered to get the grenade residue off his face, slicked back his dark hair, and donned a fresh white guayabera and tan cargo shorts. Given what he'd been through mere minutes before, he looked remarkably calm.

"So, Enrique goin' be okay?" Mafin's jaw was clenched tightly, and his arms were wrapped tightly across his chest. His head was clocking from side to side, like the arm of a metronome, in a continuous neurological tic. Paredes had seen this motion often before and knew not to be alarmed by it.

"Yeah, but he was scared shitless. The other guys almost drowned him trying to claw their way out."

"Okay, mister boat building genius, so wha' happen this time?" Paredes was often both amused and confused by Mafin's speech—his staccato Spanish, the tinny timbre of his voice, an accent that seemed to be an amalgam of various European and South American languages, the random variations in grammar and pronunciation.

Sometimes Mafin displayed a rich vocabulary and sophisticated subtlety of expression, at other times he sounded like he was speaking Spanglish or struggling with the Pidgin spoken by some of the deep jungle Amazonian Indian tribes. Paredes had known Mafin for several years and had no idea where he came from, who taught him to talk, or how he had become so powerful so fast. To everyone, he was just Mafin; no one *ever* called him Alberto.

"Enrique said the propeller shaft backed out of the stuffing box as soon as he fired up the diesel. Obviously, no one tightened down the packing gland. The sub flooded quickly, ass-down.

Shorted the batteries, so they couldn't pump the ballast tanks or run the bilge pumps, couldn't operate the diving planes. Sub hit bottom and rolled over on its side. Enrique found an air bubble in the dog house and kept his head above water, but the other guys kept grabbing at him and tearing at him, trying to climb up over him. They couldn't open the hatch because the outside launch crew had dogged it down, those fucking idiots."

"How deep down they were?"

Paredes shook his head ruefully. "How far down you gotta be to drown? Fifteen feet, maybe? It's not all that deep just off the quay. Hell, they still had the launching slings on, but the crane couldn't lift it fast enough to keep it from filling up. Then it couldn't lift it at all. You saw that sucker almost tip over. Just imagine if the crane had dropped into the water, Mafin."

Mafin's head continued to swivel, his eyes clocking left and right to keep Paredes in his line of sight. "Well, this guy Enrique one lucky son of a bitch."

"He wasn't lucky, Mafin, he was *careful*. Saved his goddamned life. He had stashed his own private pony-bottle of oxygen behind the console. Told me he knew that piece-of-shit submarine—that's what he called it, not me—was a death trap."

Now Paredes stood, walked to the sideboard and poured himself a glass of port. He gestured to Mafin with the bottle, but Mafin shook his head in disgust. "Alcohol, no. No alcohol, never. *Never!* Stuff mess me up bad, make my Tourette's go crazy."

Paredes reseated himself, took a delicate sip from his glass, stared up at the ceiling, and sighed.

"We gotta stop losing so many boats," he said. "We been doin' okay stayin' ahead of the coast guards. But all these hijackings! We getting killed right now. And now today's goat rodeo—*at our own dock! Dios mio!* Bottom line, at the moment, Mafin, we got no way to run your product."

"Not 'we,' Checo. 'You.' *You're* losing too many boats."

Mafin's voice was an inanimate monotone, as gray and flat as slate. It matched his pale gray hair, pale gray face, watery gray eyes, pale gray polo shirt and pale gray slacks. He sat rigidly in his chair, but now his eyes, recessed behind dark bushy eyebrows, suddenly began to blink rapidly. "You keep losing our boats, *you* going to get yourself killed, Checo. *Cartel de los Soles* gonna drive down here and start pullin' the trigger on you people, and you and all your delivery boys going to be fish food. And all I'm gonna do is stand by and watch. Turn our bosses on you and get 'em off my ass.*"*

"No need to be so fucking nasty, Mafin." Paredes dropped his chin, an entirely artificial gesture of deference. His arms had been crossed defensively across his chest; now he dropped his hands to his sides. Mafin read social cues poorly, but from experience Paredes knew Mafin was extremely sensitive to signals of confrontation, and he knew Mafin tended to overreact. That would not help here.

Mafin shook his head vehemently. "Listen, Checo! It's *'zactly* what's called for, you idiota! Three of our subs gone already this year, even before this disaster today."

"What's that to you? What kind of loss does your sweet little boatyard take? Maybe eighty grand each boat? You can always jes' go build another one, if you guys can manage to build one that doesn't sink at the fucking dock.

"Other hand, what's the loss of a sub to *us*? To me 'n' *Cartel de los Soles*? *Huge!* For us, huge loss of product, huge loss of market. We got orders goin' begging, man! Big orders! We been bustin' our ass to produce enough product, and none of it's getting to Louisiana. Each boat gone? *Loss of mebbe hundred million dollars street value per delivery.* And for me? Huge loss of face with the bosses. Un-*fucking*-acceptable."

Now Paredes realized that he was losing ground and that he had to fight back. He moved to face Mafin, resting his palms on Mafin's desk and leaning in toward him threateningly. Mafin lurched back in his chair, clearly surprised to be confronted.

"Just hold on, *cabrón!*" Paredes snapped. "Okay, today's screw-up, that's on us. I gotta own that one. But the hijackings? They're all on *you*, Mafin. We're just the boatbuilders and the ferry crew. *You* guys, *your* network, you're the ones gotta find out who's doing this, who's betrayin' us. The Coast Guards—I don't care if it's Colombian, Venezuelan, Mexican, U.S. or Dutch— they're not the ones killin' us. Okay, mebbe they going to grab a boat every couple of years, but that's like a blind squirrel findin' an acorn. Most times, even when they spot us, they don't catch us. Nine out of ten times we slippin' 'em.

"*But who are these new guys ripping us off?* I thought you had keep-clear arrangements with the other cartels, no? So, who the ones screwin' us over? MS-13? Some new Colombian motherfuckers? Or those scumbag Cubans? Or maybe Nicaraguans or rogue crews from Panama? Guatemalans? Mexicans, Dutch, even? *Who's doin' this to us, Mafin?*"

"I…could…not…tell…you," whispered Mafin hoarsely, still leaning back from Paredes. "You think it's all the same *banditos,* Checo? Or do we got a lot of different banditos out there? Talk to me."

Paredes turned his head to look out Mafin's window at the palm branches dancing gaily in the Caribbean breeze. He cocked his head as if lost in thought.

"My bet, I think it's a single group. And I think that group is *Cartel de Santa Cruz*. Those Bolivian bastards got a *lot* of money to spend tracking our shipments, tracking our boats from the moment we leave Venezuela. They got moles and spies everywhere. And they got good technology, Mafin, *big technology*. State-of-the-art tracking technology. They ghost us until our subs are out in open ocean, then swoop in fast.

"This last grab? Trail us with a trawler pullin' a barge with a crane on it. Send up a big meadow-mother drone, track us from five miles away and our guys don't suspect nothing. Snare our sub in a fucking *fish net, rip the loading hatch right off our sub with an electromagnet,* if you can believe that.

"To do that, they have to know our boat's got a steel hatch. *How they know that, Mafin?* Tell me that! Fuckers transfer our load to their barge in less than two hours, and *zoom!*—gone with the wind. Set our boat on fire, shoot up our crew in the water, leave everybody for dead. Now, *that* requires planning. And *cajones*. And money."

Mafin looked surprised to hear this, and it was always a bad thing when Mafin looked surprised. "How you are knowin' all these detail? Sound like one of your drivers survive that shoot 'em up, Checo. I think you ought to…"

Mafin's face abruptly locked up, his expression frozen. His speech lapsed into a labored "uh, uh, uh."

The effect was alarming, but by now Paredes knew enough not to react or intervene. When Mafin suffered a Tourette's spasm, all you could do is stand clear and wait for the seizure to pass. Paredes stood calmly in front of the desk as Mafin twisted in his chair and arched his neck, his eyes wide, his mouth agape.

Paredes knew that Tourette's syndrome and Asperger's syndrome—a high-functioning form of autism—often went hand in hand, knew that in Mafin they went iron hand in violent fist. Mafin was not plagued by the uncontrollable outbursts of profanity that sometimes characterize Tourette's syndrome, but his periodic frozen masks were a classic symptom.

On the other hand, Mafin's flat affect, inability to make eye contact, and complete social tone-deafness, were symptomatic of Asperger's syndrome. So were Mafin's intellectual virtuosity, his extraordinary attention to detail, his remarkable planning and logistical skills. Despite his handicaps, in many ways Mafin was a perfect drug driver – brilliant, cold, impersonal, hyperrational. A fiend for sweating the details.

Now Mafin's face sagged and softened, and he exhaled in a loud "*phoosh.*" Then he continued speaking as if there had been no interruption. "…ought to let me meet this survivor of yours, let *me* question him a few minutes. I can get more out of him than you clowns can."

"Not available. He took six rifle hits, torso and legs. Was blessed with six miracles. He's alive, but barely. Our guys found him drifting in his life vest, the sharks getting ready to eat 'em up. Other guys were all already chewed pretty good by sharks.

The survivor, he's in an induced coma as they try to keep him from croakin'."

Mafin began to drum his fingers on the desk in front of him, hard, symmetrical strikes with both hands, starting with the pinkies and moving in sequence to his index fingers, like a piano player banging out boogie-woogie. *"God...damn...it, Checo!* Tell the doctor—*he's our doctor, yes?*—pull that guy *out* of his 'induced coma.' I want to talk to this...*victim*...before he dies. I want...*details."*

Now Mafin abruptly seemed to change channels. He stared up at the ceiling. "I must *think*, Checo. I must...*calculate.* Tell me what you got going on right now. Tell me how soon I'm going to get another boat—ours or anybody else's. Most important, tell me when I'm makin' some motherfuckin' money. The guys up north going apeshit."

Sensing that the tension had eased, Paredes pulled an office chair up across the desk from Mafin, and now rested his forearms lightly on the front of the desktop.

"I'm going to Isla Tobias this afternoon to see them launch the new steel fully-submersible boat those guys built over there. Diesel-electric, Mafin. Supposedly can run fully-submerged for ten hours on batteries, if everything works. Their sub is short—only thirty-six feet —but it's twelve feet wide. Weird-lookin' sumbitch, but it can hold a lot of product and only requires a crew of three. They plan to sea-trial it all day tomorrow. Everything works okay, then I'm going to make them an offer they can't refuse. I'm sure they don't want to sell it, but I can make them want to sell it. Your name, *Señor Mafin,* is very persuasive, shall we say. So, we buy the sub, then we load it up and make a trip up to Progreso in Merida. See how everything works."

Mafin darkened. He squeezed the bridge of his nose and then ran his fingers down the full length of his almost comically hooked proboscis. "Why you go to *Mexico*, Chrissake? I need product in the U.S., Checo. Soon as possible. Louisiana waiting for us. Big money going begging."

Paredes shook his head regretfully. "We gotta sea trial this new boat, Mafin. We're new to steel boats, lotta stuff we don' know. How fast they are, how they handle, how they trim, how fast they submerge and surface. They may look mostly invisible on the surface, but we're afraid the steel boats might trigger a big return on a towed sonar array. But right now, it's only the U.S. Navy that has those new towed arrays, and they're only operating 'em north of Yucatan. So, we're going to drop this first trial load in Progreso, truck it up north and take it in to the U.S. through Matamoros."

Mafin fixed Paredes in a steely stare. Because Mafin tended to avoid direct eye contact, this was a most unusual gesture for him. "No. No, too slow, 'way too slow. We need to get some product up north *pronto*."

"Wait, wait, that's not all," said Paredes. "That's jus' Plan A. We also looking at grabbing a sailboat, a big boat. I'm not talking thirty-five or forty feet here, Mafin. I'm thinking sixty, sixty-five. Have our old friend Eamon Armagh do a snatch in San Juan, perhaps, Santo Domingo, maybe Kingston. Also check out Aruba or Curacao. Load it up here, maybe even load it at sea off a barge south of Cuba. Probably can get two tons of product on board if the boat's big enough."

Mafin squeezed his eyes shut. "*Armagh.* You actually want me to use Armagh."

"Well, yeah. He can get a load up to Louisiana. Knows the route, knows how to sail."

Mafin exploded out of his chair. "*You fuckin' with me?* You know I said I never wanted to see that motherfucker again. Never use him again. For *anything.* That loose-lipped cocksucker screw us over *so bad,* Checo. His leaks cost us a boat, cost us a load. I swore I ever saw him again I'd shoot his fuckin' face off."

"That's before we found out what really happened, Mafin. Yeah, he got ratted out, but he wasn't the rat. Wasn't his fault. I'm sure of that. Sure enough to trust him with another job."

"Well, I'm not! He's a snake, a whore, a spy, that Irish piece of shit! We should have killed him when we got him back here. *Poof!* Drop his dead ass deep inna jungle, good bye, asswipe."

"Look, Mafin, he's our only shot right now. Only guy we can get on such short notice. Him and Adamares."

"Ten times worse, them two together! Adamares a crazy man. Complete psycho. You really playin' with fire, Checo."

"Sure, he's a head case, but he's the one who caught the leaker." "But Dios mio, you see what he did to him?" Mafin smiled wickedly. "Very crazy shit, Checo, even by my standards. You see the pictures?"

"What, you never seen someone staked to an anthill of fire ants and then get skinned alive? The spy was a *Waryuu* and Adamares is a *Kali'na*. That kind of torture should come as no surprise. Way Adamares figured it, guy was just another victim of the tribal wars. Had it comin'."

"Still, like I say, a very crazy shit. You never know what Adamares gonna do."

"Look, just let me just arrange it, Mafin. I'll take responsibility. Armagh and Adamares sail the boat up to Louisiana, up to our place up in Grand Isle. Hit the trade winds north-by-northwest, open ocean, go like a rocket. They'll average seven knots, easy, as much as one of our diesel narco-subs. They dump the stuff, collect the cash, scuttle the boat, and suddenly, *bingo!,* our balance sheet looks a lot better."

Mafin shook his head wearily. "Hokay, you do what you gotta do. But I still be very disappointed in you, Checo. This sailboat thing is a half-assed stopgap solution, and Eamon Armagh is a big, big risk. But yeah, right now I'm agree we gotta move product any way we can. That's what the bosses expect. But this one's on you, Amigo. Anything go wrong and it's you gonna pay a visit to them fire ants."

Chapter Four

CONTAINERS UNCONTAINED

No one heard it but Beppu. All the other crew members, tired, jaded, underpaid, indifferent to any but their assigned duties, were in their cabins or in the wardroom listening to Radio Mexico, trying to tune out the sound of the storm and ignore the rhythmic rolling of the *Irakimasu Maru*.

But young Beppu Flangé heard it. As usual doing things that others thought unnecessary, Beppu was out on the container deck, crouched under the bow crane trying to avoid the sting of the driving rain, watching for anything untoward, cocking an ear and listening for anything amiss. No one else on the small container ship looked for trouble the way Beppu did, no one else found it as often.

The rest of the crew had nicknamed Beppu "PITA"—*Pain in the Ass,* because he was always sidling up to some engineer or deckhand and saying, "Hey, you wanna come have a look at this?" or "I checked the procedural manual, and it looks like that wasn't done to spec."

They also called him the ass-buster, because the problems and flaws and derelictions he so often detected invariably made more work for them or disclosed their shoddy work. But ship's captain Isao Sakai valued the constant flow of information about regulations ignored, maintenance deferred, and equipment threatening failure, and he regularly slipped Beppu extra pay—a violation of maritime union rules, but all-in-all a valuable secret deal well worth the cost.

Built in 1988, the 345-foot *Irakimasu Maru,* tired but still serviceable, was a so-called "feeder ship," meaning it transported relatively small loads of twenty and forty-foot containers from small local ports to major ports for loading onto larger container ships. It was a LO-LO container ship, a lift-on-lift-off carrier with a capacity of 600 TEUs—Twenty-foot Equivalent Units—meaning it could load as many as three hundred forty-foot containers on and off itself using its own cranes, rather than the huge shore-mounted derricks that loaded more modern and far larger container ships with their cargoes of thousands of containers. As it serviced smaller coastal ports in South America and the Caribbean, the *Irakimasu Maru* also could carry below-decks cargo, either uncontainerized bulk cargo or loads of automobiles and light trucks.

Tonight, the *Irakimasu Maru* was giving everyone a rough ride. Because its below-decks hold was largely empty and its deck cargo of two hundred containers made it comparatively top-heavy, it tended to snap roll when hit broadside by ocean swells and to pitch up sharply when hit head-on by oncoming waves. Beppu did not like the ship's motion, and as was his custom in big-wave conditions, he went on the prowl for trouble.

The pounding of the rain drummed a steady persistent backbeat on the stacks of containers. Suddenly Beppu heard a distinctly different sound, a single sharp crack, like the report of a rifle. This was followed immediately by the sound of mechanical movement, a back-and-forth grating and groaning, the worst kind of movement. Movement Beppu could feel through his feet as the ship bucked and rolled.

He walked back along the row upon row of shipping containers piled ten high, some red, some blue, some yellow, shining his torch at their attachment points and locking mechanisms, checking first on the twist locks that fastened the bottom containers to the deck, then the overhead twist locks that fastened the tall columns of containers to each other.

It wasn't unusual to see that the straight handle on a deck-level twist lock had bent or broken off, and these were easy to replace— you just backed the old handle out and screwed a new one in. But now Beppu saw a terrifying sight in the beam of his torch: one of the deck-level twist locks and its entire mounting pad had succumbed to the constant loading and unloading as the ship rolled, and had fractured, tearing the pad right out of the deck. This left the back end of the container free to slide back and forth.

Although no engineer, Beppu knew he was seeing the beginning of a failure sequence that could lead to catastrophe. The entire ten-high stack of containers now was beginning to slide and twist, channeling extreme fatigue loads on to the remaining twist lock and its mounting pad. Already Beppu's flashlight showed the striations of metal fatigue arching across the pad, with large chips of paint flecking off its surface.

Beppu sprinted to the pilothouse, raced up the steep steel steps to the bridge. Sakai, startled when sheets of rain blew in as the door was flung open, was sitting in his padded pedestal chair, reading a paperback.

"Blown lock, base container loose, port side, row five!" Beppu yelled. "Back pad completely torn out, front twist lock about to go!"

Sakai flew into action, first hitting the big orange button for the emergency klaxon, then yelling orders into the intercom.

"Deck crew to port side row five! Chains and come-alongs! We got containers shifting!"

Almost immediately a door flew open at deck level, and five men dashed out into the pouring rain. Beppu recognized Stevie and Hiko, but the others' faces were covered by their rain hoods.

The deck crew ran to the storage locker at the base of the forward crane and tugged out long lengths of heavy chain, four bright-orange come-along hand winches, and a canvas bag of large industrial padlocks. Beppu and Sakai watched as Hiko clambered up the ladder and into the crane's cab, saw the crane tremble as he powered it up. Hiko now used the crane to lift lengths of chain up and over the rogue container stack and drop the ends down to the deck on the other side. Frantically the other crew members set the come-alongs to padeyes on the deck. Beppu was amazed—and most relieved—at how fast terrified men could work when confronted with unfolding catastrophe.

Then, like an adroit howler monkey, Stevie scampered up the side of the stack, an incredible feat of agility as the ship rolled side to side through forty degrees, and deftly fastened a padlock to each level of containers. Stevie then climbed down and stood with the others on the deck, looking up to see if the jury-rigged restraints would keep the container stack from shifting and going over the side.

They wouldn't…and didn't. As the ship lurched into another steep roll, the overstressed deck pad gave way. Over the roar of the rain, Beppu and Sakai then heard the *pop-pop-pop-pop* of the fracturing twist locks that held all the outboard containers to the next stack inside, and he saw the padeyes holding the hastily tensioned come-alongs tear cleanly out of the deck.

The containers remained chained to each other, but they were no longer chained to anything else. Now the entire stack of containers began to shift and slide across the deck. There was no place, no way, to attach additional come-alongs and try to ratchet the column of containers back into proper place. To Sakai's horror, through the bridge window he saw the entire outboard stack of containers in row five slide down to the rail and teeter on the edge of the hull.

Now the *Irakimasu Maru* was hit by a steep bank of waves that heeled her steeply to port and pushed her into a twenty-degree list. A roll like this always created a profoundly unnerving sensation, but the ship always rolled back up, always righted itself. Only this time it didn't. The *Irakimasu Maru* just wallowed there in a steep list, her stacks of containers resembling the tilt of the Tower of Pisa.

From the bridge Sakai saw why the ship wasn't coming back up. Like a fat kid on one end of a teeter-totter, the combined weight of the columns was pinning the ship in a dangerous port-side list that would only get worse as the other stacks continued their march across the deck. A grim thought flashed through Sakai's mind: *my ship is about to die.*

Sakai felt bile rise. In minutes, the *Irakimasu Maru,* a relatively light and relatively unstable container ship to begin with, had gone already wildly out of balance and was rapidly becoming more so.

If the last three columns of containers shifted from the right side of the ship all the way across to port, the ship would tip onto its side and begin to flood. It would lose propulsion and steerage as its rudder and propellers were hoisted out of the water. At that point, whether it ultimately went bottoms-up or not, the

Irakimasu Maru would sink. The ship's life boat would be trapped underwater and become inaccessible.

And everybody would die.

Now Sakai saw Beppu, a blaze of color in his Day-Glo orange wet weather gear, emerge from the stairs up in the forecastle adjacent to the base of the *Irakimasu Maru's* bow crane. The captain saw Beppu scamper up into the crane's control cab, saw the crane's massive arm tremble as Beppu powered it back up.

Now, as smoothly as if he had practiced the maneuver countless times, Beppu elevated the crane's horizontal lifting beam and rotated it over the top of the stacks of containers on the *Irakimasu Maru's* forward deck. Then, in a move for which the lifting beam was definitely not designed, Beppu positioned the beam over the gap between the teetering column of containers perched at the edge of the deck and the next inboard column.

With a thunderous crash, Beppu dropped the beam into the gap, and, in a move resembling a hockey player taking a slap shot, rotated the crane rapidly against the inboard side of the unstable container stack.

The stack did not resist; the entire column simply pitched over the rail in a graceful arc, and ten containers, all still chained together, flew from the deck of the *Irakimasu Maru* into the sea.

With the fat kid suddenly removed from the end of the teeter totter, the *Irakimasu Maru* slowly rolled upright. Now Beppu positioned the lifting beam against the face of the remaining stack to keep it from moving further, and that's where the beam would stay until the *Irakimasu Maru* limped into Belize harbor. It took the deck crew five more hours to position another series of chains and come-alongs across various faces of the rebellious stack, tethering it tightly to the deck.

As the high seas abated at dawn, Sakai called the entire crew to the bridge, where he ordered the steward to break out the case of cognac that he had kept hidden in his cabin. Beppu was applauded and toasted repeatedly, and—strictly against company regulations—everyone got stinking drunk.

The ten containers that fell overboard did not plummet to the bottom of the sea. Still chained precariously together, they became a floating island, the three heavily laden with machine parts dangling beneath the seven empty—and quite buoyant—containers that remained floating on the surface of the Caribbean Sea, riding low, appearing and disappearing as this island of steel bobbed in the waves. Like an iceberg, most of the chained containers' mass was hidden underwater. It would float for months, just ten of the nearly eight hundred containers that fall off container ships every year.

Eventually the overstressed chains holding the submerged containers would fracture, and seven of them would plummet to the bottom of the sea. The remaining three, still chained to one another, would continue to bob merrily on the surface of the ocean.

Chapter Five

SEA CRUISE?

Hannes Schlossberg had been picked up by the Consulate's limousine, a fifteen-year-old Russian Zil he had purchased when the Russians closed down their own consulate in Cape Verde. It looked like a boxy old Mercedes, and Hannes said he loved it. "Wonderful car! Quiet, imposing, a little mysterious. The locals point and laugh when I go by."

After Hannes left, Delia, Christine, Colin and Cara—the Fab Four, as they now called themselves—had borrowed the Land Rover to take the ferry over to Sao Vincente and go shopping in Mindelo. Alva and I had elected to veg by the pool and were sitting in plush lounge chairs, feet propped up on ottomans, sucking up caipirinhas and savoring a rich palette of blues—the cloudless azure sky, today as clear and bright as electricity, blending into deep azure at middle distance and then fading to a pale gray near the horizon, and finally turning into a dark green-blue haze in the shaded valleys of Santo Antão.

Looking out past the other islands directly in front of us, I saw a world without end, without boundaries, limits or interruptions. I have seen my share of beaches, bays, and vistas on islands throughout the world, and I thought I had never seen a view as strikingly beautiful as this. *How had I lived over seventy-two years without seeing the Cape Verde Islands?*

"What a waste," said Alva, sadly.

I had to laugh. "What do you mean, 'what a waste?' Here's one of the most beautiful views in the world and you think it's *sad?*"

"It's not the view that's sad, Victor. But God, just look at that schooner down there—that is a schooner, right?"

Below us, a magnificent two-masted white schooner—I estimated seventy feet—slid into view, heading toward Santo Antão from open ocean. As sailors would say, she had the bit in her teeth and was thundering through swells in an effortless display of controlled power.

Alva clapped her hands. "Doesn't that look like fun? Look at the grace of that thing, just *gliding* along down there. And I'm parked up here, with nothing but the same view, day after day. Here I am, living in a veritable sailor's paradise, and I don't know how to sail. *That's what's sad.*"

"Well, hell," I said simply. "I can fix that."

She looked at me with surprise.

"What do you know about sailing?"

I gave an aw-shucks shrug.

"Everything a serious sailor needs to know, professional grade. When it comes *anything* related to sailing, I really am a know-it-all."

Alva was clearly surprised.

"You never told me you owned a boat!

"I don't, and I didn't," I said. "Not after my first few small cruising boats, anyway. When I moved up, I always sailed OPB."

"OPB?"

"*Other peoples' boats.* For years and years. Their money, my design skills, my management skills, and, of course, my sailing skills."

"In *Chicago?*"

"In Chicago, there's a bunch of very heavy-duty big-bucks great lakes racers, and I've sailed with most of them. But over the years, I moved up, became world class, if I say so myself."

"When you say, 'world class,'" Alva asked, "what are we talking about here?"

"I may have lived in Chicago, but I've sailed all over the world. I was good, sought-after even, so I always sailed courtesy of OPM."

Alva laughed gleefully. "Let me guess. '*Other peoples' money.*'"

"Bingo," I smiled. "Salaried talent. A lot of my...*sponsors* were my architectural and engineering clients, but I also got hired by some celebs and master-of-the-universe types."

"Name one," Alva giggled.

"Ted Turner. He had this magnificent maxi-class racing yacht called *Tenacious* that, after years of winning, suddenly wasn't so tenacious anymore. I worked my magic on it, gave it five more years of successful racing life. Ted Turner loves my ass."

Alva feigned indignation. "Well, Victor! You never told me about any of this! I didn't know you had a whole other side to your life."

"Well, Christ, Alva. We've barely met. And frankly, I thought you were more interested in the criminal side of my life."

"Oh, I'm plenty interested in that, believe me. But to get back to the point, are you still a big cheese in the big-bucks sailing world?"

The question brought back pleasant memories and also plenty of regrets. "Nope. Hung up my spurs about fifteen years ago."

"Why, for heaven's sake, if you were such a hot ticket?"

"Same reason I finally closed down my architectural consulting practice. I got the memo that I was getting too old, was regarded as over the hill. And I really I wasn't physically fit enough to be a crew member on an ocean racer anymore.

"And there was another important factor. All my sailing was about racing. I never, ever…just *voyaged*. Never got the chance to chart a course to some distant destination, never just noodled along with no concern for how fast I was going. Never took the time to go snorkeling at some beautiful anchorage, never got to make love to some willing maiden under a tropical moon.

Eventually I schooled myself to believe that simply making a voyage—simply *cruising*— was chickenshit. *What, just sail around? What a silly idea*! So, if I wasn't going to race, and I wasn't going to go cruising on a voyage to get away from it all, what was left in sailing? *Nothing.* End of story."

Now Alva was beaming. "Let's buy a sailboat together and sail around!"

I was floored. *"Are you out of your mind?"*

"No, no, really!" chirped Alva. "Cast off for adventure before we get too old! Take Collie and Delia and Christine and Cara and just…sail away! We would *voyage!* Go to exotic places. With my money—plus some of your money, of course—and your expertise, Victor, we could write a whole new chapter in our lives! You'd teach us everything we need to know, make yourself useful again."

I patted Alva lightly on the cheek, the way you might discipline a puppy that has jumped up on your white linen slacks. "I'm sure you'll tell me when you're serious, Alva."

"Oh, but I am serious! I know this sounds impulsive, but it pushes a lot of buttons for me. First, it's novel. Second, it's not like anything I've ever done before. Third, I would be placing my safety in the hands of an expert, which would flatten the learning curve and take some of the edge off the risk. Yeah, I'd really like to explore doing this. *Really.*"

I stopped protesting long enough to really consider the idea. Now I began thinking out loud.

"Well, I bet Delia would jump at this, probably Collie, too. But I guarantee you that Christine's out. I convinced her to try offshore sailing once on Lake Michigan, and it did *not* agree with her. I have no idea if Cara would be interested."

As I spoke, I felt something long dormant stir within me. Sure, this was an absolutely crazy idea, putting to sea with some gonzo woman and family members from whom I had long been politely estranged. But a siren voice sang out to me. *Why not? Why the hell not? What else do you have cooking in your life?* I pushed my chin into my chest, then lifted my head to the heavens. Took a long, slow cleansing breath.

"Okay, Alva, I'm willing to at least consider it, if the others are. I could look into a few brokerage listings, see what the high-end big boat market's doing. One idea strikes me immediately. We might buy a sailboat—a very nice sailboat, with quite a substantial money laundering potential—on my side of the pond, sail it around the Caribbean for a while, and then bring it over here and put it into charter."

"You mean sail *across the ocean?*" Alva's voice was a loud squeak, whether from fear or excitement I could not tell.

"Sure, why not?" I said. "People do it all the time. I'm just talking about sailing across the pond, not heading down to the Southern Ocean or sailing around the world or anything."

"*Wow,*" Alva exclaimed. "Wow, wow, wow. *That's* something to wrap my head around. How big a boat would we buy?"

"I think we have to strike a balance. We want a boat that a crew of four to six can manage, something with electric sail-handling equipment and all the safety features we can stick on it. We also would want a boat that is big enough to be sea-kindly, so we're not bashing our brains out if it gets a little rough, and also a boat that is luxurious enough to attract charter clients when we're done with our voyage.

"I'm thinking that puts us over forty-five feet, maybe even over fifty. I think I'd look first for boats made by the Dutch boat builders, like Royal Huisman or van de Stadt. Or the boats made by Nautor in Finland are excellent and hold their value. Gotta be realistic in our expectations, though. A new Swan 48 from Finland costs over $900,000, so we'd probably want to look at a used boat in brokerage."

I could see Alva was really getting into this, already imagining the logistics, sweating the details, putting pegs into holes.

"Nine hundred thousand is not a deal killer for me, not if the boat's worth it. After all, the more we spend, the more we can launder, think of that."

"I'll think of that as I do a little shopping around," I said.

As the afternoon sun dipped toward the horizon, there was an alarmed cry from the stairway leading up to the parking lot, followed by a heavy thud. I heard Cara scream, "Collie!" and leapt to my feet. When I got to the landing, I found Colin slumped on the floor against the glass wall, his legs trapped under him. Cara pushed past me and cradled his flushed face in her hands.

"I'm okay, I'm 'kay," mumbled Collie as he pushed Cara away and struggled to untangle his legs. As I reached down to help him up, I was bathed in the reek of alcohol.

"Colin!" I hissed. "Are you drunk?"

He shook his head emphatically. "No, no, no, no, no. A little…buzzed, maybe, but not drunk. Not drunk."

I turned to Cara, whose face was turning red with rage. "Cara, has he been drinking?"

She raised her hands in defense. "The only time I didn't have my eye on him was when Delia, Christine and I went in to shop for some sundresses. He said he was gonna just sit in the park and people watch."

I pushed Collie up against the glass wall of the staircase. "So, just what *did* you do? Where'd you get the booze, Colin?"

"Okay, *okay!* Across the square there was this pushcart wagon thing. Sign said, *'Try Our Native Nectar. Cape Verde's Secret Potion'* There were all these little paper cups. I did a taste test. Stuff was horrible."

Cara grabbed Collie's wrist and spun him toward her. "Just how many little paper cups did you have, Collie?"

"I dunno…a couple."

"How many, Colin?"

"Okay! Maybe three…four."

I turned to Cara. "He stinks of rum, Cara. How come you didn't notice that on the way home?"

"Hold on here! Are you blaming *me*, Victor?"

"Absolutely not. I know how vigilant we all have been in monitoring Collie's alcohol consumption. I just want to know how he snuck this by us."

Christine spoke up. "Well, that one's easy. Delia drove on the way home, and Cara sat next to her in front. They were deep in conversation. Talking about Alva, I'm sure. Colin parked himself in the back seat next to me. With no roof or windows, the wind blew the smell of his breath away from me. We had a nice conversation about the countryside, farming, and goats, and he wasn't acting drunk. I certainly didn't detect anything. But now I'm sure glad he wasn't driving. And on the ferry on the way home, he was out in the open breeze."

I was breathing loudly through my nose, and my chest was heaving. I couldn't figure what to do next, where to go from here. I released my grip on my brother's shoulders, tried to temper my anger. "When the dust clears and this guy sobers up, this family is going to have a very serious talk about this. I don't think we just have a sloppy drunk on our hands. I think we have to behave like we're dealing with an alcoholic and a sneak. We can't let this kind of shit happen ever again."

Chapter Six

FLIGHT SCHOOL

"I am not an unreasonable man, Olifante" said Alberto Mafin, once again drumming his fingers piano-player style on his broad walnut desk. It was a familiar gesture to Checo Paredes, indicating that Mafin, a deep furrow above his saturnine brows and a dark red flush spreading across the bridge of his sharply hooked nose, was feeling tightly wound at the moment.

Olifante sat in a folding chair in front of Mafin, his hands and ankles bound tightly with zip ties, his bruised right eye now almost entirely swollen shut. Paredes stood behind him, his arms crossed, his Sig Sauer pistol cradled comfortably in the crook of his elbow.

"Good thing you tell us where you hid our product," Mafin croaked. "Otherwise, I jes' shoot you, bang, in the face. Quick and clean if I was feeling…generous, you know? Or I could make it nasty if I was still pissed that some *cabrones,* some fucking *pirates*, attacked us. In open ocean. Cost me a perfectly good narco-sub. Killed a few my men and almost cost me a hundred million dollars' worth of product."

Mafin bit his lower lip and swung in an arc in his desk chair. Then he offered a wan smile. "But today my mother's birthday! And I jus' got my shipment back, so I am feeling charitable. Prepared to give you a chance to save your own life."

Paredes knew what was coming. He did not smile. It wasn't fire ants, but it was bad enough.

"First, Checo. Cut those zip ties loose. I'm sure they must chafe ver' bad, and of course Mr. Olifante would not be so stupid as to try any rash moves once we free his hands and legs. Then we are going to walk out to Eugenia. Eugenia the name my helicopter. I name her that because she is my jungle princess—she black and sleek. And fast. Aerospatiale Gazelle. I love her ass."

Now Mafin's flat smile morphed to a broad grin. Not a warm or sincere smile, but a dark and menacing smirk. "We going for a nice helicopter ride along the shore, *Mister* Olifante. We going to fly Eugenia, my helicopter, 'cross the border into Venezuela, all the way past Trinidad and Tobago, all the way to the mouth of the Orinoco River.

"We starting with a nature tour, Olifante. We going to lend you some Go-Pro video recording equipment, so you can take video of the very rare Orinoco crocodiles to share with your friends. These crocs critically endangered, you know. Hunted almost to 'stinction. But the ones I show you today are very happy, because they're getting a really good meal. You'll get to watch them feed, and if you look carefully, you may recognize what they eating. They eating Howie and Long John and Kimo, maybe some of your other guys."

A stream of urine ran down Olifante's pants leg and puddled beneath his bare feet. He began shivering and panting.

"Then we gon' turn around and go wreck hunting over near Jotajana. Know what wreck we're gonna see? Certain fishing trawler and a certain barge. They be a little hard to spot, because at the moment they upside down in the river shallows. But you can see 'em 'cause your trawler has a bright blue bottom, and if you look careful you can see the boom of that yellow crane on your barge. After we see the shipwrecks, we're going to head Eugenia home. *Andale!* Let's go."

Checo Paredes pulled Olifante to his feet, bracing him as his knees buckled and he began to collapse to the floor of Alberto Mafin's office.

Mafin's black Aerospatiale Gazelle sat proudly on the asphalt landing pad at the edge of the parking lot, polished to a luster so bright that Paredes had to shield his eyes from the reflection of the sun. A broad red stripe encircled the helicopter at waist height, and each door bore a coat of arms, five dark blue stripes slashed diagonally across a field of yellow. As Mafin, Paredes and Olifante strode up to the glistening craft, the engine began to spool up, and Mafin had to shout to Paredes to make himself heard. "Checo, reverse the numbers back to front!"

The helicopter's white registration numbers were in fact magnetic panels that could easily be transposed or removed in order to disguise the craft's identity, and. Paredes had switched the numbers around many times. As he moved away from Olifante toward the helicopter's tail, the terrified man made a sudden frantic move as if to bolt, but because he didn't know which way to turn, he simply ended up making a silly stutter-step. A sharp blow to the back of his head from Mafin's pistol butt brought him to his knees, and a sharp shove drove him face first into the asphalt landing pad.

"*Cabron,*" muttered Mafin.

As the Gazelle headed back to the west after the passengers had viewed the well-fed Orinoco crocodiles and a couple of derelict ship hulls, Mafin had to shout into the microphone on his headphones to be heard over the roar of the Gazelle's rotor wash.

"God, isn't this jungle *muy hermoso e precioso?* So, so beautiful? If I weren't so busy with my business, I'd spend all my time jus' flyin' around. No havin' to talk with people, no havin' to track down my cargo of hijacked cocaine. Just flyin' around, you know?"

Olifante sat with his head lolling pathetically from side to side, his eyes wide with fear. He was covered with vomit, having been unable to contain his bile when he saw the Orinoco crocs spinning and rolling with the half-eaten bodies of Olifante's former crew members clamped in their jaws.

"Please don' kill me," he pleaded.

Mafin spread his hands innocently. "Told you, man. *I'm* not going to kill you. You did us big favor by ratting out your partners in crime! We recovered most of the product you guys stole from us. Now all we gotta do is find some way to send to message to your cartel that they better keep the fuck away from us."

Mafin let a half hour pass as they flashed over the jungle over the Parque Nacional Delta del Orinoco toward Puerto La Cruz on the way to Caracas. Paredes sat stone-faced next to Leon the pilot, occasionally turning in his seat to watch Mafin tease Olifante. Now Puerto La Cruz came into view, the white walls of the houses flashing bright in the afternoon sun, the red tile roofs vivid against the intense green of the surrounding jungle, the docks and marinas bustling with activity.

"Hokay, Leon," Mafin said to the pilot. "Please take us up to four thousand feet and hover." He grinned at Olifante.

"Okay, man! You going to flight school! All you have to do to save your life is learn to fly! Like, *pronto*. One lesson all you need, right, *muchacho*?"

Olifante tried to vomit again but had nothing left to deliver. Instead he just retched violently.

"Now I tell you basic principles of flying, mister cocaine pirate. We at four thousand feet. Sky divers will tell you it takes about ten seconds to fall first thousand feet. Each thousand feet after that, about five more seconds. So that means your first solo is gonna be about twenty-five seconds long. But you seen those sky-diving movies, *si*? How those guys spread their arms, make themselves like a little airplane, *si*? Make airfoil with their bodies and zoom all around and do acrobatics and shit. Maybe you can fly as far as the ocean, do a graceful swan dive into the water, *si*? Ever seen those cliff jumpers in Acapulco? Or watch the Red Bull cliff diving championships on TV? Sixty-meter platform, all kinds of somersaults and twists. They going terminal velocity when they hit the water, but *they* live! You just gotta go in feet first, right?"

Olifante began writhing frantically in his seat. He stopped abruptly when Paredes turned and placed his Sig Sauer against his forehead, which now glistened with sweat.

"Now because this a *flight school*," Mafin continued, "we gotta have instructional video to show future classes, right? So, Checo, I want you to duct tape that Go-Pro camera to Señor Olifante's chest. Point it up, so it shows his face as he flying. Then let's run a camera check, make sure the feed is coming to my monitor here, make sure we're getting a pretty picture. Wanna make sure we capture our rookie pilot's entire flight so we can show everybody on You Tube how well he learned to fly."

Checo moved back into the passenger area, unfastened Olifante's safety belt and pulled him forward and wrapped several loops of silver duct tape around his body to hold the Go-Pro in place. Olifante was sobbing, but he made no move to resist. He looked into Paredes' eyes. "*No, no, no, no, please, no.*"

Mafin crouched and slid Eugenia's sliding door open, unleashing a roar of wind and sending some loose papers flying around the cabin. Paredes shook his head at Olifante. "Your own fault, you fucker. You should have thought what would happen if you ever came after us. You deserve what you get."

Without hesitation, Paredes grabbed Olifante by the shoulders of his jacket and heaved him bodily out of the helicopter. Olifante's leg hit the side of the door opening as he exited, sending him spinning and cartwheeling as he tumbled into the sky. Paredes slid the helicopter's door shut and sat down next to Mafin, who was concentrating on the images on his monitor.

As he dropped through space, Olifante was kicking and thrashing wildly, his mouth open in a long continuous scream. He fell like a stone.

"I wish you wouldn't do this shit, Mafin. It's sadistic and it makes me sick every time you do it. You should just shoot the fuckers."

"Yeah? Well, *I* enjoy it, mister chicken-liver. I love sending the message to those *cabrones* that they cannot mess with us. *That no one should ever mess with us!* This is gonna make a great YouTube. We're gonna get a lot of likes. Maybe win an Oscar."

Mafin grasped his arms tightly across his chest and exhaled delightedly.

Olifante did not make it to the ocean, did not fly or glide or discover any way to retard his momentum as he plunged to earth on his maiden flight. He was traveling at about 120 miles per hour when he crashed through the canopy of a palm tree and demolished the roof of Ali Nero-Nero's World Best Tacos fast food truck, pinning Ali Nero-Nero to his griddle, killing him instantly, and sending Ali's bright red super-spicy sauce cascading through the air and over the streets of Puerto La Cruz.

The front-page photo in the next day's *New York Times* featured a photo of Olifante's body flattened against the crumpled roof of Ali's fast-food truck. One of Ali's arms could be seen protruding from the service window. The caption under the picture read, *Cartel Wars Reach New Heights: Cruel and Unusual Punishment.*

Chapter Seven

TIME TO TAKE THE BOAT

"Eamon? Checo."

"Checo! After last time, I thought I'd never hear from you again! Where are you? I can hardly hear you. You're breaking up, man."

Eamon Armagh spoke with a pronounced Irish brogue, singsong, soft, utterly disarming.

"I'm on Isla Gazela, down at my boatyard. Down by the launching dock. Steam comin' out of my ears. That's probably what's screwing up my smart phone reception."

"What are you talking about, man?"

"I'm staring at our 'state-of-the-art' fully-submersible drug sub. It's submersible, all right. *Permanently.* Our nice new fiberglass boat, sittin' blowin' bubbles on the bottom, right here in the launching slip. Some launch day, eh? Crane lowered it part way in, it immediately took water through a loose prop shaft. Total panic. Started filling fast. Began to slip out of the slings. Crane went up on two wheels, threatened to tip over into the slip. Guys inside the sub screaming and yelling and drowning. We blew the bottom out of the sub with a rocket launcher to try to save 'em. One guy made it, couple of guys didn't."

"Wow, that is some very, very bad news."

"That's not the worst of it. You know our last load got hijacked, right? Cost us our last conventional sub, cost us a buck-twenty street value worth of product."

"Yeah, I heard something about that. All the way back in Ireland, Checo. Takes a major Venezuelan fuck-up for gossip to travel that far. I know Mafin an' me aren't speakin', but the grapevine still works pretty good."

"Well, we tracked down the hijacker captain, got him to turn rat. Ended up getting about eighty per cent of our product back. All good, right? Yay for us. So now we load the shit into that old beater we had stored in the back of the yard—actually the first drug sub we ever built here. Pretty tired, but we figure it should be good for one more trip. Tonio gets up to about twenty miles off the southern coast of Cuba and the fucker pops a sea cock. Starts takin' on water, pumps can't keep up. They barely manage to make the Ballateria's secret base, Cubans hoist the boat out before the load is spoiled.

"So, now, here's two-thousand one-kilo packets stacked on the ground. Now the Cubans, those *cabrones,* offer us this great deal. If we get another boat up there to Cuba, they'll load it for us...*taking half for themselves.* But we don't got no boats, Eamon. We got no subs in service, no way to get the load up to Grand Isle. Customer up north is going out of his mind. Like, threats. Ugly threats. And Mafin's going out of *his* mind, is all over my case. Like death threats. *To me.*"

There was a long pause as Eamon Armagh waited for the shoe to drop. "Tell me what you wanna do, Checo."

The pitch of Eamon's voice tended to lift at the end of his sentences, making each sentence sound as if he was asking a question.

"The only possible option at this point. We're going to have to grab a sailboat. I'm calling to see if you'll snag a big boat and sail the shit from Cuba up to Louisiana."

There was a long silence.

"You're pulling me chain, right? Mafin know you're makin' this phone call?"

"He knows. He also knows it's any port in a storm, and the guys in Louisiana are really storming at him."

"Well, even before our recent…*misunderstanding,* I thought we all agreed that sailboats are a bad way to go these days."

"No, choice, Eamon. We're out of options at the moment. And I actually got a boat in mind. I read in *Notice to Mariners* that the Dutch Coast Guard is about to auction a bunch of confiscated boats, and I see *Lucifer* is on the block."

"*Lucifer!* You guys gonna buy your own boat back?"

"No, you idiot. Someone else is going to buy the boat—and then you're going to pay a little visit to the new buyer."

"Do you seriously think we can get it commandeered and loaded and sailed up to Grand Isle in time to avoid a vicious little civil war?"

"We're cutting it real fine, but we gotta do what we gotta do."

"Funny you should say that, because if I do this, you know who I'm gonna hire as crew."

"Adamares Thuna," whispered Paredes.

Silence. Then Eamon Armagh slowly drew a long, deep breath. "You okay with that, Checo?"

"Oh, man, Eamon, you do like to play with fire, don't you? That guy is a major league nut case. Scares me to death. Who knows what goes on in that busted-up head of his?"

"That's true. One crazy motherfucker. But he knows how to sail, how to navigate. All that has to go through his head is to follow my orders, help sail the goddamned boat, and stand watch. I think I can trust him, particularly if I remind him that I saved his ass from Mafin and that we will kill his kid if he screws us over or goes off the deep end again. I think that under the circumstances, we have to trust him."

Armagh began tapping his cell phone screen with his finger tip. Thinking. Thinking. Trying to perform a high-speed risk-reward analysis. *Tap. Tap. Tap.* Finally he said, "You remember I told you that you couldn't pay me enough to do another job with Mafin? Or with Adamares Thuna, for that matter?"

"Yeah, you said that. But that was then, and this is now."

"So how much are you going to pay me to do another job with mister Mafin and mister Thuna?"

"Fifteen per cent."

Armagh gasped in surprise. "Well! Okay now, there's an incentive! Can you guys make your profit if you give that much away?"

"We're not hoping to make our usual profit out of this whole mess. We just want to get this customer off our back and keep him coming back. Actually, we just want to keep the customer from coming down here and killing us all."

Chapter Eight

Unexpected Visitors

At the moment, I was flooded with unexpected emotion. With...contentment. *What an absolutely terrific day this has been,* I thought. Hannes had invited the whole crew down to spend the night in Praia on the Consulate's dime, and Alva and I again had the place to ourselves.

I stood downstairs in the guest room shower washing off the salt rime and the sand from a splendid play day with the exotic Sri Lankan enchantress. It had started with some shallow-reef snorkeling—I had told Alva that my scuba-diving days were done—featuring Alva's astonishing skill with a spear gun. This would provide a red snapper, an amberjack, and a giant slipper lobster for Artur's special seafood stew tonight. I had floated languorously on the surface, watching in amazement as Alva, in her bright orange bikini, dove deep among the coral heads, expertly sending spear after spear through unsuspecting fish. Alva's aim was remarkable.

After a splendid lunch overlooking the marina in Ribeira, Alva and I had set out on Alva's inaugural sail. I had chartered a Dragon for the afternoon, and Alva fell in love with this graceful thirty-foot mahogany day sailor designed by Norwegian Johan Aker back in 1929. I also loved Dragons. With their delicate lines, narrow beams and deep keels, the boats were fast and exciting. They were forgiving for novices, but responded well to a sensitive hand on the tiller and careful sail trim.

As we tacked back and forth around the southern coast of Santo Antão, Alva proved a quick study, quickly mastering the basic mechanics of sailing—points of sail, tacking, jibing, sail trim, running, reaching, beating close-hauled to windward.

A review of all the bewildering sailing nomenclature—the standing rigging, the running rigging, all the lines that control sail trim, the names of the sails, the instruments—all required but a single quick once-over. Alva never asked me to repeat myself, to dumb it down, to explain the interplay of wind, sea and sails. She just *got it*.

Now, as the scalding water beat over my back in the shower, I realized that I was feeling better than I had in a long time, both emotionally and physically. I'd shed five pounds since coming to Cape Verde, cultivated a deep tan, was sleeping better—particularly after the hours of gentle, reassuring and exceptionally enjoyable sex with Alva—and, courtesy of Alva and the wondrous Artur's culinary skills, I was certainly eating well. I was drinking more wine and less hard spirits, and my lifelong dalliance with cigars had dropped by the wayside.

I seemed to have stumbled into new reserves of energy and stamina, of optimism, of anticipation. *Was this all because of Alva? Was it because of who she was or because of how she behaved, or because of her irreverent outlook on life?* Whatever the contributing forces were, I found myself talking out loud to myself as I shaved in the shower. "God, you old man, you're really feeling *good*."

There was a loud thump from overhead, then the crash of smashed pottery audible even over the sound of the shower. I put down my razor and cocked my head to hear better, and what I heard was loud voices, one Alva's, the other an angry male, clearly seriously upset about something. I slid on some shorts and a tee shirt and, padding barefoot, started up the stairs.

The man's voice grew louder, angrier, more threatening, the words a furious staccato. "I'll show you!" he screamed over and again. "I'll show you!" I slowed my ascent, tip-toed up the staircase and peered over the top step into the living room. I saw Alva first.

She was edging backward out of the living room toward the veranda, her eyes wide, her hands extended in front of her in defense. I could see she was terrified, but she was standing steady and erect in the face of the verbal onslaught. *God, Alva, you really do have ice water in your veins.*

Now, to the right, I saw a tall, slender Caucasian man, dressed in an expensive-looking but heavily-wrinkled fawn-colored summer business suit. Black socks, expensive shoes. His back was to me, and I could not see his face. The man had a shaved head, and his heavily-veined neck now flushed a livid red. His hands, held out in front of him as he continued to shout at Alva, shook noticeably. He was holding a pistol—a large, evil-looking automatic of some kind—police style, gripped with both hands.

He was pointing the pistol at Alva's face.

I stopped, crouched silently on the stair. Alva's voice was low, but I had no trouble hearing her. I was amazed at her calm.

"Stop shouting at me," she said. "I can hear you. I'm listening to you. Just be calm."

"*Calm?* Oh, you think I should be *calm?* I'll tell you when I'll be calm. When I see your body lying at the base of the cliff. I'll be calm when you take a dive, Alva."

"Who *are* you?" Alva asked. "I have never met you, or I certainly would remember you."

"Who am I?" the man screamed. "I'll tell you who the hell I am! I am South Saharan Venture Partners, Premier Investors' Circle, Account Number 00424! That's who I am, Mrs. Lloyd Patel!"

The gunman was spitting and frothing, now shaking his head wildly from side to side. I feared he might discharge his gun unintentionally.

Alva remained composed. "00424…Oh! Yes! Mr. Tanner! Lucas! This is a strange way to finally meet in person! Of course, I am very familiar with your account, and I really very much regret the losses you suffered when the fund closed down."

Now Tanner was shrieking. "*Regret the losses? Fund 'closed down?'* 'Your husband, your fucking fast-talking snake oil salesman, conned me out of *three million dollars*! Suckered me! Screwed me! Your husband ruined me, bankrupted me, destroyed my life! Me and a whole lot of other people. Then he just up and kills himself, 'ta-ta, so long, too bad for all you suckers I wiped out.' Well, Lloyd may have escaped punishment, but you're not. *You…are…going…to…pay… the…price.* Back up."

"No," said Alva.

"*Oh*, yes," Lucas Tanner yelled. "You're going to walk your black ass back to the edge of the terrace, and then I'm gonna enjoy watching the Alva Batek cliff diving act."

"No, Lucas. That's not what's going to happen. You want to *punish* me, you're going to have to shoot me. In the face, while looking at me in the face. You ever shoot anybody before, Lucas?"

"You think I won't?"

"No, I don't think you can. Don't think you have the nerve to be a killer."

"Yeah? Well, you, you arrogant bitch, are in for one hell of a surprise. I got nothing to lose, but I look around here and see *you* got plenty to lose. And you are just about to lose it."

I realized instantly what I had to do. I edged silently back down the stairs on my hands and knees. When I felt the floor under my feet, I spun back into the guest room and moved to the magnificent display of wall art hanging over the bed.

Alva's interior decoration for the guest room included two matched Muramasa samurai swords dating, she'd told me proudly, from 1584—a lavishly engraved katana long sword Alva had bought at auction from the Japanese National Museum, and a shorter wakizashi side sword, the kind often tucked into a samurai's obi at the hip. Both were mounted simply on open rosewood hooks over the guest bed. I grabbed the wakizashi, slid off its scabbard, gripped its graceful, curved handle with both hands and headed back toward the stairs.

In the course of my life, I have weathered many fraught events, moments when my muscles tensed, my pulse pounded, and my breathing came hard and fast. Like the time when the ten-story apartment I was hired to save began to topple in Kathmandu, or when we dynamited the weakened foundation from under a northern Italian bell tower. Or the time I stepped off a sinking sailboat into a life raft during a storm off the west coast of South Africa.

But nothing like this.

As I squeezed the sword and prepared to act, a flood of raw adrenaline coursed through my body. I heard a thunderous roar in my ears, and it seemed like every synapse in my body was firing at once. I was totally and completely *wired*. I had never experienced anything like it.

Even in this overwhelming moment, I marveled at the exquisite combination of the balance and heft of the sword I held in my hands. I did not know the proper way to hold a samurai sword, so I simply grasped the handle with my hands together, as if it were a baseball bat. I crept up the stairs, listening as Tanner continued to scream at Alva. Now he was simply shouting, "You're gonna pay! You're gonna pay" over and over again, and Alva was repeating, "Be calm, Lucas. Just be calm."

Tanner was still pointing the pistol in Alva's face as I tiptoed up behind him. When Alva saw me holding the sword, she inhaled deeply, pointed at the ceiling, and screamed, "Look up there!" Tanner, surprised at the volume of her cry, froze momentarily, glanced up at the ceiling, then sensed me behind him and started to turn.

I did not really aim as I rushed at him, just jabbed with all my might, trusting the heft of the sword to do whatever it could do. The thrust of the blade pierced Tanner's neck behind his right ear, just under his jaw. I was astonished at how smoothly and cleanly the sword cut through his flesh. Smooth as a hot knife through butter, the blade shot through the back of Tanner's head and emerged through the center of his mouth, like a wicked steel dragon's tongue, amidst a gusher of blood.

Dropping his gun, Tanner reached up and grabbed hold of the sword's extraordinarily sharp blade, cleaving huge gashes in his palms and neatly amputating his left thumb. He did not scream, could not scream, because the blade had severed his vocal cords.

He spun wildly around in several tight circles until his knees collapsed and he toppled forward onto his face. Still protruding from his lips, the tip of the wakizashi blade dug into the bamboo flooring, propping Tanner's face several inches above the floor and making him look like a piece of beef on a kabob skewer. Still drunk on adrenaline, I straddled Tanner, grabbing him from behind by his shoulders and spinning him over on his side just as his bladder and bowels released and covered his fawn-colored suit with dark stains.

Tanner was still alive, his eyes bulging, his knees pumping spastically, his arms clawing wildly in the air. Alva, her face ashen and her eyes wide in shock, had the presence of mind to reach over Tanner's thrashing body and pick up his pistol. Before I could stop her, she racked the slide on the pistol—*where did she learn how to do that?*—bent down, placed the muzzle of the pistol against Tanner's shirt front, and squeezed the trigger. Tanner's back arched in one electric spasm, and he then fell still. Alva straightened and threw the pistol down toward the crimson stain burgeoning on Tanner's shirt front. The gun bounced off the sword blade still projecting from Tanner's mouth and skittered across the floor, ending up under the couch.

The threat relieved, Alva now recoiled, covered her face in her hands, and dropped to her knees, her face contorted in anguish. Without saying a word to me, she toppled on to her side, and, suddenly wracked with sobs, pulled her legs up into the fetal position.

As for me, the adrenaline jolt abated as quickly as it had struck me. I felt a sudden weak emptiness, a kind of vacuum. My breathing stopped completely, then resumed in spastic gasps. I have no idea how long I just stood there, looking at Alva curled up on the ground. An intense wave of horror extinguished my uncontrolled fury, and my knees turned to water.

As I collapsed to my knees beside the fetal Alva, I heard a wrenching groan burst from my mouth, although I was not aware of uttering it. My head dropped to my chest, and I croaked a series of deep animal grunts. My prior thoughts from the shower once again flashed through my mind: *What an absolutely terrific day this has been!*

Cleaning up was a long, ugly mess, costing Alva a perfectly good blanket. Now wearing rubber gloves, I trussed Leon Tanner's shit-stained body up in the blanket and cinched him up into a cylindrical bundle—"like reefing a mainsail, Alva"—before hauling him up the stairs and into the parking lot. I found the keys to Tanner's rental car, a tired old white Opel, in the ignition, and wrangled Tanner's body into the trunk.

When I returned to the living room, gagging in spasms and my knees weak, Alva moved into me and hugged me—hard and long.

"A fine friend you are," she whispered with a wan smile. "All you had to do was drag a body up some stairs, while I was left to mop up all this shit and blood."

Then she burst into tears again and, shuddering and trembling, pulled herself even more tightly into my embrace.

By the time Artur and Gracia, who'd arrived after the clean-up and knew nothing of the afternoon's drama, served up Artur's seafood stew, both Alva and I had regained a semblance of composure, but both of us left our meal half finished. "I'm a little under the weather, Artur. Maybe you'd better excuse us. Why don't you and Gracia head home, and we'll clean up the kitchen after ourselves."

Once alone, Alva and I tried to discuss the implications of the afternoon. This was hardly a calm, rational discussion. I had knocked back shot after shot of ouzo and now was pretty much smashed. As I struggled to put coherent sentences together, I realized I was shaking my head back and forth like a metronome.

"My God, Alva, I'm a killer! I'm just a fucking killer!"

Alva reached across the table and gripped my forearm—*hard*.

"Get hold of yourself! *You are not a killer!* You had to kill someone because *he* was a killer."

"But I *am* a killer," I spat out. "I just killed someone. Without a moment's hesitation, without giving him a chance. What kind of...*monster* does that make me?"

"You are *not* a monster—any more than I am a monster just because I just shot this bastard when he was down."

The two of us now lapsed into silence, drawing deep ragged breaths. After a few minutes, I pushed out a cleansing breath, shook my head to try to clear away the fog.

"We gotta think this through. Does this invasion really change anything, Alva? Do you think killing this crazy man puts an end to your risk? Are other people going to come here to kill you?"

"I honestly don't know, Victor. As a single insane incident, I don't know if it means much, unless Tanner told a lot of people that he was coming here. But how likely is that, really? I mean, would he really tell people, 'Hey, I'm going to Cape Verde to kill the wife of the shitheel who defrauded me of my life savings?'

"But that *is* the question, isn't it?" Alva continued. "Was Tanner acting alone, or is there some sort of conspiracy going on to get back at me, to punish me? If there is, I don't think it would be masterminded by a deranged wimp like Tanner. More likely it would be someone like John Boyajian, or, even more likely, Ashi Fukashi."

"Who're they?"

"Boyajian is a fund manager in London who took a big hit in Lloyd's deals. Fukashi was another victim of Lloyd's who might like to kill me. Yakuza. Former partner of Lloyd's, lost a lot of face when he found out Lloyd was robbing him blind."

"Christ, Alva, with guys like this out for revenge, did you really think you would be safe here in Cape Verde?"

Alva furrowed her brow, as if entering a debate with herself. "Well, I sure thought so. When Lloyd committed suicide, I basically grabbed all the money and ran. Hid my tracks, worked hard on not leaving any clues. Came to Cape Verde because it has no extradition treaty with the U.S. I set Hannes Schlossberg up as my front, or my beard, or whatever you call it."

"How long have you been hiding out here?"

"I'm not 'hiding out,'" Alva snapped. "I've simply been living a quiet, reclusive life while keeping my eyes open."

"For how long?"

"It's been nearly five years now. Five years with no incidents or major alarms. Hannes—who is a very savvy guy—and I both thought Cape Verde would be a pretty secure safe house. Said he couldn't think of any better place. I don't know, Victor, maybe it's still safe. But now, in light of Tanner showing up out of the blue, I guess it's not impossible to track me down after all. Maybe some of Lloyd's other victims, all fired up with a need for revenge or eager for blackmail, might also begin showing up at my door."

Alva looked intently into my eyes. "Look, Victor, I can't ask you to keep standing around here indefinitely, guarding me with a samurai sword twenty-four-seven. Maybe this really is the best time to go on a sea cruise, you know?"

It felt like a cool breeze had suddenly washed across my face.

"Yeah, well, I gotta say that the idea of going sailing is a lot more attractive all of a sudden. Maybe I'm just turning chicken."

Now Alva took my cheeks in her hands, squeezing gently. "You, Victor Harding, are not a chicken. You are my hero. An incredibly quick-thinking hero. You're a knight in shining armor, a maiden rescuer, a..a…"

"Try seventy-two-year-old retiree who just stabbed someone to death in the mouth with a sword."

That image struck Alva as funny. "Yeah, that too." She tried to stifle a giggle, then cracked up again, sending another spray of Rioja down the front of her caftan.

"Look, Victor, don't get me wrong. I'm not making light of this. Obviously, it's going to take a while for us to process all this. Please, please don't go dark on me."

The mental image of 'going dark,' of curling up unseen in some lightless hidden corner, was curiously comforting to me. I wanted to hide out from the world, to bathe in cool, quiet darkness. I wanted everything and everybody off my back.

"So, what should we do, Alva?"

"First, I just want to make this whole episode disappear, so we can get on with our lives."

"Yeah? Well, speaking of making things disappear, we got a body in the trunk of a rental car in your parking lot. I think that's our most immediate problem."

"Not as big a problem as it would be in, say, back at your house in Green Lake, Wisconsin. This is Cape Verde. Things are different here. We can get this done quickly."

"How so?"

"The crime rate in Cape Verde has actually gone down in recent years, but that's mainly for petty crime, mugging tourists, and like that. We have some gangs and cartels on Santiago Island, particularly in the capital, in Praia. Those guys play rough sometimes. People disappear. Bodies get found. Bodies don't get found."

"And Lucas Tanner's body is going to get found in Praia?"

"Probably not until he decomposes a while and creates a stink. Unless we leave the keys in his rental car's ignition. Then whoever steals the car probably will find him sooner."

"Just what *is* your plan, Alva?"

"As soon as time permits, we draw a quick mustache on you, Victor, hide you behind sunglasses, buy a pair of workman's overalls for you on our way into Praia. Then you, wearing your workman's gloves, drive the Opel onto the Praia ferry and enjoy a nice sea cruise across the channel for a few hours. I will be behind you on the ferry in my car to give you a ride home. We will not meet or talk on the ferry. You drop the car in an alley in Praia Sud, wipe it down carefully. On the way home we toss the overalls in the trash—trust me, someone will retrieve them and put them to good use—and when we get back, we get drunk and have sex. Sound like a plan?"

"Okay by me. One question," I said. "Do we tell the others? After all, as long as they're here, if there are killers on the loose, they're in danger, too. Aren't they entitled to protect themselves?"

"Maybe, maybe not. We don't actually know if there's more danger. If Tanner was a one-off, we don't want to get everybody all worked up for nothing. Maybe Delia would keep her cool, but from what I've seen of her so far, Christine sure couldn't. She'd unravel, for sure, get all panicky. And given all Collie's been through with the attacks on him last year in Wisconsin, I honestly don't know how he'd respond to this. And I think our sweet soft-souled Cara might come unglued, too. Besides, I'm not sure what any of them could do even if we do tell them.

"Until we can lock in our sailboat plans and arrange to get ourselves out of Cape Verde, my vote is that you and I keep this under wraps. I do think it makes sense to tell Hannes and maybe have him arrange for security guards around the property. Also have him do some sniffing to see if he hears something's in the wind. If he thinks we're making the wrong decision about not telling the others, I'm sure he'll say so."

"Hannes?"

"Jawohl."

"This is Alva and Victor on a speakerphone."

"Ja, I can tell. But Alva, you sound…upset."

"Well, we have a serious situation here, and we need your advice. Maybe your help."

"Ja, okay, you have my attention."

Alva's voice quavered. She coughed to clear her throat, regaining her composure.

"Hannes, we had an intruder at the house this afternoon. One of Lloyd's old clients. English guy named Lucas Tanner. Lloyd and I fleeced him big time—like over three million bucks—about eight years ago."

"What did he want?"

"He wanted to kill me. Or, more exactly, he wanted to force me to kill myself. He had a gun aimed at my face. He was trying to force me to jump off the cliff."

Hannes gasped, then exhaled loudly. "I gather he did not succeed in getting you to jump off the cliff."

"Ah, no." Now Alva's voice was calm, steady.

"So, what happened?"

"Victor was downstairs when this guy barged in and began screaming at me. Screamed he was going to make me jump over the side. He was totally out of control. Victor heard the screaming, crept up the stairs behind him, and came to my rescue."

"Was there a fight?"

"Not really. Victor crept up behind him and stabbed him to death with the samurai sword from my guest room. A lot of blood and shit on the floor, but neither of us was hurt."

Hannes' voice dropped to a hoarse whisper. "*Lieber Gott!* When did all this happen?"

"This afternoon, after Victor and I got back from sailing. The rest of the family is on the tour around the island you arranged, and they're still at their festival dinner in Praia. They won't be back 'til late. So it was just Victor and me. It's still just Victor and me."

"So, what have you been doing since the attack?"

"We have cleaned up the house, stuffed the body in the trunk of his car. We worked fast, but don't worry, we did a very good job. Don't know if Tanner told anyone he was coming here, but if any authority ever came sniffing around, there'd be nothing for them to find. Now we've had dinner, sucked down a lot of alcohol, and figured it was time to call you. Anyway, please don't ask me where or how we plan to get rid of the body, because I won't tell you."

"Well, thank you for that little bit of deniability, Alva. And you are calling me now because why?"

"Because now we haven't the least idea what to do next. I think maybe we may be in shock or something, because we're just standing around here, feeling numb. And dumb."

When he is deep in thought, Hannes has a habit of lifting his head, then nodding a couple of times as ideas come to him. I could picture him nodding now. He spoke very slowly, as if ticking action items off on his fingers.

"First, do not—I repeat, *do not*—under any circumstances contact the police. They're useless and they're corrupt and they really like giving ex-pats a tough time. I'm sure they would love to blow this up into a big ugly story, harass you, maybe charge you with manslaughter or something. I, in my capacity as Swiss consul—and with the benefit of my diplomatic immunity—hereby assume full jurisdiction over this matter.

"Next, lock the front door and do not open it for any reason until the security detail I'm sending arrives and you receive a phone call from me saying they've arrived. Within two hours I will have a squad of consulate security staff stationed in your parking lot, and they will remain there, twenty-four seven, until I discharge them. The guards I'm sending are very competent and very tough, but they're not very friendly. Don't bother trying to befriend them or cook them hot soup or anything. They'll take care of themselves, and they'll take care of you."

He paused, working to figure out the order of march.

"Next, get on the phone with Lufthansa and book tickets for all of you out of Cape Verde, leaving soonest. They have a good early morning flight that goes to Zurich, but if you can't get on that one, fly directly to Frankfurt. They'll be lots of connections to New York from there."

Alva interrupted him. "No," she said firmly.

"Pardon?" said Hannes. His voice had gone up an octave.

"I mean, yes, we should book tickets for everyone else, but not me. *I'm staying.* We don't know if anything else is going to happen, if there will be any more threats or revenge visits. In any case, I refuse to be chased out of my own house. Once I've hired my own security service, it'll free up your squad to depart. Okay, Hannes?"

I'm the one who spoke next. "No," I said. "I agree that the safest bet is to get the rest of the family the hell out of here, but I'm staying, too. I'm staying as long as Alva stays. I'm going to stay until we buy ourselves a suitable boat in the Caribbean and Alva and I can leave together for our sea cruise. I'm also suggesting that Alva keep this house under guard while we're away."

Hannes' sigh was long, exasperated. "I can see I have no choice, no voice in this matter. But Victor? Alva? *Please move fast on this.* Maybe there's no danger, maybe there's huge danger, especially if this Tanner chap was collaborating with other of Lloyd's victims."

I noticed that he was polite enough not to refer to them as Alva's victims.

At 1:00 AM there was a loud knock at the front door. "Who is it?" I called, samurai sword in hand.

"I am Captain Klaus Lindenmayer, a security officer of the Swiss Consul to Cape Verde. Technically, we are Swiss Guard, even here in Cape Verde. We have been assigned here on instructions from Herr Schlossberg. We have some people out here who say they are your family. Are you expecting family?"

"Yes, please let everyone in, and please step in yourself."

When I say Captain Lindenmayer was all business, I mean *all* business. Twice as big as a house, buttoned-up, buttoned-down, combat-booted, heavily armed with both an assault rifle and a Glock 19 at his hip,. I felt a wash of relief just looking at him, and I heard Alva exclaim, "My heavens, just *look* at you!"

Collie pushed past him, waving his arms. He clearly had drunk a considerable amount of alcohol at some point recently. "Victor, what the *fuck* is going on here?"

I pressed Collie's arms to his sides, made a stern shooshing noise. "Okay, family, we were attacked here today. Guy busted in, tried to force Alva to jump over the cliff."

Christine turned white as a sheet, and her knees buckled. Cara caught her before she hit the floor and guided her to the couch. *"What...who?"*

"Former client of Lloyd's," said Alva, raising her eyebrows and looking pointedly at the Swiss guard as if to say *Ixnay on the etailsday.* "He suffered losses in one of our overseas funds and he was obviously very upset with me." She spoke with complete calm.

"But what happened?" This was Cara revving up. I needed to quiet this down, wanted to be very careful about what we said in front of someone who was, after all, a kind of cop.

"I'll give you all the details when you're all settled and Captain Lindenmayer has returned to his outside duties. Let's just say that we got the intruder out of here, but not before some very frightening moments. Captain Lindenmayer, these are indeed our family members, and there are six of us. Me, I'm Victor Harding.

This is my brother, Colin Harding. My sister, Christine Harding, and her spouse, Delia Chamberlain. Cara Spaaks-Harding, Colin's wife. And, of course, this is Alva Batek. It's her house. No one else should be let in without you people calling into us first. That said, sir, let me excuse you to return to your men. We're very grateful for your help."

"Nür die Ruhe," said Lindenmayer. In German, literally that means 'nothing but quiet.' When most Swiss and Germans say it, roughly translated it meant *Peace.* With all my heart, I wanted to believe him.

The Wisconsin contingent, minus myself, was gone by noon the following afternoon, angry and exasperated that Alva and I would not provide them with all the gory details of the attack. In order to spare them all those gory details and provide them deniability, and also to spare them the image of me as a sword-wielding slasher, all we would say was that we had managed to kill the intruder and devised a plan to dispose of his body.

Collie in particular was furious. "We're all in this together!" he shouted at me when informed that everyone but Alva and me were, as he put it, 'being evicted.' "You're always preaching this noble sermon about family bonding, and then first time that bond gets put to a real test, suddenly it's everyone for themselves, good-bye, y'all, be seein' you."

It was Delia who calmed him down, standing in front of him and actually pushing at his chest with her hands. "Put your petty self-righteousness away, Collie. This isn't about defending the Alamo. There's no point in circling the wagons against an Indian attack when we don't know if and when there's going to be an attack, or even whether there are any more Indians."

Collie turned to Cara for support, found little. "I agree we all should get out of town," she said softly, "like right now. The only thing I don't agree with is Victor staying here. He doesn't offer any more protection than we do. For that matter, Alva should come, too. I don't know how you two senior citizens handled that first guy, and I don't want to know. But I don't think you two can count on holding the fort if a bigger assault comes."

Alva and I stood our ground, at least kind of. Alva agreed to stay in the house and not go anywhere for the immediate future. We agreed that I would stay another week and then fly to Aruba to begin boat shopping. The rest of the sea cruise crew would join us from Wisconsin when the right boat was found and fully outfitted.

Hannes' guard detail would stay on until Alva eventually joined me in the Caribbean, then a contract security service would take over patrolling the property—at Alva's expense.

It turns out Alva and I did not have to drive Leon Tanner's rental car into Praia for disposal. Hannes Schlossberg apparently whispered a few choice words in Captain Lindenmayer's ear, and, as if by magic, the Opel quickly disappeared. Not a word about it was spoken to us.

After Lucas Tanner had…*became gone*, Hannes' guards were patrolling the place, and my family had departed, Alva's and my hopes for peace and quiet lasted less than a week.

Chapter Nine

Take Two

I was facing the counter in the kitchen, toasting a bagel in the toaster oven, marveling that you could get a perfectly acceptable everything bagel in Cape Verde. Alva had yet to appear for breakfast. I heard the squeak of a rubber sole behind me, turned, and jumped back in surprise as I found myself staring at the business end of a very curious-looking weapon, a matte milky white rectangle, about three by four inches, maybe an inch thick. It had a hole in the end, which I took to be the opening of a gun barrel.

Holding this funny-looking gun with both hands, police-style, was a tall woman in a black Lycra jumpsuit standing in the middle of our living room. The hands holding the weapon were covered in white powder. She had a white-dusted rock climber's chalk bag strapped to her waist, and she wore black rock-climbing shoes with white rubber soles.

"How did you get in here?" I sputtered.

She showed me her chalk-covered hands, wiggled her fingers.

"One guess, mate." She had a pronounced midlands English accent. "So, here's your fancy-ass Swiss guards just standing around outside, right? All together in a nice tight little circle! Like maybe it's a darts club meeting down at the pub or something!

"I been watching 'em since four AM. No one thought of policing the perimeter, no one bothering to look over the edge of the cliff. *Incredibly incompetent.* So getting in was just as easy as pie, mate. I walked down the road a quarter mile, eased myself down, did a lazy lateral across the cliff face and then an enjoyable free climb right up to the patio. Guards still happily chatting each other up out there as I came up over the edge. So here I am, and *bingo!,* Bob's your uncle."

"What?" I said. "Bob who?"

"What, you never heard of 'Bob's your uncle?' To Brits it means, like, piece 'o cake. *Easily said and done. No worries.* Now, put your fucking hands on your fucking head."

With time to size up the intruder, I now noticed various things—besides the fact that she was holding some kind of gun—that argued against making rash, heroic moves. She was nearly six feet tall, powerfully muscled, evidently very, very fit. She had a long black pony tail pulled tightly back from her pale face, which was curiously asymmetrical—her right cheekbone was high and round, but the left side of her face was flattened and scarred, as if it had crashed into something unforgiving at some point, like maybe the stones at the base of a cliff. I now could tell that the intruder had a glass left eye and had to clock her head around to survey the entire living room. She refocused on me.

I fought for time. "Interesting weapon," I said.

To my surprise, the woman smiled. She looked down at her strange, rectangular weapon. "Like it? It's a ghost gun. Can't be traced or registered, you see. I made this one completely by myself. No manufacturer, just my own clever little CAD design that I whipped up on my iPad and assembled out of plastic parts I molded up on my home 3-D printer. If you care, it's nine-millimeter parabellum. Just like a Glock. Holds three rounds."

The woman said this with evident pride.

I wanted to keep her talking. "Why is it square like that? Looks just like a bar of soap."

"I designed it to look like a bar of soap, which was the whole idea. After I push the folding handle back up into the closed position, don't look much like a pistol any more, does it? Trigger's hidden, all you see is this soapy-lookin' rectangle. Not a bit of metal in it, nothing to trigger metal detectors. I'm thinkin' of patenting the design. Lucas doesn't know I made it, doesn't even know I have it. He hates guns."

I continued to stare at the gun. "Doesn't the plastic melt from the heat of firing bullets?"

"Sure it does. Gun's good for about eight shots before the barrel warps or the trigger sticks. It's only good for a few close-in shots, then I'll chuck it and print me up a new one. This one's brand new. Ready to fire. *Ready for business.*"

Her tone changed abruptly. "Speaking of business, where's Lucas?" she said.

"Who?"

"Lucas Tanner, my husband. Where is he?"

I worked to buy time as I slowly brought my knee up to press the panic button mounted on the bottom of the kitchen counter. The day after the first Tanner invasion, Hannes had a security service install what the technician called a simple SHAWS—a *silent house alert warning system*. Most customers refer to it as a Panic Button. It consisted of several plastic wireless push-on-push-off switches, one switch mounted just inside the front door, another under the kitchen counter where I now stood, one in each bedroom, and another outside under the parapet at the edge of the veranda. No sirens or whistles. A push on one of the buttons simply illuminated one of six red LED lights on the master panel by the stairway indicating where in the house an emergency had arisen.

"Stop!" the woman barked. "What are you doing!"

"To be honest," I croaked, my hands still on my head, "I am crossing my legs because I am pissing my pants. You're scaring me to death."

"That's the idea, you old fart. It's supposed to be frightening. Now, where's Lucas?"

"I believe Lucas is in Praia," I said as matter-of-factly as I could. I expected her to ask *What's he doing there?* That was what I would have asked in her position. Instead, she surprised me.

"Is he alive or dead?"

I was not about to risk a cute answer. "Lucas is dead," I said simply.

Her shoulders sagged, her chin dropped. She inhaled deeply. But her expression remained unchanged as she looked back up at me.

"I thought probably," she said. "You kill him, or Alva Batek kill him?"

"I killed him. Had to. He was going to kill us...well, kill Alva."

She seemed oddly detached, her tone flat. "Well, you know what that means."

"No, what?" I said, my hands still on my head.

"Means both of you gonna die," she said simply. "Now you call Alva fucking Batek up here. No fast moves, boyo."

I saw a flash of turquoise disappear behind the jamb of the doorway leading down to the bedrooms. Alva's dressing gown. I slowly turned toward my left, and the woman's gaze followed me. That meant she was now blind-sided, that the side of her head with no peripheral vision could not see Alva stepping out into the living room holding her spear gun.

The woman had no time to react when Alva's spear gun went *ka-ching,* no time to dodge as the spear penetrated both her forearms, pinioning her arms together as she gripped the ghost gun two-handed. The woman did not scream, she merely uttered a deep guttural grunt and spun to face Alva.

The ghost gun spun out of her hands, bounced off the bamboo floor and skidded toward Alva, who fielded it as cleanly as any major league shortstop. Alva did not take the time to marvel at the ghost gun's unique design; without a moment's hesitation, she squeezed off three rapid taps on the short free-standing trigger, resulting in three surprisingly quiet shots straight into the woman's face. As the second Tanner intruder pitched to the floor, Alva gave an anguished wail.

"Enough! I cannot take any more of all this!"

We—the Swiss guards, Alva and I—were circled around Mrs.

Tanner's body in the parking lot when Hannes roared up in his Russian Zil sedan and screeched to a stop in front of us. As he scrambled out, the guards came to attention with their hands clasped behind their backs, their heads hung.

Hannes was livid, totally out of control. *"Unglaublich!"* he screamed at his men. *"Scheiss dreck! Ganz weg vom fenster!"*

Alva looked at me for translation. "'Unbelievable, complete shit, you guys were totally out of it, totally out the window.'"

Hannes spun in a tight circle and slammed his hands down on the hood of the Zil. He inhaled deeply as he struggled to regain his composure, then looked at Alva and me and reverted to English.

"A rock climber! Dear God in heaven! Alva, Victor, I am so ashamed! There is no possible apology."

Alva stepped forward and put her hands on Hannes' shoulders. "Hush, Hannes. No apology is called for. We got outsmarted, that's all. None of us thought we'd have to protect ourselves against a *rock climber*. Thank God I had my trusty spear gun handy. Thank God that woman was blind in one eye. Yeah, from now on we're going to tighten up security, we're going to do better. Let's all just suck it in and get it together, okay?"

Captain Klaus Lindenmayer's lower lip was trembling, and his eyes glistened with tears.

Of course, Hannes wanted us to accompany him to the consulate and then catch the next plane out of Cape Verde. And, of course, Alva would not hear of it.

"I'm not ready to go yet, Hannes. I still need some more time to collect myself. Yes, I am now scared good and proper, and believe me, I am not taking this lightly. But I insist on staying in my own house until Victor and I have the whole sea cruise thing locked down. Until then the only question is whether we use guards I hire or continue to use your guys. Either way is okay with me, you make the call. I'm not out to bust Lindenmayer's ass or get his squad disciplined."

In the days after the attack, Alva seemed calm, cool and collected. I couldn't believe it. Not after witnessing her first anguished reactions to the Tanners' deaths.

As for me, this second intrusion compounded my conviction that the whole world had spun completely out of control and pulled me into synchronous orbit with it. Alva seemed to be holding it together for the moment, but now my wheels came off. In the days after the Swiss guard carted Mrs. Tanner's body away for invisible disposal, I found I could not settle myself. My hands now trembled constantly, my shoulders periodically shuddering with spastic heaves. I got diarrhea. I could not stand the slightest touch, rocketed to my feet at the slightest noise. I could not hold food down but still managed to drink myself into insensibility every night. And even then, I could not sleep. Victor Harding was suffering from sensory overload, and Victor Harding needed relief.

I began to research sailboats for purchase and charter, and burying myself in a topic I knew well and a world where I was on top of things, where I was in control. I found some nice boats in the Caribbean—all at truly extraordinary prices—and imagining myself at the helm or purchasing a lot of fancy equipment to outfit the boat helped to take the edge off. I was ready to get the hell out of Cape Verde.

Chapter Ten

Nuptials and Travel Plans

"So, Alva can we agree that it's finally time to pull freight?" I asked by way of pillow talk.

"Pull what?"

"Pull freight. Leave. Vamoose. Skedaddle."

"I'm working up to that conclusion," whispered Alva. "I've definitely got intruders on the mind. Who knows who else may be out for revenge? I think it's time to bite the bullet. I really have been thinking a lot about how to do this, Victor. I can install Artur and Gracia as interim tenants and have Hannes arrange to pay them a regular stipend to watch over the place."

"I've been thinking that maybe he could help us out another way, not just paying Artur and Gracia's rent."

"Like what?"

"Is Hannes licensed to perform marriages and issue Swiss passports?"

Alva burst into laughter. "Victor, what *are* you talking about?"

I rolled over and turned on the bedside lamp. "Okay, hear me out. We are going to do our sea cruise, right?"

"As far as I'm concerned."

"Okay, me too. But at some point, that cruise is going to be over. We get our boat over here, put it into charter, use the charter business to launder money. Or, if we decide to sell the boat, to launder the proceeds of the sale. But then what do we do? Do we just go our separate ways? Or revert to a strictly business relationship and conduct miscellaneous laundering transactions from opposite sides of the Atlantic?"

Alva's eyes opened wide, and she began blinking rapidly. I continued to pound on, aware I was plunging into deep water.

"Look, we've already agreed that you can't stay in Cape Verde, right? And even if we decide we want to explore being together in the long run, I'm sure as hell not going to take up permanent residence some place where assorted people keep showing up with guns."

"Explore being together in the long run?"

"Okay, okay, I know maybe this sounds wacko, but just *listen*. Am I safe in assuming that Alva Batek is on some FBI radar screen and customs and immigration watch list?"

"Probably a good bet."

"So Alva Batek cannot return to the U.S., not without creating some forged papers, which would add another crime to her existing list of crimes. But there's no reason why some little old lady holding a Swiss passport can't get a US tourist visa, right? And suppose that little old lady enters into a perfectly unremarkable late life marriage and changes her name, becoming, let's say, Brittany Harding. Or Courtney, or Tiffany."

"Victor, are you proposing to me?"

"I am proposing a green card marriage, one perhaps marked by true love—we'll know a lot more about that after a lengthy sailboat voyage. But also supported by simple expediency, as well as the opportunity, if you liked, to live out your days in Green Lake, Wisconsin in the bosom of a very offbeat family of philanthropists and criminals. Not to mention the embrace of your very offbeat semi-criminal daughter."

"Good God," whispered Alva Batek, her eyes glistening. "You're serious, aren't you?"

"That depends on where you and your head are. How does any of this sound to you?"

"Actually, it sounds heavenly."

———

As usual, Hannes Schlossberg could not have been more accommodating. An accomplished multi-tasker, he first assumed the role of Maître—that is, a Swiss lawyer—and produced an ironclad pre-nup agreement protecting both Alva's and my assets. He also agreed to serve as executor of both of our estates and assure that Alva's assets went to Delia and mine were split between Christine and Colin.

Next, as a Swiss banker with power of attorney, he took over financial management oversight of both Alva's and my new Cape Verde offshore accounts. After that, in his capacity as Swiss Consul, Hannes performed a brief civil marriage ceremony that united Alva Batek and me in wedlock legal in both Cape Verde and Switzerland.

In his capacity as magistrate, when it was time for Alva's legal name change, Hannes called for a time out, making a 'T' gesture with his hands.

"Alva, I don't know what you had in mind for your new married name, but I want to weigh in here. Perhaps you had something dramatic in mind, like Anastasia or Ermintrude, but I suggest you adopt a name that is very close to your present one. There may well come a time when you are confronted by some hostile authority figure. If, when asked your name under fraught circumstances, you hesitate or hem and haw for even a moment, you are going to trigger immediate suspicion.

"Let me suggest a name that is so close to your present one that it will trip easily off your tongue. And even if you trip up and say 'Alva' by mistake, it will sound so similar to your new adopted name that your slip won't be noticed. May I suggest that you become Elva or Ella Harding, or, at most distant, Ellen Harding. To a computer, the change of any single letter is of fundamental consequence, but to the human ear, the difference may be almost indistinguishable."

"You've done this before, haven't you, Hannes?" Alva laughed. "Let's go with Elva."

Hannes smiled warmly. "Having agreed on that, let me say that in other interactions you can use whatever name you want, but I know you as Alva, have always known you as Alva, and I'm going to call you Alva unless I'm called to testify in a court proceeding."

"Me too," I said. "You'll always be Alva to me. Unless a U.S. customs agent puts a gun to my head."

Hannes cracked his knuckles. "Okey-dokey, *alles in Ordnung.* Everything is in order. I will now don my Swiss Consul hat once again and issue a new Swiss passport to Mrs. Elva Harding."

Later, as he handed Alva the shiny red passport embossed with a gold Swiss flag, Hannes turned somber. "I must tell you, as a government official, that I do not like green card marriages."

Alva laughed. "Hannes, are you lecturing us on moral grounds?"

"No, my dear, I'm speaking on the grounds of risk to you and Victor both. As a general proposition, sham marriages are a *bad idea.* The U.S. immigration authorities take a very dim view of them, and not only could you both be subject to criminal charges, but Alva would be at serious risk of immediate deportation if the fiction is revealed. If those tight-asses suspect your marriage is a sham, they will investigate your life and your 'marriage' very tenaciously. They can be incredibly invasive. They'll badger your family, friends, employers, neighbors, *everybody,* asking if your marriage is the genuine article.

"In addition, to apply for a green card, you won't only have to produce a marriage certificate. They'll also want to see joint bank accounts, tax records, life insurance policies with each other as beneficiaries, family photos, and such like. And even if this 'Swiss lady' eventually is awarded U.S. citizenship, she would be forever at risk of losing that citizenship if the ruse is revealed."

"No problem," I said, a bit self-righteously. "Because it's *not* a sham marriage. It's a marriage of convenience. Something lonely older people often do to escape late life solitude. This is not some cash deal scam, Hannes. It's a way for us to be together legally in the United States. There's no predicting how long our marriage might last, but the plan is for us to live together in a family enclave. We are a group, moreover, that are more than a family. We also operate a variety of business enterprises together."

"Yeah, let the immigration Nazis investigate their asses off," said Alva. "This is about more than keeping up appearances. Victor and I will be living together as a couple in his house, socializing and celebrating holidays as a family, and going to the movies together. If we also spend our evenings grinding the numbers on our offshore accounts, that's nobody's business but our own."

Alva turned to me, smiling from ear to ear. "But it sure seems ironic, Victor. Here I am an American citizen chased out of the U.S. and now living in Cape Verde who is becoming a Swiss citizen in order to become a U.S. citizen with another name so that I can live in America. Ah, the things we do for love."

"Is that what we're calling it now?"

Chapter Eleven

DREAMBOAT

Before I departed Cape Verde for the Caribbean, I bought Alva an Iridium Extreme satellite telephone, complete with the Emergency Responder Package and a solar panel and an indestructible bright yellow Pelican carrying case.

"Not a very romantic wedding gift, Alva, but very practical both for our sailing adventures and for various other conversations we might want to remain confidential, if you catch my drift. This thing will bounce calls off marine satellites—not commercial telephone satellites—all around the world, and you'll be astonished at how clear the reception is. The subscription costs ninety-one dollars a month. I'll foot the bill."

"Oh, Victor!" Alva exclaimed and hugged me more tightly than I, a lifelong non-hugger, was comfortable with. "It's just the most *darling* present! That nice onyx-like black case on the phone, the cute little aerial, all the little LED numbers on the front, and that sweet yellow Pelican case that sets off my skin to such fine effect."

I smiled, having never had conversations like this before—silly, tender, deadly serious in their implication. "I trust we will put it to good use, Alva."

A week after she took me to the airport, I called Alva in the middle of the night on the satellite phone. It took her a long time to answer, because she had to figure out where the persistent buzzing was coming from. From the sound of it at my end, Alva fiddled with the phone until she finally pushed the receive button.

My voice echoed menacingly around Alva's room. *"This is the voice of doom."*

"No, it's *not!*" Alva giggled. "It's the voice of the first satellite phone call I have ever received. It has nothing whatever to do with doom."

"Hi, Alva," I said.

"Why are you calling me in the middle of the night, Victor?"

"I think I may have found it."

Alva obviously was not fully awake. "Found what?"

"Our dreamboat. Actually, a *most* interesting boat. Interesting history that suggests I can get it a great price."

"Where are you?"

"I am speaking to you from Curacao in the Netherlands Antilles. Just down the Caribbean from Aruba and Bonaire. Very Dutch. Nice Place."

"Okay, okay, I'm awake. Let me pour a glass of Lillet and get settled here. I'm going to want all the details."

"You got a computer handy?"

"Always, my dear, always. Presently covered with spread sheets, including current reports on your sixteen new offshore accounts with the Victor Kim Private Bank here in Cape Verde and your new master account at the Schadevogel Bank in Zurich. You're already doing quite nicely, I must say."

"Alva, pay attention. Screen up the site for Yachtworld. It's the world's biggest sailboat brokerage site and then enter *'Oyster 62.'* When you find the various listings for boats for sale, look up the one that says, 'to be auctioned by the Dutch Caribbean Coast Guard'."

I heard the click of Alva's keyboard. "Oyster 62. Sounds like an aphrodisiac or a French champagne. Let me see here, I'm just...*holy shit!"*

"Pretty nice, hunh?"

"Victor, it's gorgeous...but it's *huge!* Isn't that way too big for us?"

"Remember, Alva, that we will have a crew of four—you, me, Colin, and Delia. That's enough to set proper watches without wearing anyone out. As for the sailing part, it will not be too big, not after I install electric winches, electric sail-handling equipment, a couple of auto-pilots, satellite-linked navigational chart plotters, and a major-league computer with complete redundancy. That and a bunch of other stuff."

"And is our...*crew* going to be able to manage this thing even in rough weather?"

"Yep. I have every confidence. Oysters are known to be very sea-kindly."

"Why does it have two steering wheels?"

"It has two *helms,* Alva, because when a boat is heeling it is much easier to steer from the high side, the side the wind is coming from. Now, Alva, go to the pictures on the site and look at the interior pictures, see what real sailboat luxury looks like."

Victor heard Alva gasp. "My God! It's beautiful! Is that maple woodwork?"

"Yep. Many Oysters are built with mahogany interiors, but this was a full custom job. Maple, with rosewood inlays."

"God, look at the living room!"

"We call it the main salon, Alva, although some people call it the saloon. And that 'office' you see next to the full queen-size bed in the master stateroom is the navigation station. And how do you like the galley? Full stainless appliances, double oven, microwave, air fryer, dishwasher, the works. Three heads—that's bathrooms—separate shower stalls, washer and dryer. All the comforts of home."

"My, my, *my*. What year is this thing?"

"2014. Actually, it's sixty-three feet long, not sixty-two. Fifty-five-foot waterline. Eighteen-foot beam. Draft eight and a half feet. Displacement 71,000 pounds, Ballast is…"

"*Victor.*" Alva cut me off. "Victor, stop. Except for the length, all those numbers mean nothing to me. Tell me something I can relate to, something that *matters.*"

"Okay, *okay*" I said testily. "This is a very high-end English boat. It was custom-built for an extremely wealthy casino owner. Oysters come in various colors. This one's white. Not as sexy as the black ones, but it doesn't show dirt."

I waited for a laugh, got none. "This boat is luxurious, inside and out. All its fittings and equipment are absolutely the best there are., and by the time we set sail, I will have equipped it with every safety feature known to God and man. Top of the line in all respects. High-quality six-man life raft—the best of the best, six different EPIRBs..."

"What's an EPIRB?" Alva cut in.

"Stands for *emergency position-indicating radio beacon.* It's a kind of broadcast radio beacon. When an EPRIB is triggered, *everybody* receives the signal—coast guards, airplanes flying overhead, land stations, other boats. Believe me, the cavalry mounts up pronto. Very reassuring item of gear to have on board, gets the good guys to come save your ass.

"And best of all, we also have Oscar."

"Who's Oscar?"

"Oscar isn't a he, it's an *it.* It's a brand-new bit of safety technology I helped to prototype. Oscar is a state-of-the-art marine collision-avoidance system, an automated monitoring system whose 'eyes' are thermal and color cameras positioned on the top of the mast. They feed information about what they 'see' to a computer 'brain' down at the nav station powered by artificial intelligence."

"Is it like radar or sonar or something?"

"Completely different. We'll also have both radar and sonar aboard, but unlike them, Oscar does not send out a signal that bounces back. It actually is more like a super-sophisticated camera that constantly takes pictures in real time and compares what it's seeing with a library of stored images."

"Images of what?"

"Well, primarily images of water under different conditions. Oscar has millions of 'pictures' of all kinds of wind, wave and water already loaded, so it can identify any condition it's seeing.

"Oscar also captures pictures of a lot of the crap that's floating in the water— rafts of floating sea weed, logs, derelict or unlit boats, containers that have fallen off cargo ships, sleeping whales, anything floating that neither radar nor sonar will detect. When it comes to identifying what it is seeing, particularly things that are dangerous, Oscar just keeps getting smarter and smarter."

"Okay, I'm stoked. This is all pretty amazing. So, what's this dreamboat likely to cost us?"

"At brokerage, Oyster sixty-twos in good condition, say 2004 or 2005, go for between eight hundred grand and a million. A good 2014? Between one-and-a-half and two million.

"But this boat was confiscated by the Dutch Coast Guard, and it has a checkered background. It was previously used by a cartel to transport drugs. So this is a distress sale, We might be able to steal it for six. We stick a buck-fifty worth of equipment into it, and we have a hell of a boat for seven-fifty or so. I'm off to talk to the Dutch Caribbean Coast Guard this morning, see if they'll consider a behind-the-barn deal, a pre-emptive bid. Saves them the hassle of conducting an auction. No harm in trying."

"None, indeed. That's been my motto for my entire life. Good night, my dear. This has been fun."

The following night, Alva's satellite phone again rang in the middle of the night.

"I won't keep you long." I'm sure Alva could hear the excitement in my voice.

"What's up?"

"*We got it.* No auction will be needed. The Dutch Coast Guard is pleased to be spared the cost of doing further advertising and then conducting the auction."

"What's it going to cost us?"

"Five forty-five, plus a $30,000 'private expedited-service fee,' payable in cash."

"That's *outrageous*. Only five forty-five? Victor, you go back and pay that man a bigger bribe so that no one has a chance to trump our ace."

"Yeah, I'm outraged, all right. Worry not, Alva. The deal's locked in, deposit paid, bribe already handed over in cash. I've got a good feeling about this boat. Just one thing."

"A problem?"

"Not really, but the boat is presently named *Lucifer*. Yuck. I know it's considered bad luck to change a boat's name, but we gotta change this boat's name. Alva, think of something."

Chapter Twelve

CUT TO CURACAO

Alva Batek stepped through the customs doorway at the Curacao International Airport, looking for me. She scanned the waiting crowd, and when she did not see me, a *frisson* of annoyance washed over her face. This family gathering was supposed to be a big deal. *The great sea cruise embarkation.* Then, among the throng dressed in shorts and short-sleeved shirts, Alva saw a strangely familiar figure—a woman dressed in a long red cloak that draped to the floor, with a dramatic hood shadowing and completely hiding her face. She was holding a hand-lettered sign that said, 'Mrs. Elva Harding.'

"Surprise," called Delia. "Hi, Mom. Welcome to family time in Curacao."

"Don't get too comfortable in these fancy digs, y'all," I said across the dinner table, "unless, Christine and Cara, you want to stay here awhile after Alva, Delia, Collie and I sail off across the ocean. All the hard-goods provisioning is complete, and I'm having the perishables delivered the day after tomorrow. All our additions and alterations to the boat are done except for gold-leafing the new name on the transom."

"Which is…," asked Cara.

"Well, we immediately bagged the existing name, *Lucifer*. The fewer associations we have with the devil, the better."

"So, what is it going to be now?" Cara pressed.

I nodded to Alva. *Your reveal.*

"Well, Victor and I were having a tiff in which he was displaying his customary arrogance. I told him to get the fuck down off his high horse. He said, 'I damn well will stay up on my high horse as long as I want.' We looked at each other, then broke into laughter. 'I think that's it,' Victor said. '*High Horse* it is, I said.'"

"Check." This was Alva, deadpan.

"What? *No way!*" This was Collie, in response to being humiliated once again.

"Actually, I see I was wrong," said Alva. "It's not check, it's *checkmate*. I overlooked my bishop parked over in the corner. The king is dead, long live the king."

"Damn it, Alva, you are *cruel*. You should let your opponents win every once in a while, just to preserve their self-esteem."

"That's not the way I play. I warned you, Collie. I don't play charity chess."

Collie stood and looked out at the torrential rain pouring down on our veranda. "I'm not having fun," he whinged, swinging his arms theatrically. "Who wants to be trapped inside in a hotel in Curacao?"

Two hands shot up. Cara and Christine were reclining on our luxurious couch, content to lounge and read. I was sitting at the dining table, tinkering with the ghost gun.

"Colin, come over here and check this thing out. It really is an ingenious piece of work. Look how easily it breaks down, like one of those wooden Chinese puzzles. Just push this little square button on the bottom, and everything slides open. *Good engineering.*" "What's the big deal? A gun made to look like a bar of soap. Oh, my, smite me dead."

"Jest all you want, you jerk, but this gun is really clever. Look at how the whole handle swings up against the bottom of the frame to cover the trigger, so there's no need for a trigger guard. And look how the magazine ejects straight out the back. And she managed to make it a nine-millimeter. Man, that's a feat! This 'bar of soap' has a lot of stopping power, Collie. Useful little self-defense piece. Only one problem."

"That being?"

"We don't have any ammo for it. All Mrs. Tanner's bullets ended up in her face."

"Well, just buy some more. Must be a sporting goods store around in downtown Curacao somewhere, and nine-millimeter is a real common load."

Delia stood and sidled over to the table. "What are you going to do with it?"

"Well, I've been thinking about that. I think we should keep it. Keep it concealed, but hold on to it in case of emergency. Another form of self-protection for one of us. You know, *'Casper the friendly ghost gun.'*"

Everyone laughed.

"The question is who wants to carry it?"

"Well, count me out," said Alva. "To me it's just a little homemade toy likely to go off by accident and blow someone's genitals off. Besides, my recent experience with guns—with *this* gun, actually—has not been pleasant."

Colin was starting to speak when Delia cut him off. "I'll take it. I want it."

"Well, maybe *I'd* like it," he snapped. "Why do you always have to get *your* way?"

"Momentum," said Delia, and picked up the gun. "In life, Colin, if you push, you win. Besides, you're the one who was just ridiculing this 'bar of soap,' you turkey. Me and Casper the friendly ghost gun gonna live together."

Collie's pout was almost ludicrous. He looked like a ten-year-old who didn't get the bicycle he wanted for Christmas. "Well, what about the other guy's gun? Where's that?"

"I threw it over the cliff," I said matter-of-factly.

"Why in the world did you do that? That would be much better protection than this fucking bar of soap."

"It seemed like the thing to do at the time. Call it an act of passion."

"Well, did you ever think that I might want it?"

"No, I did not think that you might want it, that any of us would want it. But Collie, if you want to climb down to the bottom of the cliff to retrieve it, it's all yours."

In addition to all the gear for boaters, swimmers, and outdoor party animals, the Camping World store in Curacao was outfitted just like the one in Oshkosh, Wisconsin—right down to the kayaks, canoes, tents, hunting boots, plaid wool shirts and an entire room filled with all kinds of firearms. Delia stood next to Collie, shaking her head dismissively. "Boys and their toys," she sniffed.

"This coming from someone who charges those same boys two hundred thousand bucks for a piece of fancy costume jewelry," I responded, which earned me a painful noogie on my upper arm.

Collie immediately began eyeing a used Sig Sauer nine-millimeter, and I brought him down to earth. "You couldn't carry this, Collie. Wouldn't make it through airport security. Besides, we already have two guns on the boat, dad's old Luger, which I have concealed under the chart table drawer, and the stainless-steel Ruger carbine hidden in the lazarette. I think we've got enough firepower."

We did buy a twelve-pack of nine-millimeter parabellum rounds, and Collie was just about to buy a miniature cleaning kit for the ghost gun when I stopped him. "No point, Collie," I said. "By the time that gun's been fired enough times to need cleaning, all the heat from firing it will have begun to melt its plastic innards. We fire it maybe ten times and it's time to throw it away. Meanwhile, the question is, where does Delia conceal it? If a situation comes up where she actually needs it, you know she's gonna get searched."

"I've been thinking about that," said Collie. "I was looking at all the various kinds of Pelican cases they carry here—specialized cases for carrying your guns, cases for photographers, cases to carry delicate instruments, the works. I see they even have a case for emergency responders with a three-level, organizing tray that looks sort of like a fishing tackle box. A lot of little compartments, just perfect for all that indispensable shit women carry—sunscreen, deodorant, skin products, dental floss, mascara, tampons, meds, Preparation H."

Delia laughed. "As I've said many times before, Collie, you really are an asshole."

"No, really. We could buy one of those EMS cases to make Delia a rough-tough ocean-going toiletries case, cut a square in its foam bottom to fit our ghost gun, then drop the EMS insert on top of it. Unlikely a searcher would lift all those partitions out to search for a false bottom, right?"

"Ingenious," I said.

"Overkill," said Delia.

"You got a better idea, Miss I-know-everything?"

"Well, certainly simpler. And a *lot* cheaper."

"Enlighten us," said Collie sourly.

"I already have a flexible, clear plastic toiletries bag with a zipper top. You can see everything that's in it just by holding it up and looking at it. Don't need to dig through a lot of compartments. We simply add one more item that can be seen in plain sight."

I did my patented gimme-gimme gesture.

"A box of tampons. Me, I use the Tampax Pearl eighteen-count box. Throw a few out, and *shazam!* Just the right size for Casper the friendly ghost gun. Tell me, Victor, what color is a box of Tampax?"

"Blue, with white letters."

"See? Everybody in the whole world, males included, already knows what a box of Tampax looks like, and no male enjoys handling feminine care products, right? So, our hypothetical searcher—who's likely to be a guy and likely to be in a hurry—sees the blue-and-white box in my see-through toiletries bag and doesn't figure it's hiding a firearm. Highly likely he doesn't even unzip the bag and rummage around in there, because he can see there's no gun in there. I think this is a better plan."

"Checkmate," I said.

Chapter Thirteen

High Horse Meets Eamon Armagh

Mickey Chung straightened up from his crouch on *High Horse's* stern boarding platform and looked down to admire his work. "Aw done now, Missa Harding," he called down the aft hatchway. "Dissa first-class job, you bet. In two-hour, gold leaf—*gode reef*—be all dry and hard. Last forevah."

I eased myself out of the aft stateroom, climbed up through the recessed cockpit, clambered across the plush cushions in the helm station, and eased myself down next to Mickey on the boarding platform.

"Mr. Chung, that is very, very fine work. I hope you won't mind if I add a bonus to your fee."

Mickey Chung feigned modesty. "Oh, no, Missa Harding, I cudnah possibee take no tip…" Then he broke into a broad grin. "Hah! I joking!" he cackled. "Gimme da money! I love money!"

I clapped him on the back and straightened just as Alva, Delia at her side, called down from the parking lot overlooking the pier where *High Horse* bobbed quietly in regal splendor. "Victor! Collie! The truck is here with the last of the fresh provisions! Will you help me wheel all this stuff down?"

As I prepared to hop off the boat and grab a couple of dock carts, I was approached by a genial-looking middle-aged carrot top in sailing shorts. He was trim, with liberally freckled, hairy legs—red hair, naturally—protruding from his cargo shorts, large hands, an easy smile, a bristling shock of bright red hair sticking out from under a green baseball cap with 'Eire' embroidered on it in white script. The collar of his dark blue polo shirt had been neatly pressed and his horn-rimmed glasses were clean. All in all, he looked very put together. He spoke with a distinct Irish brogue. "Permission to step aboard, sir?"

Apparently, my impatience showed, because the man shrugged apologetically. "So sorry to bother you—I hate it when people think they can invade others' privacy whenever they have a mind to—but may I ask what that chap is doing up at the top of your mast?"

A fast way to build rapport with me is to talk tech, and I beckoned for the man to join me in the cockpit. Together we peered up at the rigger dangling in a bosun's chair at the top of *High Horse's* eighty-six-foot mast. "He's just finishing an Oscar installation," I said, as if this was the most common activity in the world.

"An Oscar! I heard about them for the first time just a couple of months ago. I had no idea what they looked like."

"Well, thar she blows," I smiled. "State of the art, at least until next week when some new iteration renders it obsolete. Still, this model will be enough for us once I add a supplemental transponder that will allow us to be tracked wherever we go. I'm Victor Harding, by the way."

"Eamon Armagh. Great pleasure to meet you. So, Oscar stands guard for you 24/7?"

"If I have it turned on, yes, and I intend to keep it turned on."

"How's it work?" Armagh continued to stare at the shiny globe at top of the mast.

I gave him the same wonders-of-Oscar lecture I'd given Alva.

"Wow," said Armagh. "Talk about buying some peace of mind. I had never heard about anything like this, and I've been a sailor for years."

"Well, this just came on the market in the last couple of years. After I closed down my architecture practice and hooked up with a couple ex-Raytheon guys, I gave them the performance parameters, and they dove into the tech. First version was developed for round-the-world offshore racers. If one of those boats hits anything at twenty knots, the results could be catastrophic. We'll only be sailing seven or eight knots on *High Horse,* but we'd still rather not hit anything, ever."

The redhead cocked his head, smiled warmly. *"High Horse.* Now there's a nice name."

"Thank my wife for that. It's her description of my mental attitude. That's her and my sister-in-law up there in the parking lot, waiting for me to lug boxes of produce."

"Well, I shan't keep you, but I must say I'm mightily impressed with your *High Horse.* I've been admiring it for several days now, and the harbormaster says soon you will be gone, so if I wanted to see it up close, I'd have to act fast. Besides this Oscar machine, looks like you've got nothing but the best aboard—bigger winches, Seago life raft, Brooks & Gatehouse autopilot. Man, you don't fool around when you're paging through the equipment catalog."

I felt a rush of pride. Nothing like being praised by an expert.

"And lots of good stuff below, too. Five supplemental EPIRBs, inflatable collision mats, Helly Hansen full flotation suits, even a Kifco diesel water pump. That was twenty grand all by itself."

"Wow," said Armagh. "Redundancy upon redundancy."

"You can't be too careful, or too prepared for the unexpected."

"Indeed. That's a heavy-duty bit of kit you've put on your fine boat. May I ask where you're sailing off to? Looks like you're provisioning for some serious voyaging."

"Tut, tut, Mr. Armagh. Not an appropriate inquiry in a foreign country. No offense."

"None taken. Sorry to be nosy. But before I head off, might I take just a quick peep below? This is such an exquisite boat."

"I must disappoint on that score as well, Mr. Armagh. First of all, we've got supplies and provisions spread all over down below and we're still mapping out storage plans and diagrams. Second, and I hope this doesn't seem rude, I make a point of never letting people I do not know down below. I hope you understand."

"I respect your caution, Mr. Harding. Can't be too careful these days."

"I can tell you this. Except that it's finished in maple rather than mahogany, our interior is just like any other Plan B Oyster 62. You can see what we look like just by looking up any old Oyster 62 brokerage listing."

"I shall do that!" said Armagh brightly. "Thank you for your time and hospitality, Mr. Harding. If our paths cross again, I hope you'll let me buy you and Mrs. Harding a drink. Ta!"

Armagh climbed from the cockpit and strode away down the dock, a distinct roll to his gait.

This guy spends a lot of time on boats, I thought, as I wheeled two dock carts—pushing one and pulling the other—up to where Alva and Delia stood surrounded by boxes of various shapes and sizes.

"Who was that?" asked Alva. Her tone was not warm.

"Some Irish guy. Interested in Oscar."

"What did you tell him?"

I bristled. "I told him about Oscar."

"Did you tell him anything about us or our plans?"

"I did not. He asked to look below, and I said no. Politely, but firmly. Look, Alva, we're justified in being on our guard. Still, he seemed like a nice enough fellow."

"Frankly, even looking at him from a distance, he made me a little uncomfortable," said Alva. "Reminded me of that old Bob Dylan song, the one that goes *And you know something's happening, but you don't know what it is, do you, Mr. Jones.*"

It's not often one sees Delia Chamberlain at a loss for words, so I found her shock and awe gratifying when she first climbed down into *High Horse's* salon.

"Holy fucking Jesus."

"I gather that means you find our boat...acceptable."

"My God, Victor, it is simply *gorgeous*. You said most Oyster 62s were finished in mahogany. This isn't mahogany. Or ash."

"No, it's light maple. Custom order. Probably cost the buyer an extra fifty grand. The buyer, rich Bolivian dude, also ordered custom upholstery, custom sheets and bedspreads, and custom LED lighting, not to mention major upgrades on all the technology. Buyer also installed a custom galley, basically a full gourmet kitchen—and yes, those are granite countertops."

Chapter Fourteen

RULES, ROLES AND RESPONSIBILITIES

"Y'all, I would like you to grab a beverage of your choice and join me around the salon table. Time to go to school."

I had stacked the four binders in the middle of the table—the blue one, the white one, the red one, and the black one, parked next to a thick green book.

"What are these?" asked Collie.

"These," I said, perhaps rather too proudly, are 'what's what,' 'where's where,' and 'how's how' of *High Horse*. While we are going to be sailing this boat, we also are going to be *running* this boat, tending this boat, navigating this boat, feeding ourselves on this boat, and washing our underpants on this boat.

"Consider this meeting 'High Horse 101.' You will get whatever further instruction you need—and, if you're interested, any other instruction you want—when we're out there on the open ocean. You all ready?"

I was pleased there were no wisecracks or rolling eyes. It was time to get down to business.

"First of all, the binders, which are going to be kept in the shelf above the chart table. The blue one is our equipment inventory and manuals. In there I have indexed all our ship's mechanical and electrical systems and their instruction manuals. In the back pocket are all the warranties, purchase information, and like that. This binder will make lots of good reading for your spare time. I am available for tutorials.

"The white one is our provisions list—canned, dry, frozen for our freezer, fresh and liquids. This will have to be kept up date as we plan meals and consume supplies. There is a cabinet diagram in there for where we'll store provisions. We'll probably do a big restock in Barbados before the big pull across the Atlantic to the Republic of Cabo Verde.

"The red binder is our maintenance log—what items get scheduled, tended to, repaired, replaced, or maintained. This covers everything on board that does something. The sails, the engine, the winches, the controls, the instruments, the kitchen appliances. *High Horse* is in good shape and should not require a lot repairs, but there is a good bit of routine upkeep and cleaning up. A clean ship is a happy ship, and all that.

"Finally, the black binder is the ship's log. At all points, we're going to know where we're going, where we are, where we've been and everything that happened while we were doing all that. If you're asking how we know that, the answer is simple: our GPS—global positioning system. I, and I alone, will maintain the log, and I also will be navigating manually, using charts. You are welcome to read the log whenever you want, but please do not make any entries without asking me.

"I am not out to win the Captain Bligh award, but if I make a request—let's not call it an order—please take it as more than a casual suggestion. There will be times when responding quickly and without a lot of questions might be very important. Also, in talking to authorities, other boats, vendors and suchlike, I speak for the boat. It's not helpful to have a lot of different voices.

"As for maintenance, Collie, I'm putting you charge of that. We can collaborate on planning and priorities, but the hands-on work will be largely yours unless you need multiple pairs of hands.

"Now, eating. We're not going to do hardtack and sea biscuit. We are provisioned to eat well and drink well. Because I have a lot of experience with long ocean cruises, I did the provisioning for our first leg, food and drink. But I didn't know your tastes, so I played it conservative. Now is the time to state preferences and make requests, so we can eat the stuff we really like. This trip is supposed to be fun.

"Look, I don't mean to be a sexist pig, but I am not a very good cook, and, having lived with him, I can tell you Collie isn't either. Delia, let me ask if you and Alva can team on food planning and preparation, at least for major meals. The men—meaning whatever man is off-watch—will clean up and do the dishes.

I picked up the green book. "This is *Cooking at Sea,* written about thirty years ago by Barton Priebe. It is unquestionably the greatest nautical cookbook ever published. Great recipes and desserts, also great tips."

I pulled a piece of paper out from Priebe's inside cover and handed it to Alva, who solemnly read out a list of handy tips as if she were the town crier.

Collie had finished his second beer and was fidgeting.

"One more item, and then we're done," I said. "Before we go anywhere on the open ocean, we need to get our ducks in a row about setting watches. We've all have to get into a regular routine."

Delia showed me that million-dollar smile of hers. "Is this like all that six bells and eight bells and yo-ho-ho stuff they're always talking about in those pirate movies about the Spanish main?"

"Well, yes and no. A crew of four people will stand two-person watches, alternating every four hours. Alva, I choose you as my watch partner. Collie, you and Delia will work together.

"Okay," I said, "one last thing."

"That being…?"

"Our extra crew member. The autopilot."

"Like on an airplane?"

"Really quite different, Collie. On *High Horse,* it's basically just an electronic steering machine that will hold the boat on any course you set it for. If the boat begins to stray off course, the autopilot steers it back. I'll show you how to use it. Easy-peasy. It's not infallible, so you still always have to have somebody near the helm, but it does spare the helmsman from having to steer all the time.

"Helmsperson." Alva again.

"I stand corrected."

Chapter Fifteen

WATCH THIS

"Okay, guys" I said. "Time to get to business. Transmission in neutral?"

Collie laughed, slightly too loudly, I thought. "I don't know nothin' 'bout no transmission, Mr. Down-to-business. But the gear lever there is in the middle of the…thingy, so I'm guessing the *sailboat's* in neutral."

Delia gave Collie a fierce noogie to his upper arm, and he recoiled in pain. "Let's get serious, mister clown show."

Collie and Delia had been on each other's cases ever since they arrived in Curacao, sometimes in jolly jest, equally often with real barbs attached. I was getting sick of the friction.

"Collie, when I call out, '*Now,*' move the gear level to forward and turn the helm slightly to port—not too much, please. As the boat edges away from the dock, I'll cast off the stern line and hop aboard. We will all then be voyaging. *Ta-da!*"

Alva tore off her broad-brimmed sun hat, waved it gaily, and gave out a loud whoop. "Oh, Victor! I…am…so…*excited!* Here we go!"

As we passed Sabana Westpunkt on the tip of Curacao three miles to port, I called out to Delia, who was seated behind *High Horse's* windward helm, "Time for some basic on-the-job training, folks. Some equipment and operational techniques we've got to get you up to speed on."

Alva pinched her face into a pout. "Oh, don't be a drag, Victor. We're all just settling in."

"Well, *unsettle*. This boat is no Dragon-class day sailor, Alva, and there is some very important stuff you need to know, some skills you all need to try. This lesson is not optional."

Delia flipped me off and crossed her arms over her chest. The rest of the crew sat politely as I showed them the ropes…also the sails, the sheets, the instruments, the two helms, the winches and winch handles, and all the other stuff on deck.

"Tomorrow, I'll take you below and teach you all the electronics and navigation equipment. We need to get to the point where everybody can do everything, if only to save your own neck."

Now I said. "Later on, I am going to show you how to deploy the life raft, which is in the white hard-shell case up there just behind the mast. It's easy, because it has to be. Gotta be able to abandon ship in a hurry if need be."

Alva shivered and smiled wanly. "I just hope I never have to be with you in that raft. Bobbing around in an orange bathtub with a tent on top is not my idea of fun."

———

In a vinyl pocket next to the huge Barient main winch was a heavy tool, perhaps twenty inches long, brightly polished with two black handles mounted one over the other. Collie pulled it out and examined it. "What's this thing?"

"A double-grip winch handle. For the big primary winches, although it will also fit all our other deck winches."

Collie hefted it. "God, it weighs a ton. But it doesn't look like the winch handles I saw on sale in the marina store. They just had one handle."

"If you're ever going to be hand-cranking our big Barient primary winches, you're going to need two hands."

"But our winches are all electric."

"Belt and suspenders, Collie. If we should ever lose electric power to our sail handling equipment, we still need a way to trim the sails."

Collie grabbed the two handles and swung the winch handle in a circle over his head.

"Careful!" I warned. "You clonk someone on the head with that thing, and there's going to be a fractured skull."

"Sorry," muttered Collie sheepishly and slipped that handle back into its pouch. "But God, Victor, This boat is such a *beast*. And everything on it is...*beastly big.*"

"Do you regret coming on this trip with us?"

"*Hell, no!* I love everything about it. It all just takes some getting used to, that's all."

"And we're going to spend considerable time getting you used to it. Next time we dock, I'm going to give everyone a full orientation of all the boat's equipment and systems. I want to show you how our chart plotter and radar work, get you up to speed on all the radios, teach you how the inflatable emergency collision mats work. If for some reason I'm incapacitated, our survival may depend on your knowing how to do all this stuff. Am I scaring you?"

"Yeah," interjected Delia, "but it's good scary. I know we can't be complacent and simply rely on you to do everything. Especially if a whale eats you and we have to do everything ourselves."

"That's the spirit. Good on you. Good girl."

"Do not, I repeat, *do not*...ever call me a girl."

I put my serious sailor face on. "Let's ease off to a close reach. Alva, why don't you take the helm from Delia? No point bashing our brains out beating close-hauled to windward."

"But I love bashing my brains out! The pounding, the spray, this wonderful giant just muscling her way through. Makes me feel like I'm the captain of the universe."

"Well, captain," I said, "may I tell you something in all seriousness?"

Her face clouded.

"No, no, this is *good*. I'm not about to dump on you. I must say that I think you have the makings of a very good sailor, a real natural. When we were sailing around on the Dragon, you showed a sensitive feel for the wind and seas and a really superb touch on the helm. I very much enjoy watching you sail."

Alva beamed, leaned over and gave me a peck on the lips.

"Sometimes you're sweet. Have you noticed anything else about me?"

"Uh, no. People don't notice what they don't notice."

"Well, mister wise-ass, you should have noted that I do not tend to get seasick, at least not so far. I don't think you have to worry much about me turning green and barfing all over the place."

"I had indeed failed to observe that, Alva, but I am happy to hear it—if it proves true in heavy weather. It's a drag to sail a boat all by yourself for a couple days while your crew is lying groaning in their bunks."

Chapter Sixteen

MOTION ON THE OCEAN

"Alva, Delia, do you see that dark band over there?"

"Sort of nasty-looking, I'd say."

"What you're seeing there is a squall line. It is a line of storms—often thunderstorms—that boils up at the leading edge of a cold front. It means we've got about fifteen minutes before some serious weather kicks us in the teeth."

"Should we go down below?"

"I would recommend just the opposite. Let's all get our safety harnesses and rain jackets on, clip our safety lines to the binnacle, and wait to see if this is going to become anything serious. I'll stay at the helm."

Alva turned to me from her perch deep in the leeward cockpit. "Why don't we just go down where it's nice and dry, make a batch of sangria, and wait for whatever kind of storm this is to just blow through?"

"First of all, if this front produces big waves and steep crests, you're going to get thrown around plenty down below. Feel like you're inside a kettle drum. There are better handholds up here than down there. I think more people get injured belowdecks than they do on deck.

"Equally important, guys, so far, all of you have shown yourselves to be relatively impervious to sea-sickness, but you haven't really been tested yet. If this squall turns into a gale, I guarantee that you will be tested. The best trick for avoiding seasickness is to keep your eyes firmly on the distant horizon.

You can't do that while vomiting your guts out down below in the head."

Alva clapped her hands in frustration. "You told me this boat was going to be safe!"

I stepped behind Alva as she stood at the helm and enfolded her in my arms. "It *is* safe, my dear seagoing rookie," I said softly. "This boat is not going to sink. But that doesn't mean that things aren't going to get rough."

"How rough?" whimpered Alva.

"Probably not very," I said, now looking at the squall line through the binoculars. "There's a long fetch between swells, and the wave crests don't seem to be stacking up. That suggests that there's not a lot of wind, so maybe we won't get thrown around too much.

"Here's the part you may not like. The waves are coming at us from the forward quarter—at a diagonal from the port bow. If this storm heats up, that means the boat is going to corkscrew through the waves. If you've ever seen any of those World War II newsreels of destroyers fighting their way through steep bow swells in the Atlantic, you've seen what the worst may be like."

"Victor, you are scaring the shit out of me." This was Delia.

"I'm not trying to scare you. I'm trying to teach you what you might expect. And I've changed my mind. Alva, I want you to stay at the helm as we move into this storm. After I reef the main and furl the jib down to a little storm trysail, I'll come back here and stand right behind you. I want you to experience steering in a squall, but I don't expect you to weather a storm by yourself. Maybe this squall will blow right through, and you can handle the boat until it passes. If this thing lasts awhile, don't worry—I'll certainly spell you."

"As I believe I've mentioned before, Victor Harding, you can be such an asshole."

"And you, Alva Batek Harding, are an asshole's first mate. Now go and get your foulies and your safety harness on. This is going to be great training."

The cloud front proved to be a short, severe squall, not a protracted storm or a gale or any other major weather feature. Alva stayed at the wheel for three hours in soaking rain with water cascading off her sou' wester rain hat and foul weather gear as *High Horse* danced through a bank of thunderstorms. Almost immediately, she realized how the boat wanted to move—how to keep it from ramming its bow straight into an oncoming wave, how to ease the boat off the wind with each wave until the bow lifted smoothly and the body of the wave slid under the hull.

Alva not only did not get seasick, she soon relaxed her iron grip on the helm and let her body go with the flow. She began to smile, then to grin. She was *loving* this roller-coaster ride. Given all the pitching and rolling, for my part, I was feeling more than a little queasy, although I kept lunch down and managed to disguise the flip-fops in my stomach. The squall abated abruptly, although the swells continued to surge under us, sending *High Horse* galloping forward, then easing the boat back, then throwing it forward again.

"You want me to take the helm?" I asked.

"No, I'm fine. But if you wanted to crack a fine Bordeaux, that sure would be nice."

"Amen." That was Delia.

As I sat opposite her in the cockpit during our watch the following morning, it appeared to me that Alva, now perched comfortably behind the helm, was experiencing a moment of deep peace. The sun had not yet crested the eastern horizon, but the buttery glow of imminent sunrise now limned the dark line that separated sea from sky. *High Horse* was not completely becalmed, but rather was tip-toeing gently across a mirror-smooth ocean, the swish of flowing water a soft susurrus along the side of the hull. Occasionally the autopilot made a soft *brrr, brrr* sound as it made small corrections to *High Horse's* course. The knotmeter on the console said we were headed toward Aruba at all of one-and-a-half knots.

All this was fine: it allowed Alva an easy extra hour on watch, had meant an extra hour of off-watch time for Delia and Collie. I was pleased: *Things are going well,* I thought. *We are settling in quite nicely. Collie is not acting out as much as he did when we first left Curacao, has backed off on the sarcasm that is so typical of him whenever he is unsure of himself.*

Then, just as the dawning sun peeped over the horizon, our quiet solitude was interrupted by an urgent electrical alarm, a sound that sounded just like the *Meep! Meep!* call of the Road Runner character in the old Warner Brothers cartoons. I had instructed everyone about what this sound meant.

Alva shot to her feet. "Victor! Victor! Oscar alarm! Oscar alarm!" I watched her whirl around in a circle, looking for whatever had triggered Oscar's warning. At first neither of us saw anything. Then, far off the starboard bow, we saw a dark area on the horizon.

As we stared harder, the dark spot became several spots, then more spots, and then the spots became low, glistening domes. Alva grabbed our fancy gyro-stabilized binoculars from their rack on the binnacle and adjusted the focus.

"Victor! Whales! A pod of whales!"

"Collie! Delia!" I yelled. "Come up on deck, you're going to want to see this!"

As they came up, I ducked down below to see what was appearing on Oscar's screen, then came back up and stood beside Alva, draping my arm reassuringly over her shoulders.

"Let me see those binoculars," I said calmly. "Yep. Large pod, and they're headed toward us. And I can see at least one calf. No, there's another. Oscar is identifying them as humpbacks—isn't it amazing that this machine can do *that,* that from its library of images it can determine what breed a whale is from a mile and a half away?

"Alva," I said, "fire up the diesel, but leave it idling in neutral. I want to be able to motor away from them if we have to, but I don't want to startle them with prop noise if I don't have to. For the moment, let's just move the helm to starboard and see if we can ease away from them under sail."

With all four of us now on deck, for several minutes we sailed slowly in complete silence. Now we could hear the chatter of the gulls flying over the pod, could see the flashes of white as the gulls dove and climbed and dove again, begging scraps of krill that spilled from the humpbacks' gaping maws. "It looks like they're having a picnic!" Delia chirped gleefully.

Suddenly a dark, pointed snout emerged from the surface in the middle of the pod, followed by a huge gray mass glistening in the rays of the early morning sun. This strange shape, which resembled a granite obelisk like the Druids might have carved, rose higher and higher until it stopped, motionless, its tip perhaps fifteen feet out of the water. Then at its base a huge dark eye blinked.

Alva recoiled in horror. "Victor! *What in God's name…?*"

"That's a humpback, all right, probably a bull, and this move is called spy-hopping. Orcas, gray whales and humpbacks all do it. Basically, he's coming up to have a look around."

"Can it see when its eyes are out of the water?"

"*Oh, yeah*. Whales are color blind, but they see as well in open air as they do underwater."

"Well, what's he *doing?*"

I lowered my voice, as if maybe the whale could hear me. "He's trying to figure out if we're friend or foe. Whether we're a threat to those calves."

Slowly, slowly, the whale's massive head began to sink, as if it was being pulled down from below by some giant underwater winch. The whale disappeared, and the water where it had popped up smoothed over.

"Well, I guess he decided we mean no harm," said Alva.

"Don't be too sure...," I started to say as I happened to glance straight down into the water along the port side of the boat.

I was horrified by what I saw.

"Grab hold!" I yelled. "He's coming straight up under us!"

High Horse pitched wildly sideways as the entire body of the humpback rocketed from the water inches from the port side of the boat, as if launched by a catapult. It was huge, unbelievably huge. The shiny black body arched and twisted in mid-air, sending a fifteen-footlong pectoral fin whipping along the deck toward the base of our mast. There was a loud *twang!* as the fin struck the shroud supporting the mast and sent a harsh vibration throughout the boat.

If he lands on us, I had time to think, *he's going to break this goddamned boat in two.*

He didn't. The whale's enormous body crashed back down into the ocean right next to the cockpit, sending a sheet of water cascading over the boat, and he disappeared into the depths.

Now *High Horse* rocked wildly from side to side, her mast swinging like an eighty-six-foot pendulum high above our heads. Alva screamed in terror and dropped to her knees on the cockpit sole. Even as her cry still echoed, the whale's gigantic flukes suddenly appeared thirty yards behind the boat. They rose gracefully out of the water and then slapped the surface with a report that sounded like a cannon shot. Alva screamed again.

"Okay, we gotta get out of here!" I shouted. "That was a bull, and I bet he's the pod's dominant bull. I'm guessing he was not playing tag with us for the fun of it. That dude is *hostile*."

Hoping we'd escaped undamaged, I turned to Collie. "Go forward and check the port shroud, see if that mighty whack he gave us did any damage."

I slammed the gear lever into forward, shoved the throttle lever full ahead, and spun the helm to starboard. *High Horse's* stern squatted with the sudden application of power, and the Oyster pirouetted in her own length, throwing Delia to the deck. I felt my legs start to slide out from under me, but I kept a firm grip on the binnacle and managed to keep my feet.

Behind us, the bull popped to the surface and slowly, deliberately rolled onto his side. He slowly raised a long ridged flipper high into the air and slapped it down on the surface with a sharp *bang!*, triggering still another scream from Alva. Now, looking for all the world like a submerging submarine, the whale's back began to revolve, and the beast sank slowly beneath the surface.

Alva and Delia and I gaped at each other in stunned silence, Alva on her hands and knees, Delia clutching the compass binnacle in a death grip, and I still breathless with fear. A minute passed, then two, then three.

Now, heading away from us, a dark shining dome broke the surface, arching higher and higher until it paused and then started to subside. In a froth of foam, the whale's enormous flukes, water cascading from their back edges, again lifted slowly from the ocean, hesitating in the sky in a moment of amazing grace. With a final dismissive *thwack*, the whale again slapped his tail hard on the surface...and disappeared from sight.

Trying to appear calm, I phooshed an involuntary sigh of relief. "Well, I guess he showed *us*."

"How can you joke about this?" snapped Alva. "He almost killed us."

"Yes, yes indeed, he did. But he didn't. I think we're okay, but he sure as hell *warned* us. There's all this talk on the nature shows on TV about the 'gentle giants of the deep.' Well, not when they're protecting their families. I think that bad boy meant business."

"Victor!" A frantic yell from Collie from the base of the mast. "That fucking whale tore the shroud right out of the deck! It's gone all slack! I can see the mast wobbling!"

I yelled for Alva to take the helm and scrambled forward to the mast. Sure enough, the base plate for the upper shroud, the thick stainless-steel cable that basically holds the mast upright, had been completely ripped out, leaving four ragged holes in the deck surrounded by shards of fractured fiberglass and a ripped-up section of teak decking.

Fortunately, *High Horse* had additional shrouds attached lower down on each side of the mast, and the bases of both the forward and aft lower shrouds hadn't been compromised. They provided at least a little support to the mast. Still, we were in deep trouble. With the upper shroud torn loose, the top half of the mast was left pretty much totally unsupported, and we were at real risk of a dismasting.

"Colin, unclip the extra jib halyard and bring it around to me on the port side!"

"I have no idea what you're talking about!" screamed Collie.

A halyard is a rope used to raise a sail. In addition to the main halyard behind the mast used to hoist the mainsail, *High Horse* had four other halyards leading from the top of the mast to the bow, used to hoist the boat's various jibs and staysails and spinnakers. When unused, they are simply led down to the deck and clipped to the bow pulpit.

I sprinted up to the bow, unshackled a spare halyard, and tugged it around to the port side, where I clipped it to the toe rail next to where the shroud base had been torn out. As the rest of my crew watched helplessly, I moved back into the cockpit, whipped the halyard around an unused winch, grabbed the big double-handed winch handle and cranked for all I was worth.

My jury-rigged shroud worked well enough: when once again under tension, the mast stopped oscillating around the sky, and I suddenly found that I could breathe again.

I collapsed back onto the soft cockpit cushions. "Jesus, Mary and Joseph, guys, we just dodged a major bullet. But that's it for sailing until we can reach port and get the shroud repaired. Once we furl all the sails, we're in for a few days of nice, quiet motoring. The good news is that y'all are going to get to visit Aruba. They have excellent repair facilities there."

Alva pulled herself up next to me on to the cockpit settee. She was blinking rapidly and trembling uncontrollably.

"Delia, I think Alva may be in shock. I think this calls for some medicinal brandy."

Delia brought a fresh bottle of VSOP and a bunch of crystal tumblers up to the cockpit and poured everyone a hefty tot, including Collie. In the confusion of the moment, I didn't notice that she left the half-empty bottle open on the floor of *High Horse's* recessed cockpit.

I clinked my glass firmly against Alva's.

"To Oscar," I said.

"Oh God, yes! To Oscar!" Alva whispered.

"Victor! Emergency! Help! I need help!"

As the time neared for Alva and me to come off watch, I had asked Delia to go below and fetch Collie so that they could stand their watch together. Now Delia's voice was panicky. I bolted belowdecks, through the salon, into the port forward stateroom, where I found Delia crouched by Collie's inert form. He was crammed face down into the front corner of his bunk, his head pressed between the cushions and the side of the hull.

"I can't wake him up! He won't wake up!"

I pressed past her, grabbed my brother by the shoulders and spun him on to his back. His eyes were closed and his jaw slack. He was drooling. I felt for a jugular pulse and immediately found one, strong and regular. I also detected the strong reek of brandy. I called up to Alva in the cockpit. "Smelling salts! Get me the smelling salts! They're in a blue glass jar in our medicine cabinet!"

It was only a couple of seconds before Alva handed me the plastic inhaler, which I jammed into Collie's nostril and gave a healthy squeeze. Smelling salts—pungent ammonia inhalant compounds that smell like stale pee, only worse—trigger a strong involuntary inhalation reflex and stimulate a rapid return to consciousness in people who have fainted. They worked splendidly on Collie. He waved his hands wildly in front of his face, opened his eyes wide and sneezed loudly as he popped up into a sitting position.

"*Wha'? Wha'? What? Whutha fuck?*" Now he shivered as if trying to shake off an attack by gnats. I took him by the shoulders and held him fast. I glanced around his bunk, and, buried at his feet, found what I was afraid I'd find: an empty brown brandy bottle signifying that while no one was looking, a half a bottle of finest VSOP had gone down Colin Harding's hatch.

I felt an explosive and all-consuming rage, classic 'seeing red.' In our entire lives, Collie and I had never once had a fight—not a physical one, anyway. Now I utterly lost control and slapped him hard across his face, an outraged seventy-two-year-old guy walloping the hell out of a blind drunk sixty-eight-year-old guy. The blow resonated like a starter pistol, and Collie was spun against the wall of his cabin.

"You bastard!" I screamed. "You drunken son-of-a-bitch! Is this the thanks we get for taking you with us? To have you turn lush on us when we're out in the middle of the fucking ocean, just when you're scheduled to go on watch?"

Collie raised his hands, whether in apology or to ward off another blow I couldn't tell. His voice cracked. "I'm sorry, Victor, I never intended…"

I shouted him down. "I don't give a shit what you *intended*, Colin! The *impact* of what you did was to insult your family. You potentially put all our lives in danger. I don't care if you're sorry, and I don't care if you have PTSD or are a helpless little bunny or whatever. Everybody cut you a ton of slack the whole time you went through your own private shitstorm, and you thank us by climbing into the bottle, time after time after time. Cara may put up with this shit, but I've had it. The moment we reach land, you're off this boat."

"Now, hold on a minute…," he started.

"No, *you* hold on a minute! Here's what's going to happen, *baby* brother! It's gonna take at least a day for us to motor to Aruba to repair the mast. Your only job during that time will be to sit down and shut up.

The moment we dock, I'm going to take your duffle, heave it on the dock, and excuse you from future service. What happens then, I leave up to you. You can fly back to Milwaukee into Cara's forgiving arms or stumble into the nearest taberna in Abaco and drink yourself into a stupor, I don't care. I'm sick and tired of playing nursemaid, particularly when your lack of self-control puts us all at risk."

For this pompous speech I received a sharp smack across the back of the head from Delia. "Whoa, killer! Let's just rein it in here, okay? Nobody elected you sheriff, nobody appointed you judge and jury."

"Actually, you *did,* Delia. You all did. Since all of you know exactly *nothing* about ocean sailing, you all entrusted your safety to me. This isn't a little family banquet where there's no harm in going a little too heavy on the cocktails and you can sleep it off in the morning. Oscar can warn us, but he can't save us if no one is minding the store. You should be just as angry at Captain Brandy here as I am.

"Please fix Colin here some coffee and try to sober him up. Meanwhile, I'll stand a double watch, either with you or Alva, you two choose. And yes, Colin still leaves the boat in Aruba."

———

We motored in silence. Delia was positioned stone-faced at the helm, staring silently at the horizon. The rest of us sat in the cockpit, blanketed in an electrically-charged silence. Alva made a show of reading an old Anaïs Nin novel. Me, I just sat there with my arms crossed, staring at the top of Collie's head, which hung low over his knees. I was drawing tight, shallow breaths through clenched teeth; Collie was taking rasping sniffs that sounded like a cross between panting and sobbing. We maintained this intensely uncomfortable tableau for over an hour.

Collie eventually tired of acting contrite and shifted to acting sullen, shaking his head and flicking his thumb against his middle finger. I had hoped I might calm down, regain a sense of perspective and forgiveness, extend an olive branch. But when I sensed that Collie had abandoned genuine contrition and now was copping a surly attitude, I found myself seething, glad that I would not have to sail with my brother across the Atlantic.

One ocean is enough, I told myself. I didn't need another between my brother and me.

Chapter Seventeen

Deep Trouble

"It's not all that complicated, Mr. Harding, and the damage is really not all that serious, although cosmetically it sure looks ugly when a chainplate gets ripped right out of a deck. But there are several different ways to skin this cat. Depending on your needs and budget and time constraints, we can make the repair quick and dirty and fast—but certainly strong enough—or we can do perfection. Better than new, in fact."

Dennis Horgan's voice was a soft purr behind his bushy Walrus-style mustache. His exuberant hand gestures, in contrast, made him look like he was directing an orchestra, although it was only the two of us staring at *High Horse's* deck. He was small and wiry, and he barely came up to my chin, yet he exuded competence.

"Tell me about quick and dirty and fast."

"Okay, we fix just the one chainplate. The deck core is pretty much intact, thank me sainted mother, so we don't have to cut a portion out of the deck out and sister in a whole new cored deck repair, complete with proper non-skid pattern molded in. The impact simply sheared all four stainless bolts in two and pulled them right through the deck. That must have been some whack.

"Anyway, just left four fairly neat holes. The backing plate is still in place inside under the cabin furniture. So, for the fix, we put a slurry of fiberglass on the deck to fill the bolt holes, buy a big strong chainplate assembly at the ship's store, bolt it all together. Bingo, safe as houses."

"Cost? Time"

"Two days, say thirty-five hundred dollars. But I won't be proud, and it'll cost you in the long run."

"Why's that?"

"Why not proud? Because Varadero is the best yard in the Netherlands Antilles, and we pride ourselves on impeccable quality. What I'm describing is a jury-rigged repair that will work fine and get you on your way, but down the road any surveyor will look at it and significantly reduce the value of the whole boat because it's been damaged, the repair is a jury-rig job, and the chainplates are not the same on both sides. The Oyster is a super-premium boat, and buyers—and charterers—will expect everything to be bloody perfect. Like I said, im-fucking-peccable."

"Okay, what's involved with making it...*im-fucking-peccable?*"

"You insured?"

"Is the fix cheaper if I'm not? Am I better off paying you cash?"

"I'll knock ten per cent off for a cash deal, sure. I hate all that insurance paperwork."

"So, what's the damage if we do it...*impeccably*, but do it for cash?"

"Six days and twenty-eight thousand dollars."

"Oof! Explain *that one* to me."

"Well first, I'm proposing quite a major project. I want to use a different chainplate design, because this boat has taken a hell of a shot and its structural integrity, particularly on the side of the hull. My assembly will be longer than the original chainplate in order to distribute the rig loads more broadly. It'll look gorgeous and be stronger than anything Oyster ever built. Surveyors will look at it and nod, 'oh, yes.'"

"Yeah, but twenty-eight grand?"

"That's because we'll have to do *both* chainplates. Make your beautiful boat symmetrical, you know. Make the boat impeccable. You'll get your money back whenever you resell it."

Varadero rushed it for me, then cut me a deal: five days, twenty-five five, payable in U.S. currency—to which I had to add the cost of putting our whole crew up at the Ritz Carlton Aruba, Delia's choice, while the im-fucking-peccable repairs were completed. Let me not be waspish here: we all were having a great time at the Ritz and dining well.

Collie and I shared a room, but he was accepting his banishment from the boat stoically and was considerate enough to avoid lapsing into a passive-aggressive war with me. We did not discuss his drinking; I was content to leave the AA intervention to Cara. So for five days we all sat by the pool and drank a lot of Ritzy rum drinks, except for Collie, who made a pointed show out of ordering tricked-out Virgin Marys a la Ritz.

As Dennis Horgan and I stood next to the completed *High Horse* at the dock, he clearly *was* proud, and he should have been. Our Oyster 62 looked factory-fresh, and the yard had waxed and polished the entire boat. You could not tell repairs had been made. I tipped him two thousand dollars.

The night before we were to depart, after we'd finished provisioning and re-packing, we treated ourselves to a final bon voyage dinner downtown, featuring foodstuffs we were unlikely to cook on board. It was five hundred dollars well spent.

As our cab drove back into the marina, we had to detour around a shiny black helicopter—I recognized it as an Aerospatiale— with a wide red stripe around its waist. Some fat cat had chosen to turn the parking lot into his own private helipad, a bit of Caribbean arrogance I did not find surprising.

As our cab reached the head of the dock, the other cab we'd called for Collie rolled up, this one to take him to a bargain-basement hotel downtown. After a final night at in Aruba, he'd be off to Chicago the next day as we started our sea cruise toward Cape Verde. I gave him a manly big boy handshake, helped him load his duffle into the cab, and said we'd be checking in regularly on the satellite phone, reminding him that he should keep his cell phone charged and on twenty-four hours a day.

As the rest of our merry crew strolled down the pier, I felt a stab of annoyance.

"Damn it, guys. You left the lights on."

"Not me," Alva said. "Must have been you. More evidence that your aging brain is turning to mush."

We all continued down the dock to the T-head where *High Horse* bobbed quietly. "I'm going to miss the Varadero Aruba Marina, Victor. I like it here more than Curacao."

"Amen to that," said Delia.

"I'm tired of both of 'em," I grumped. "If we're going to voyage, let's *voyage,* for Christ's sake."

I stepped down into the cockpit and moved to unlock the companionway hatch. "God damn it, Alva! You also left us unlocked! You should just put out a sign, '*Hey, come on aboard and steal everything.*'"

Under the halogen dock lights, Alva shrunk back. "Victor!" she whispered hoarsely. "Get off the boat! Get off the boat!"

"*Don't* get off the boat, Victor," said a lilting voice with a soft Irish burr. The voice came from inside the cabin. "Come below, all of you. *Join me.*" As I turned to flee, a huge form rose from the shadowed cockpit settee and planted itself in front of me. I felt the terrifying pressure of a pistol pushed up under my chin.

"Down," the gunman hissed. "Go down." Now he waved the pistol at Alva and Delia. "*Tu tambien.*"

I slid the top hatch open, lifted out the drop boards, and stepped slowly down into the cabin. Seated across the salon with a half-filled glass of dark wine in front of him sat Eamon Armagh. He was wearing a black seaman's cap and a crisp white short-sleeved shirt. He looked like a purser on a cruise liner, except for the semiautomatic pistol resting on the table in front of him.

"Hello, Victor, Alva. Miss Delia. Nice—*noyce*—to be seein' you again."

Alva's outrage overrode her judgment. "How'd you get in here?" she shouted.

Armagh calmly held up a key chain. "Easy. I used my personal key."

In an instant, all the pieces fell into place, and now I saw it all, realized exactly what was happening.

"This was *your* boat. *Lucifer* was your boat."

"Correcto-mundo."

I pressed my hands on my forehead. "And you're hijacking us."

"For sure, you *are* fast on the uptake," said Armagh, his Irish brogue now even more pronounced. "Yes, *Lucifer* used to be mine, or at least my cartel's, and Adamares and I are indeed commandeering your craft. First off, we are going to sail it to Cuba, fill *'our'* boat full of cocaine, and then we're going to take an uneventful sail to the good ol' U.S.A. You'll forgive me if I don't tell you the exact location."

Alva collapsed back onto the companionway steps. "My God, you're going to kill us!" she croaked.

Armagh spread his hands in mock exasperation. "Ah, here we go, the same old screamin' fit. *Pirates of the high seas!* Hijackers steal the sailboat, kill the crew, sink the boat. That's a bad rap, Mrs. Harding. To be sure, I do know of one boat that got scuttled when the Mexican Coast Guard was closin' in on 'em, but the owners lived to sail another day. Probably collected their insurance, too, I bet.

"I personally know of no other sailboat used for trafficking drugs that ever got scuttled. By *anybody*, much less me. Sure, the cartels sometimes shoot each other up in land battles, but we drug couriers, we tend to avoid murder. Mainly to avoid the capital punishment, you see. So just relax, Alva—*may I call you Alva?* As long as you folks behave yourselves and don't alarm Adamares here, you're in no danger. We're just going to take a wee detour from your planned itinerary, is all."

Now Armagh looked around, surprised. "Where's the other bloke?"

"My brother? Headed back into town. He's…ah…not coming with us."

There was a long pause.

"And what's all that about?"

"We had a major falling out, and I decided I did not want to make a sea cruise across the Atlantic Ocean with him. He has been…*excused*…from the crew."

"I think not," said Armagh.

"What the hell does that mean?" I bristled.

"It means actually, *yes, I want him to come with us.* We are going to want him as crew. So, phone him, Victor. Get him back here. *Now.* Tell him it's, you know, *urgent*, but not an emergency. Try not to alarm him, okay? No need for this to get exciting."

I was surprised at how automatically and easily my next word came to me.

"No," I said firmly.

Eamon Armagh obviously was not used to being confronted. He rose from the settee and leaned his hands heavily on the table. He pushed his face toward mine. "What's that you say?"

"I said, 'no,' as in 'no'. He is absolutely not coming."

Adamares Thuna stood and tensed. A very frightening guy when aroused.

I held my ground. "You aren't going to want him as crew. First of all, he's a complete sailing novice, so he doesn't add anything to our crew skills. Second, we've discovered that he's a man with a severe drinking problem. I'm not going to sail with that, and I won't let any of the rest of us sail with that, either. If you want to make a big deal out of it, you'll be making a big mistake. But you'll have to make it now."

Now Armagh, confronted with a highly-charged dilemma, sighed and stared up at the ceiling. The truth was that he didn't really need an additional crew member who would only use up a lot of space that he wanted to fill with bundles of cocaine and whose only real use was to stand watches. On the other hand, his authority had just been challenged, and if it was not firmly reasserted, Eamon Armagh risked losing face.

He smiled at me. Not a warm smile. "Are we in a tug-of-war then, Victor?"

"We are not, Eamon. I know who's got the pistol. But this boat is not sailing anywhere with my brother on it."

Eamon looked down at the floor, looked up at me. "So be it," he said calmly.

Now Armagh turned to Delia. "Ah, Miss Delia. Miss Delia Chamberlain, yes?"

Delia's eyes grew wide. *What was coming next?*

"We know all about you, Delia. Or actually, Checo Paredes, who runs our boatyard over at our base, well, *he* knows all about you. Now, I don't know shite about jewels, but Checo moves a lot of gems t' various parties all around South America and Spain, and he sure knows all about *you,* Delia Chamberlain. Winnin' all them big prizes, and all."

Armagh smiled warmly. "So, Checo's orders, you are not going to be going on the sea cruise, either. Checo's going to entertain you on our island while the rest of us make our trip up north. First, because as Victor has just pointed out, we can use the extra space on the boat. Second, because I suspect Checo has ransom in mind.

"But think of this part as reassurance, Delia! As…*life insurance.* If Checo and Mafin are going to ransom you, that means they won't be killin' you, right? And if they're not killin' you, that means we'll not be killin' *the rest of you*, because that would screw up the ransom arrangements, *aina?* I can assure you that you will be well treated, Delia. No jail cell or handcuffs, okay? You'll probably be staying in Checo's apartment, and there will be a sentry outside the door, but you will receive cordial hospitality. So, that said, why don't we everybody just relax?"

"*Relax?*" I shouted. "Are you fucking nuts? Just how is this whole ransom thing going to work, anyway? How do we do the ransom payment? How do we get Delia back?"

Armagh smiled reassuringly. "Provided the cocaine drop goes smoothly...everything else is going to go smoothly. I'm not the ransom manager, but here's my guess for how I think this should go down. At the same time we leave Aruba in this here sailboat, Mafin's helicopter is going to fly Delia from Aruba to our secret island base. Which is Checo's boatyard. She will be kept in friendly custody while we complete our sea cruise. You, Alva, Adamares and I are going to sail to the southern coast of Cuba, where we are going to retrieve half of a huge load of cocaine that got stranded when the narco-sub that was taking it to Louisiana began coming apart at sea.

"After we load the sailboat in Cuba, Delia is going to continue to cool her heels with Checo while we sail to the cartel's usual U.S. drop location, which is on the Louisiana coast somewhere west of New Orleans. My guess is that we'll be sailing for ten days or so, maybe less. At our camp in the U.S., we will let you use your fancy satellite phone to arrange for delivery of whatever ransom amount Mafin and Checo demand. Cash, of course. Mafin doesn't accept checks or wire transfers."

At this, Armagh actually smirked. I wanted to slug him, an urge easily resisted.

"The ransom details are not my business, Victor, I'm basically just a bus driver, *aina?* But I suspect that Mafin will then have some of our shore team drive you to New Orleans, where y'all will connect up with your 'personal payment representative.' Probably at some hotel or another. Once the payment has been completed, you and Alva will be allowed to go. Then we will contact Mafin and Paredes to say the deal is done, and they will helicopter Delia right back to where they picked her up—the Varadero Marina at Aruba. There she will be released, and it's good-bye and good luck. Delia will have to take care of herself from there. Now, is that so hard?"

"Our sailboat?"

"Silly question, Victor. You should be content to escape with your lives."

As we tried to take all this in, Armagh really did appear relaxed.

"So when all is said and done, Checo and Mafin are gonna get their ransom, right, and I'm surely tempted to try to acquire this fine boat. Especially now that you've put all this fancy new equipment on board. God, Victor, lovely stuff! Finest kind! But my reacquiring my own property—that's only fair, innit? I mean, sure and it wasn't exactly mine—the cartel's the one what originally bought it, but I made so many trips in it that it *felt* like it was mine. Anyway, I didn't willingly *give* it to the Dutch authorities, did I then? And I'm assuming you've got it fully insured, am I right, Victor?"

I nodded.

"Did your marine surveyor note anything funny?"

"Of course he did, Eamon. He couldn't help but notice that all the furniture in the front half of the yacht had been taken out at some point and then replaced. It was done well enough, but it clearly was not factory original."

"Anything else?"

"We both noticed that at some point *Lucifer* had been floating higher on her lines, that a new freshly-painted water line was four inches above her true water line."

"And I'm assuming you knew what that meant."

"Of course. Meant the boat had been used for drug running, was going to be loaded so heavy that it would float below its proper lines. Anyone looking at her and seeing no painted water line—like, let's say, some Coast Guard types—would know immediately that she was overloaded. A drug mule."

"Ah, well, what that shows *me*, Victor, is that you knew what you were buying. Smart lad! Bet you struck a good price with the Netherlands Antilles Coast Guard, *aina?* But then I bet you turned around and got it insured for fair market value, am I right? Bet you didn't tell your insurer that she'd once been stripped out and once had a drug runner's waterline. So, one way or another, it looks like you're going to come out all right."

I had to ask: "Why did you put the furniture back in?"

"Well, the cartel sorta had a change in...*policy* about the best way to run cocaine. Sailboats were...obsolete, see? Slow, at the mercy of the winds, not a whole lot of cargo capacity, and everybody's coast guard had caught on to the repainted water line trick. Mafin and Paredes moved to LPV-IMs and LPV-OMs."

He saw that I was drawing a blank.

"Don't know what that means, Victor? *'Low Profile Vessel – Inboard Motor'* and *'Low Profile Vessel – Outboard Motor.'* In other words, narco-subs. Drug subs. Paredes' yard began building 'em, even sold a few to other cartels. Narco-sub design is changing fast, *aina?* Paredes wanted to keep up. So the decision was made to sell *Lucifer,* so the yard put the full interior back in. I wanted to buy it back from the cartel, on an installment plan, like. But Mafin, who enjoys fucking me over, he said no.

"We had a big argument about it that was settled when the Dutch Coast Guard snatched *Lucifer* from our slip in Curacao. They got the boat, but they didn't get me. I thought that was the end of *Lucifer's* story until Mafin recently lost several of his LPVs to hijackers. Big loads, *big* losses. And then our newest sub—carrying a *very* big load—suddenly started falling apart in open ocean. Our lads were lucky to make it to Cuba. We struck a deal with our Cuban... *friends* to retrieve half the load, basically to go halfsies with them—*how's that for a ransom, Delia?*—but now Mafin needed a way to get our share of the load to America somehow.

"You are that somehow. Aha! Heist our old sailboat! I followed the notice of auction—and your rather shady purchase—with great interest. See, Victor, I was interested even before I saw you fiddling with Oscar."

As we spoke, I had been standing with my palms raised to signal surrender and submission, even while things grew increasingly tense between Eamon and me. Alva's hands still covered her face. Delia stood completely expressionless.

Armagh made a pooh-pooh gesture. "Oh, put your hands down, Victor, for Christ's sake. This isn't some western cowboy movie stick-'em-up, after all. Come, have a seat, you folks. Let's just dial it down a notch or two, okay? But yes, please do keep your hands where I can see them, now and in the future."

Armagh rose, walked over to the galley sink, threw the rest of his wine down the drain. He rinsed his glass, walked over to the liquor cabinet, and filled his glass with Irish whiskey. "Just a little celebratory tot before headin' off for a sea cruise, what? Victor, Alva, can I offer you a little something? Miss Delia, a nip before we bid you adieu and you fly over to Checo and Mafin's place?"

Armagh continued to stand in the galley while Alva, Delia and I sat on the salon settees. "All right then, I know you folks are already fully provisioned and fueled, so we can set off immediately. Delia, Mafin's chopper up there in the parking lot will fly you over to enjoy the tender mercies of Checo Paredes. It's that black bird with the red stripe. I can assure you, Delia, that Checo is quite the gentleman and that you will be treated respectfully."

"What do I get to take with me?" asked Delia.

"Well, I'd take pretty much everything you brought on board," smiled Armagh. "It's highly unlikely you'll ever see this sailboat again, so I wouldn't leave anything you'll want behind. Please do get your belongings together, darlin.'"

As Delia went to her stateroom to gather her things, Armagh turned to us. "Before we weigh anchor, we should do a quick orientation, and then I've got a couple of questions. First, this is Adamares Thuna. Some people just call him 'Tuna,' like the fish, but he hates that. You want to make friends, make the effort to use his proper name. My colleagues think he's crazier than a shithouse rat, but what he really is…is incredibly loyal. To *me*. Because one time I saved his son from being' carved up into little pieces by the MS-13 gang. Good story, remind me to tell it to you sometime. The point is, I give an order, *any order,* and Adamares follows it, no questions asked.

"Adamares does not speak much English, but he understands a lot of English, see what I'm sayin'? Think of it this way: *what he hears, I hear.* So let's keep the conspiratorial whispering to a minimum, okay? I'm not saying you shouldn't talk, I'm just saying don't get cute, all right?

"Underway, we are going to stand staggered four-hour watches. Some would disagree, opt for longer watches with more sleep in between, but that's how I'm gonna do it. First watch is going to be Alva, Adamares, and Adamares' gun. Adamares, by the way, is proficient in the use of firearms and decent in hand-to-hand combat. He also is a superb sailor. He can hold a course. He never trips, stumbles or falls. He doesn't fall asleep.

"Victor, you and I will take both the graveyard and dog watches, all right? Alva, I know this is a sexist insult, but I'm going to have to ask you to cook for all of us, or at least keep us fed. You can keep it simple, but none of us wants to eat anything Adamares or I cook, I promise you.

"Now, a couple questions. First, do you have guns aboard?"

"One," I said, "a stainless-steel Ruger carbine. It's secured on the underside of the aft lazarette hatch." *And, of course, I thought, my father's old Luger secreted in the hidden drawer under the chart table.*

"Next," said Armagh, "how many EPIRBs do you have aboard?"

"Six," I said. "One for the boat, one in the life raft, and four little units attached to the life vests." *Oh, and I'm not mentioning the military-frequency unit nestled next to the Luger under the chart table.*

"Satellite phone?"

I nodded. "An Iridium Extreme. It's in that yellow Pelican case."

"*Very nice.* I'll ask you to hand that over to me, Victor. Next, and this is an important question, so do not bullshit me here. On your lovely new Oscar instrument—have you installed a supplemental GPS, transponder or other tracking device?"

"Yes, I have," I admitted.

"Shit," said Armagh. "I was afraid of that."

"*What?*" asked Alva, spinning toward me in alarm. "Afraid of what?"

I shook my head in dismay. "He's going to turn Oscar off. Doesn't want any way for us to be tracked, so we're going to sail blind."

"Sad, but true," said Armagh. "No reason to leave a trail of bread crumbs. But still, sailors managed without Oscars for thousands of years, *aina?* Next, have you two filed a sail plan with anyone or provided an itinerary? Friends? Family? Coast Guards?"

"Only with our relatives in Wisconsin in the most general terms. We did not specify routes, ports or arrivals in detail."

"Well, that's a bit of load off me shoulders, for sure. Okay, so now Adamares and I are going to stow our gear, and then it's hi-di-ho, off we go. Victor, you and Alva can keep the aft stateroom. I will take the forward port stateroom, and Adamares will take the starboard stateroom. So, before we shove off, do either of you have any questions you want to ask me?"

We had no questions.

Delia appeared with her open-topped boat bag in her hand, a stylish black leather cross-body pack strapped diagonally across her chest, a large yellow sun hat on her head and an extra pair of sandals in her hand. "My mother never taught me how to pack for a ransom," she smiled. "Will there be a drycleaning service?"

"C'mon, Delia," laughed Armagh. "I'm going to introduce you to Leon, Mafin's pilot. He's ex-U.S. Army, can fly and maintain any helicopter in the world, so you're safe flyin' with him. He doesn't talk much, but he's a lot better company than Mafin. Checo Paredes will meet you at the island. Enjoy your flight."

Leon looked pretty scary: six-five, military buzz cut, deeply-set eyes and pock-marked cheeks. No chin. Huge hands. Absurdly large feet in combat boots. But a soft, gentle voice.

"Please watch your step as you climb in, Delia. Door's a trip hazard. You can either sit in back on the bench seat or up front with me in the copilot's chair. You'll get a much better view that way. If you put on the headphones, I'll describe what we're seeing as we fly over."

As one would expect, Delia sat up front.

Chapter Eighteen

SMALL TALK

"Why won't you talk to me, Alva?" Armagh's brogue was almost a purr.

Alva, Eamon, Adamares and I were all stretched out—stretched out but not *relaxed*—under *High Horse's* elegant pale blue bimini top as the sloop eased over a moderate swell along the northern coast of Venezuela.

We men all wore tee shirts and shorts. I was wearing a broad-brimmed straw fedora, Armagh a New York Yankees baseball cap, Adamares a sombrero of sorts crudely woven out of palm fronds. Alva was bundled up in loose trousers, long sleeves, a huge sun hat and oversized sunglasses. She claimed to be defending herself from the sun, but I knew different: she was *hiding*. Under the circumstances, Alva did not want to show any skin, literally or figuratively.

"Because I don't trust you, Eamon," said Alva.

Adamares snorted.

"Oh, Alva, I am deeply hurt. I know these are stressful conditions, but if I may say so, to me you seem quite able to handle yourself. Why should I be alarming to you?"

"Because you *are* alarming. Because you don't ring true. Because your silky Irish brogue comes and goes, Eamon, waxes and wanes...like the *fookin'* tide. Because sometimes you sound like butter wouldn't melt in your *fookin'* mouth and at other times I sense you could shoot me just as easily as look at me. Because you're part of a *fookin'* cartel of monsters and murderers and thieves."

Adamares snorted again, and Armagh joined in his laughter. "Come on, Darlin', tell me what you really think."

"No, seriously. Sometimes you sound like you're from Dublin, and sometimes you sound like you are from Miami or the docks in New Jersey. I can't tell the blarney from the bullshit, Eamon. Excuse me...*bullshite*."

"Well, I do spend a lot of time in all those places, as well as in my wee cottage out on the Dingle peninsula in Ireland with me gal Moira," grinned Armagh.

"Also Cartagena. See, in my line of work, you have to be able to adapt, to *adjust*. You know, make the most of where you are, love the one you're with, when in Rome, talk like the Romans talk."

"*My line of work*," mimicked Alva. "And just what is that? Cartel heavy? Carrot-top drug lord? Funny career path for an Irisher."

Now Armagh shook his head. "Nah, all that shite's way above my pay grade, Alva. I'm not cartel chieftain, don't even directly work for any of the other major cartels, for that matter. I did work for Sinaloa some years ago, but them times are dead and gone, just like Sinaloa is. Anyway, I don't launch drug wars, don't enslave the Indians, don't blow up police buildings, don't bribe politicians. Don't use drugs meself. I'm just contract help."

"I don't understand," I said. "Just what the hell are you then?"

"Victor," said Armagh with exaggerated patience, "I am a *mercenary*. A mercenary drug *courier*. More than a foot soldier, less than a boss. And my man Adamares here is a mercenary's mercenary. I am a supply chain expert, a go-to person in...*transportation logistics*. It's just that what I transport happens to be illegal substances. In the beginning, it used to be in sailboats—I quite enjoyed that—but now my job is piloting narco-subs. Stinky, smelly, leaky narco-subs. Except this trip, of course."

Adamares snorted again, amused by Eamon's stilted language. Clearly he understood most of our conversation.

"I am employed by Mr. Paredes. He runs the boatyard where they build narco-subs. Alberto Mafin owns the boatyard, but Paredes runs the boatyard. He's a pretty decent guy, Paredes.

Now *he* works for this guy Mafin. Mafin is *Cartel de los Soles*. The 'sun cartel.' Mafin is a very, very scary guy. I have met him face-to-face exactly once, when we had our *disagreement* about buying the sailboat, and that was enough for a lifetime. I don't ever want to see Mafin again, and if I'm lucky, I won't.

"As long as the drug deliveries get through—as long as *this* delivery gets through—I suspect both Mafin and Paredes will leave me and Adamares pretty much alone. At least until some future trip, when Murphy's Law—forgive me for slanderin' the Murphy clan, Holy Mother—seems bound to rear its ugly head again."

Armagh turned to Alva, reached over, and lifted the brim of her sun hat, forcing her to look him in the face. He eased into his most saccharine brogue.

"Still, *that's* the point, Alva darlin'. Over the years I've earned respect for my ability to get coke deliveries past them what would bring us low, and I get paid a nice pocketful of money to do just that. On the other hand, if recent trends persist and *Cartel de los Soles* keeps losin' boats and shipments, I'm going to receive a lot of unwelcome attention. Maybe a bullet. You know, 'murder the messenger.'"

I grasped Armagh by the wrist, in hindsight a stupidly silly macho gesture. "I wish that you hadn't told us Paredes' and Mafin's names, Eamon," I said. "That can't be good for our survival prospects."

I was pleased that I was able to keep my voice modulated, particularly in light of the spasms that were roiling my gut. Let's be clear: I was terrified.

Armagh jerked his hand away and shook his head vigorously in denial. "Ah, will you just come down off it, Victor! *God!* All the old wives' tales, all these tall tales about the drug trade! Listen, if I don't have to kill you, I won't kill you. I don't shoot people for the hell of it."

"But you have shot people," said Alva.

"*Of course, I've shot people.* Sometimes in the blink of an eye, *Bang!* right in the face, without a moment's hesitation, if that's what the situation called for. I've been in gun battles and fire fights and ambushes. And yeah, people died. But I am not ruthless, Alva. I'm not brutal. I'm just a businessman who happens to make his living as a criminal. Something you wouldn't know anything about."

Alva choked and coughed a mouthful of ginger ale directly into Eamon Armagh's face. I couldn't help myself: I broke into laughter.

"Oh, Eamon, you just took a very long walk off a very short pier."

To his credit, Armagh did not explode or lash out with his fists. "All right, then," he smiled menacingly. "I guess you'd better be letting me in on the joke."

I took a moment to try to settle my stomach and catch my breath.

"The joke is that whatever pesos or Bolivars or whatever your criminal activity has put in your pocket over the years, this lady's criminal activities have put a *helluva* lot more in her late husband's.

"You think you're a smart criminal, Eamon? You think you've seen it all, know all the angles? This little Sri Lankan gnome, who bootstrapped herself up from the slums of Colombo, has you beat six ways from Sunday. And she made her fortune without gun battles and firefights and murdering innocent bystanders."

Armagh cocked his head quizzically, like a German shepherd hearing a dog whistle. "You'd best explain, Alva."

Alva, realizing we had set a hook and given ourselves some leverage, gave Armagh a sly look.

"Maybe later, Eamon. Maybe later."

Chapter Nineteen

Welcome to Isla Gazela

Delia later told me that when Mafin's helicopter touched down on a helipad in the corner of the marina parking lot at Isla Gazela, and Leon ushered her out into the steaming jungle evening, Checo Paredes was waiting.

He seemed every inch the freshly-showered, impeccably dressed, lacquer-haired Latin gentleman of wealth: lime green slacks, white guayabera shirt with elaborate chest embroidery, highly-polished huarache sandals with elaborately woven toes. He did not affect air-kisses or even say welcome, but she said he did give her a long two-handed handshake.

He spoke slow soft, lightly-accented English, with a slight lisp. No pauses, no grammatical stumbles. No doubt about it: this man had been to *school.*

"I knew what you'd look like, Delia, because I have that article in *World's Finest Gems* magazine about you winning the *Coeur d'Or* award all those times. And all about your rather…*colorful* prior life as a famous model. Article suggests you really got around. Your picture, happily, does you justice. You, if I may say so, are quite the piece of work—and your pieces of work are quite the pieces of work, too!"

He threw back his head and guffawed at his own joke.

"I assure you that you will be treated with respect while you are here. Here, let me take your bag. I'll have all your things moved into my apartment—thank you for packing light. Don't worry, I'll be moving out—and we will keep a sentry posted outside your door to keep you feeling safe. Tomorrow after a nice breakfast we can all start negotiating your...*repatriation fee.*"

"All?"

"Indeed. You are going to have the pleasure of meeting Mr. Mafin. When you do, please mind your manners. Mafin is...a little eccentric, and he has a short temper."

"And *repatriation fee* means ransom?"

"That's what it means."

"I get it."

Delia told me that at this point she had blessed Checo Paredes with her warmest smile.

Checo smiled back. "Call it whatever you want. You will not find us difficult to bargain with, Delia, as long as you don't try to play us for fools. We know what you're worth, and I trust you'll agree with our opinion of what you're worth. No low-ball estimates, please, no playing silly games. We'll be the ones calling the shots."

"And when the deal is done, just how will I get out of here?" Delia had responded.

"*After* the deal is done, meaning after our cocaine delivery to the U.S. has been satisfactorily completed and after we collect the ransom from your representative in New Orleans... then we put you on Mafin's helicopter and have Leon fly you to a nearby island of your choice—back to Aruba or to Bonaire or to Curacao. Your call.

"There is a bridge off this island, but the road just leads deep into the jungle, so we won't be driving you anywhere. That also means...*if you were entertaining any thoughts of escaping from the island*...you should forget it."

"What if there's a hitch in the ransom deal or the drug delivery?"

I winced when Delia told me she'd said this, appalled at her chutzpah. *Why couldn't she just shut up sometimes?*

She said the smile never left Checo Paredes' face. "You should sincerely hope that there is no hitch, Delia."

As for us sailors, we soon found ourselves about a hundred miles south of Cuba. There was a soft glow on the eastern horizon, and a bank of cumulus clouds reflecting copper and rose hues hung like drapes down to the surface of the ocean. Dawn was near.

Eamon Armagh carried the yellow Pelican storage case into the cockpit, popped the latches, and removed Alva's satellite phone. "*Niiice*," he whispered. He removed a scrap of paper from his pocket, punched the numbers written on it into the phone, and waited for a connection.

As the call bounced up to the satellite, bounced back, and finally clicked through, Armagh walked up to the bow, turned his back to us, and began speaking animatedly, waving his free hand in the air. I could not make out the words, but I could tell Armagh was speaking Spanish. He sounded fluent. And angry. Evidently an argument was underway. Armagh began punching the air with his hand and shaking his head violently. When he finally walked back to the cockpit where Alva, Adamares and I waited, his face was scarlet. He sighed loudly.

"These Cubans. Such *arseholes*. Still, when you've been thrown over a barrel, you might as well roll with it, *aina?* Okay, friends, here's what's going to happen. Victor, you and Alva are not going to be allowed to touch Cuban soil, and for some reason that includes remaining on your own boat when it's tied up to a dock that touches Cuban soil. So, you get to stay out here on the ocean for half a day or so.

"Some Cuban chaps are going to meet us out here in international waters in their sport fisherman. Alva and Victor, you are going to transfer over to that boat, and several of their other guys are going to come aboard to take me, Adamares and *High Horse* into the Cubans' secret encampment. Their lads, those fookin' bandits, are goin' to load half the coke our leaky narco-sub had been carrying into *High Horse,* keep the other half.

"My guess is our load's going to be about a ton and a half. That's a lot, but then again *High Horse* is a damned big sailboat. That much won't sink us. Most of the product will be packed forward of the mast, but to keep the boat from gettin' all silly out of trim, they're going to have to place some on the floor of the main salon and a bunch in the aft stateroom, as well. We'll be taking one of the heads out of service and filling the space up with product. We will not be welcoming any guests—like, let's say, any Coast Guard types—below for the duration of our journey, if you catch my drift.

"I don't know how many lads, in addition to Adamares and me, they'll have workin' on loadin' us up, so I can't tell you exactly how long we're gonna be. Sorry. You're going to be out beyond anchoring depth, so you and several of your Cuban buddies are just going to be putt-putting around in circles in their forty-footer with the GPS on until we get back. Once we return, you'll transfer back to *High Horse*, and *bingo!,* we're off to Americky.

"Victor, before the sport fisherman gets here, I need you to do a couple of things for me. I don't expect trouble, except that in my line of work, I always expect trouble. First, would you make sure the Ruger carbine stored in the aft lazarette is loaded and that the safety is off? And unfasten the lazarette's storage latches, please."

"Second," Armagh continued, "Adamares' little blue duffel, the one with the leather handles—would you store that securely in the port cockpit locker with the top unzipped? Please don't muck around inside, just put it where Adamares or I can get to it in a hurry.

Third, Victor, please take the Luger—the one you have so cleverly hidden under the chart table and think I don't know about—load it, wrap it in a rag, rack a round into the chamber, and store it in the binnacle next to the gear shift lever. Never hurts to have a little extra security, and you can't be too careful. Belt and suspenders."

The 'sport fisherman,' which hove into view shortly after dawn, was a wreck. It was a Mainship 40 cabin cruiser, easily thirty years old, with cracked gel-coat everywhere and rust streaks running down from all its deck rails and fittings. The high tuna tower was made out of galvanized pipe and plumbing fittings, rather than neatly welded stainless steel, and I shuddered to think of all the extra weight that the boat was carrying high above the waterline.

The long fishing outriggers were made out of something that looked like bamboo. Still, both its diesels ran, although both coughed and stumbled and smoked heavily. And there was ample space in the cabin for Alva and me to get out of the sun and large windows for us to savor the breeze and keep our eyes locked on the distant horizon.

Armagh and Adamares greeted the leader of the Cubans, a self-important little creep with a Joseph Stalin mustache who spoke too loudly and seemed to be in a great hurry. As soon as he and two other soldiers clambered aboard *High Horse,* Adamares threw the Oyster in gear, and they motored off to the north.

The crew left on the Mainship to 'guard' the *Yanquis* consisted of three young men dressed in olive-drab fatigues with military pistols strapped to their waists in homemade holsters. The leader of this motley crew was Horacio, smooth-faced and handsome, with a proud chin and dazzling smile.

"Hi, guys," he said in completely serviceable English. "I speak the language, okay? Community college, Mexico City. Straight A. So, no whispering or sneaky hand signals or like that, okay? Let's all just be cool and make the best of this, okay? There is…no, there *are* cold beers in the fridge—yeah, the fridge actually works—okay, but hey, don't eat our lunch, okay?"

Five hours later, I saw the top of *High Horse's* mast pop above the northern horizon and nudged Alva, who had been dozing, awake. It was mid-afternoon, and shimmers of heat rose from the glassine surface of the ocean. A dense bank of cumulonimbus clouds was gathering to the west, only now beginning to stack up into a range of towering thunderheads. I hoped the boat exchange could be made before we were deluged. The less excitement and distraction, the better.

Now *High Horse's* hull appeared over the horizon, and I could see that the boat was laboring under her load. She rode bow down, pushing a much heavier bow wake than usual. Her sails were furled, and I could hear her diesel pushed to full throttle. Now I could see Armagh and Adamares in the cockpit, flanked by two very serious- looking soldiers in fatigues and pillbox hats. They held pistols in their hands, with their automatic rifles slung over their backs. The self-important Joe Stalin lookalike was absent.

As the two boats drew close abeam, Armagh gave a wave to Horacio up on the Mainship's flying bridge and then gave me a wink, a broad smile, and a thumbs-up. Adamares flashed a victory sign, then gestured for Alva and me to hop back across to *High Horse.*

As Alva landed lightly on the side deck, Armagh moved to help her and whispered quietly into her ear, "Alva, get below. *Now.*" She pushed by him and down the steps in one fluid motion.

Now Armagh moved to steady me, although I had not tripped or slipped, pulling me firmly to his chest. "Ambush," he said softly. "Be ready to drop."

Now I saw Adamares move nonchalantly to the locker where his duffel had been stored and casually open the hatch cover. At the same time, I saw Armagh squat slightly and reach into the binnacle storage locker.

"*Hola!*" Armagh suddenly yelled brightly, and in one smooth gesture he spun first right, then left. His shout blended with the sharp report of the Luger—once, twice—as each soldier's head exploded next to him. He dropped to a knee on the cockpit sole and flipped open the aft lazarette to grab the carbine.

Confused by the unexpected action, Horacio looked down at us from the Mainship's flying bridge. "Hey!" he yelled. *"HEY!"* Then his gaze fastened on the small football-shaped object arcing through the air toward him. Adamares' toss was a little off, but the grenade nonetheless clattered to the back of the Mainship's large aft cockpit. Before it could explode, Eamon emptied three taps from the carbine into Horacio's chest. With a look of horrified surprise, he groaned loudly and dropped from view.

Tigar and Raoul dashed out from the Mainship's cabin just in time to be devoured by the explosion of Adamares' grenade. Tigar was hurled, in several pieces, high into the air and over the transom into the sea. Raoul vanished in a curtain of flame as the Mainship's fuel tank exploded.

I had been lying on the cockpit sole with my hands over my head. Now I jumped to the helm, slammed *High Horse* into gear, and swung her away from the raging inferno of spilled diesel fuel on the ocean's surface.

"Good, Victor, good!" I heard Armagh yell. "Good man, good thinking!"

Then he yelled, "Alva, you can come up now! You're not goin' to be dying today!"

As Armagh, Alva, Adamares and I stood under the Oyster's bimini top and watched the sportfisherman's death throes, I held

High Horse away from the inferno of diesel flames spreading steadily across the ocean surface. Even from forty yards away, the air reeked of the combined stench of burning diesel fuel and melting fiberglass. The Mainship was settling by the stern—evidently the tank explosion had breached the hull, and the sportfisherman was going down fast.

As the top of the Mainship's transom neared the ocean's surface, there was another sharp explosion that blew the flying bridge's upper control station high into the air. Adamares broke into a broad grin.

"Propane tank," he chortled. "Go bye-bye."

I felt a very strange sense of elation, not a reaction born of my rational faculties, but rather a deep surge of power, of electrical energy radiating from the core of my body out through my limbs. My fingers spasmed, my toes tingled. I began to tremble. No doubt about it: I was *charged up*, and I wondered if my sensations signaled I was going into shock.

Just as the bow of the Mainship pointed to the sky before the sportfisherman's final plunge, a sudden cloudburst deluged the scene of the aborted pirate attack. There was a deafening clap of thunder, causing us all to jump in surprise. "What is it, God?" screamed Armagh. "You're a movie director now? Didn't you think our scene had enough drama?"

I moved away from the helm and stood behind Alva, trying to shield her from the sheets of rain whipping across the ocean's surface. Suddenly she began shivering violently and sobbing in loud, gasping hiccups.

"Adamares," I said, pointing to the hatchway, "take Alva below. Hot tea." I pantomimed a pouring motion. "Put bourbon in it. Alva, I'll be down in a minute."

Now I returned to the helm and turned to Armagh. "Talk to me. What the *fuck* just happened? I mean, I know what happened, but *what happened?*"

Armagh hastily returned the carbine to its storage clips in the aft lazarette, thrust the Luger into his pocket, and dropped heavily to the cockpit settee. Suddenly his face was drained of color. Now he too was trembling.

"We are *so* lucky to be alive, Victor. So, so lucky! *Here's* what happened. I was in a tent with Colonel Flanisti knocking back some truly spectacular Cuban rum. Adamares was watching a couple of Cuban grunts load bundles of cocaine into *High Horse*. As the Cubans were almost done loading the coke, one of them asked Adamares, in Spanish, if he spoke any English.

"Adamares didn't know what to make of the question, so he said no. Then, in front of him, *in English,* the two Cubans began talking about the ambush, about how they would wait until we four were all together in the cockpit of the Oyster before opening up on us. As we were motoring back out, Adamares sidled up to me and whispered one word. *'Emboscada.'* I knew what that meant, and I knew immediately when and how they'd ambush us.

"And before you ask me, Victor, *no, I did not expect all this to happen!* These clowns went way off the reservation. Congratulations, you've just seen the beginning of a *Soles Cartel-Cuban* war. At least these particular Cubans. This is going to get real ugly, real fast."

"But all those preparations you had me make before they arrived…"

"Simply prudent thinking, Victor. When I said 'you can't be too careful' before, I was just talking some blarney, you know. Not really expectin' trouble, just trying to put you on alert. The ambush was life imitating bullshit."

Chapter Twenty

BREAKFAST AT MAFIN'S

A pleasant buffet had been spread out in the shade on the veranda outside Mafin's office—mixed fruit, shirred eggs with bright red picante sauce, green salad and Brazilian cheese bread, laid out together with a pitcher of iced tea and an urn of steaming coffee.

Alberto Mafin had dressed up for breakfast. Once again, everything about him was gray—his slacks, long-sleeved shirt, sandals, even the frame of his sunglasses. But today everything was starched and freshly pressed, which Delia later told me she interpreted as evidence that Mafin regarded this as an important meeting.

Delia was dressed in a beige safari suit. In her hands she clutched her open-topped carpet tote bag. She had held tight to this colorful bag from the moment she had been taken captive. Now in Mafin's conference room, Paredes moved to take it from her and put it on the sideboard, but Delia shook her head firmly.

"No, I'll just hold onto my bag, thank you very much. I didn't want to leave it in my room. A woman's prerogative. Lady stuff, you know."

Paredes shook his head politely and gestured for Delia to hand him the bag. Delia did so without hesitation but kept up a steady stream of chatter to distract him.

"Just a couple of changes of clothes, Checo, my cross-body pack, which is empty, plus my toiletries bag—meds, sunscreen, shower cap, special shampoo, makeup remover, Tampax, sun cape, spare sunglasses…"

"Please stop prattling, Delia. Don't make me be a rude man."

Checo turned the carpet bag upside down on the desk, spilling all the contents. He riffled through Delia's clothing, looked quickly into the cross-body pack and put it back, and then picked up the clear plastic toiletries bag. He turned it over in his hands, held it up to eye level, squeezed it, then shook it. Then he scooped up all of Delia's clothes, crushed them together with the body-pack and the plastic toiletries bag, and stuffed everything back into the boat bag.

He never unzipped the plastic bag. Never closely examined the cross-body pack which held her passport and American Express card in an inside zipper pocket. Delia later told me she felt like she'd been pulled out of a vat of boiling water.

"It's all right, Checo," she said amiably. "I'll repack everything properly later. Do you need to do a body pat-down or a cavity search or anything?"

Checo seemed offended. "No need to insult me, Delia. A strip search won't be necessary."

———

Delia later told me that at the buffet table, Paredes stepped back, and then gestured for Delia to step back, too, to allow Mafin first access to the food spread the length of the table. Mafin shook his head dismissively at the fruit and eggs and in his thickly-accented English said, "you know I can't eat that crap, Paredes."

He plucked five pieces of the bright yellow cheese bread from the earthen platter, poured himself an oversize mug of black coffee, and plunked himself at the head of the table. Without waiting for Delia and Paredes to serve themselves, Mafin began stuffing large pieces of cheese bread into his mouth.

When everyone was seated, Paredes said, "Alberto, allow me to introduce Delia Chamberlain."

"I don't have to allow nothing, Checo. I know who the fuck she is. I read the planning report Armagh wrote before we grabbed the boat, including her financials and that article in that glossy jewelry magazine. Fancy-ass fat cat, blah, blah, blah. Oh, my, I am *so* impressed!"

"Well, she *is* very famous," said Paredes. "Equally important, she's the sister-in-law of the guy we hijacked the sailboat from. Her family wants her back bad, and they got plenty money, too."

"I know that also." Mafin did not make eye contact with Delia, did not bother introducing himself, did not invite her to speak.

Delia, not about to be muzzled or ignored, spoke anyway.

"Okay...*gentlemen*...let's get down to business. What are you demanding?"

Mafin, evidently amused by Delia's effrontery, smiled. "What you offering?"

Delia smiled back. "Depends on what form you want payment in and how you want it delivered."

"No entiendo," said Mafin. "What you mean?"

"We are agreed that I am going to have to pay some kind of ransom for my release, *si*? The question is how and how much."

"'Splain."

"I can arrange to pay my ransom in cash, hand-delivered to your people in the U.S., or by bank draft, or international bank notes or letters of credit. Or, if you prefer, using gold. I am a famous goldsmith, you know, so I have easy access to gold, of course, plus a supply at my atelier in Wisconsin. Once you choose which form of payment you want, all we have to discuss is how to make the payment and where to set me free."

"No," said Mafin. "First we discuss how much."

"Okay," Delia said. "Like I said before, what are you demanding?"

"Million dollars."

"Bullshit. No way. No possible way. My international bankers in Switzerland—*my cartel*—will never go for that."

"You wanna die?" There was not a trace of humor in Mafin's expression.

"You want a *very* serious SWAT team to visit you here on your cute little island? Execute a well-armed cease-and-desist on your whole operation here? You think my… *protection*…can't track you down, Mafin? Can't take you down? I thought you said you knew everything you were dealing with when you kidnapped me. Anything bad happens to me, and you and everyone here are in for a world of serious hurt."

"You bluffing."

"*Try me.* Or try this instead: a reasonable win-win counter-offer. So that no one has to die, I am willing to call my people in the U.S. and have them deliver...a single six-kilogram ingot, just over thirteen pounds, of 24-karat fine gold. Easy to transport, easy to conceal.

"The current market price on the world spot gold market is between $78,000 and $82,000 per kilo. So, Mr. Mafin, a single six-kilogram ingot will probably gross you about $480,000, give or take. How much you net depends on how much you have to discount to your fence. To me, that seems like a pretty reasonable ransom offer, one that doesn't require you to push your luck."

"You bluffing."

"No, I'm negotiating, as one experienced crook to another. Doing business, calmly and reasonably. Here's what I propose: you and Mr. Paredes may listen in as I make my arrangements on the phone. I will be talking to my brother-in-law in Wisconsin, so I'll need an international connection. He'll probably need a day to put his end together and another day and a half to drive the ingot to...what's good? New Orleans? I assume you can easily get a couple of your gang to drive to New Orleans, right?

"At the agreed time, you have Leon fly me back to Aruba in your shiny black helicopter, right back to the same marina where you picked me up. I climb out. Your people can cover me with a gun, if it makes you feel safer. Then *my* chartered helicopter lands next to your helicopter. In New Orleans, my brother-in-law hands your guys that ingot—he'll probably have it in a locked metal box—and they then call your dudes to say they have the ransom. I climb into my charter and fly away. After that, your people can do anything they damn well please."

Mafin seemed surprised that the details had been thought through in such detail. Delia folded her hands primly on the dining table.

"Agreeable to you?"

A long pause, then Mafin nodded. "Hokay."

Checo Paredes' jaw dropped, and his eyes opened wide. He could not believe what he had just heard, some woman calling the shots to Alberto Mafin.

"One more thing, Mafin," Delia said. "Anything bad that happens to any of my family on that cocaine run will trigger violent retribution. You better take good care of my family, Pal, or you are all dead. No shit, Sherlock."

At this, Delia Chamberlain rose from the table, dropped her napkin in the middle of her plate, picked up her boat bag, and headed back to Checo Paredes' apartment.

Chapter Twenty-One

ON THE HIGH SEAS

"Alva, she look like hell."

Adamares and I were seated in the salon, slugging hot coffee and trying to dry off after standing our watch in the driving rain. I was still trembling, although I could not tell whether it was caused by chill from the soaking rain or the jolt of realizing I'd been marked for a hideous death.

My body certainly was reacting to *something,* but I was surprised to realize that my mind seemed clear. My thinking had taken on a lucid focus, my perceptions honed into a calm sharp edge. I felt like I had my shit together. I felt…*in control.* Of what, I had no idea, but to my relief, I was aware my mental processes seemed to be hitting on all cylinders.

Armagh was standing at the bottom of the steps leading up to the cockpit, looking up and watching Alva, wrapped in her bright orange wet weather gear with a hood pulled tight around her head, as she wrestled with the helm. She had her hands full as *High Horse* bucked and tossed through the waves breaking over the bow.

Armagh shook his head ruefully. "She shouldn't be up there at all, much less taking time at the helm in this weather. I know she insisted on pulling her weight, Victor, but we shouldn't have let her. It isn't just that she looks tired and miserable; she looks…*shellshocked.*"

Adamares nodded in agreement.

"Well," I said, "she *is* shell-shocked. And so are the rest of us. She's just showing it more. Look, Eamon, Alva expected to be going on an exciting sea cruise, but being hijacked and targeted for murder is surely not what she had in mind. Me neither. And clearly you weren't expecting your Cuban pals to turn on you either."

Adamares again nodded agreement.

"Well, you got that right, Victor," Armagh said softly. "This thing turned into a full-blown shit storm, and I almost got caught out. I bought into the Cubans' 'we're-all-in-this-together' load of bull, and if it wasn't for Adamares' phantom English skills, we'd all be dead.

"Good news is that's going to be some time before the guys on shore realize something's gone wrong, so I think we're probably in the clear, at least for the next few hours.

"But who's to say who and what these guys might send after us? Other than the Mainship we blew up, I didn't see any boats at their camp capable of chasing us down, but that doesn't mean they don't have friends somewhere nearby with an ocean racer or a helicopter to put in the air."

Armagh rose and went over to the map of the Caribbean Sea and Gulf of Mexico taped to the cabinet above the chart table. He took a pair of dividers from the drawer in the chart table, set them to the scale on the map and, starting with his guess about our present position, began measuring off various courses and distances.

"I think if we just keep going northwest, we can't get far enough away from Cuba to keep some of our buddies' buddies from zooming along Cuba's north coast and intercepting us before we can get out of range.

"So let's fool 'em. I want to shift course to south-by-southwest and make a big loop over toward Mexico, toward Cozumel. Then we hug the Mexican coast until we hit the Gulf of Mexico and continue westerly for a couple of days before we swing north to Louisiana."

"Mes'can coast guard," said Adamares flatly.

"Sure and it's a worry," Armagh said, "but it's a better risk. I don't think the Mexicans are the sharpest crayons in the box, and at least they're not out to murder us. Those fancy new towed sonar arrays the U.S. Navy gave 'em are useless against a sailboat, and they probably won't expect a couple of gray-hairs to be running a load of product up under their noses. What's more, I don't think they'll be looking for a drug boat—of any kind—comin' in from the east and not from the south."

"How much will the altered course extend this trip?" I asked.

"My guess is maybe a week. Depends a lot on the winds and how soon we get clear of this damned storm. We keep beating to windward like this, and it's going to be a long, slow slog. If the wind backs to the southwest, which is the prevailing pattern, we'll be on a nice beam reach and go like a bat out of hell."

I sighed, looked up at the ceiling, and slapped my hands on the salon table.

"I guess I have no choice but to bow to your smuggling expertise, Eamon, but if we're taking this longer route, I'm going to insist on some changes in how we do things."

"Do you think you're in a position to insist on anything?"

"Don't be an asshole, Eamon. Just listen, okay?"

Armagh shrugged. "Okay, okay. What needs changing?"

"Alva should be relieved of all watches, starting now, and we three move to a four-hour on, four-hour off watch schedule with a two-hour overlap. Won't kill us. Alva's already doing all of the cooking, and we are taking advantage of someone who is seriously overstressed. We can let Alva take the helm if and when she wants, but she shouldn't have to. Furthermore, it's better if Alva is never on the deck alone. *Ever.*"

"Okay by me," said Armagh.

"Ay, *que bueno*," said Adamares.

"One other request," I said. Armagh raised his eyebrows.

"I want you to turn Oscar back on."

"No can do, Victor," Armagh said firmly. "*No can do*. I'm not sending out any signal that can be traced or tracked, and you told me you'd added a transponder to the Oscar masthead array. That's as good as telegraphing a message to the entire drug interdiction universe, 'Hey! Come get me!'"

I felt my bile rise and pointed a finger at Armagh's chest. "You know something, pal? One way or the other, you are determined to get us killed."

Armagh just smiled. "Victor, you are a pompous prick."

The wind shifted, the sky cleared, and the waves turned into long, graceful swells that lifted *High Horse's* bow, slid smoothly under her long hull, hoisted her stern, and then propelled her down the back of the wave like an arrow shot from a bow. This was the Oyster at her best, powerful, easily managed, exhilarating. Even overloaded, she was a picture of grace. Now we were able to shake the reefs out of the sails and move under full sail, causing the boat to heel down to the lee rail, but pick up another two knots of boat speed.

Everyone was in the cockpit as the sun moved toward the western horizon, and a bottle of Zaya rum had buoyed our spirits, as well as calming Alva's nerves. She still looked exhausted, but some color had returned to her cheeks, and she had emerged from two days of sullen silence to participate in conversation again.

"Were you able to sleep?" I asked.

"Finally. And finally without death-and-destruction dreams. I'm better, Victor. Thank you, dear heart, for asking."

Armagh moved over and sat down next to Alva on the settee. "So, Alva darlin'. Before our recent excitin' events, you were going on and on about your laundering skills. Supposin' you was managing *my* money. Just supposin' now. What would your approach be? What *vee-hickles* would you be using?"

To his astonishment, Alva reached up and pinched Armagh on both cheeks. She smiled wickedly. "Depends," she said.

"On what?"

Alva ticked items off on her fingers.

"On how much you're starting with, where it's being held or invested now, what vehicles you're using for holding and laundering, how many passports you're holding, how much confidentiality you want, how liquid your assets are, how much control you want over day-to-day management versus how much leg work you'd want me to do, how much investment risk you're willing to take, how long you're going to keep doing this suicidal drug running thing, whether you want to bring your Irish lady into the circle, and whether you know a Swiss lawyer who can serve as liaison with a very discreet Swiss bank. As I do."

Armagh smiled. "Hmmm," he said. "Well, that's a lot goin' on. Can you move money rapidly from country to country?"

"I think we've discussed this in connection with your silly death threat. I move large amounts all the time," said Alva brightly, "using my own special means and methods. Actually, the bigger the nut, the better. Call it...*monetary momentum.* As in, 'in for a dime, in for, say, ten million dollars.'"

"Are you federally insured, like, say, the FDIC?" Armagh laughed.

"I won't scoff at you, Eamon, because I know you're just joshing. My brains and my experience are my insurance. Look, Pal, no one's forcing you to dance to my tune. For years I've acted strictly to my own account. I'm not panhandling for clients, but if the sums are significant and you respect my fee structure, sure, we could talk.

"Remember, we're not just talking about investment management here. We're also talking about *consulting* fees, the laundering strategies and tactics needed to transform funds into a form that could be invested legally and moved easily without having to constantly bounce your resources from...*vee-hickle* to *vee-hickle*."

"A full-service launderer, eh?"

Alva winced, unwilling to joke when she was going for the close. "I guess you could call it that. It's the results that matter, Eamon, not the label."

"What is your fee structure?"

"Dunno. Never had one before. I guess once I established offshore accounts for you the way I have for Victor—and that part would be done as a consultant on an hourly fee-for-service basis—I suppose an annual fee of three per cent of total funds under management would be fair. I think that's an industry standard. Also, if there are fund acquisition or processing fees, you would pay those. Cost of doing business, you know."

"Oof," said Armagh raising his eyebrows. "Sounds like this could get costly."

"And this is all assuming that you have the table stakes to begin with, Eamon. Cost of entry. The minimum amount required to get into the game with me. I am not willing to screw around for chickenshit."

"And what would your table stakes be, Alva?"

"Never thought about that before either, Eamon, because I always had enough to create some real economic clout with banks and funds. My guess is that we'd need about ten million dollars in order to get folks to take you seriously, treat you respectfully."

Armagh's smile faded. "Mother o' God, there's a proper nut! I thought I was doing pretty well, but I don't have that kind of cash on hand."

"Yeah, well, that amount would make for a pretty lumpy mattress, wouldn't it? Stashing cash can be a major pain in the ass. So, can you lay your hands on five mil? Wire me those funds, and we could start with some high-leverage games and play for high-rate short-term returns. If I told you that I'd guarantee your low buck five million ante would be worth ten mil after a year, would you play?"

"I'd definitely be interested in talking more about that, Alva."

"One condition, of course. I'd have to have absolutely free use of the funds for that year, complete control, and you'd have no right of withdrawal or liquidation during that time. I'm a consultant, not a neighborhood bank."

"Did you impose that condition on Victor?"

"I'm married to Victor. I don't impose conditions on my marriage."

"Yeah, but you were managing some of his money before you two got married. Did he have to jump through all these hoops in order to play with you?"

"Eamon, I'm offering you a favor. If you don't want the favor, just say so. My daughter is Victor's sister-in-law. The rules are different for family. Look, I'm not going to twist your arm. I mean, are we talking seriously here, Eamon, or just spitballing? Is this whole discussion all just more of your blarney?"

"You got any references?" Armagh smiled.

"Sure. Victor here. He's only been with me six months, and I have done very well with the relatively illiquid funds he brought my way. I think he appreciates both my creativity and my determination to make him rich. Well, at least richer. He's never going to be in my league, wealth-wise."

"You mean make both of you rich. You're married."

"Pre-nup," smiled Alva. "Our funds are segregated. Keeps us both honest, in a manner of speaking."

"Well, got any ideas?" Alva rolled on to her stomach on the foredeck, hiding her face from sight, and making it look like she was simply sunbathing rather than try to hatch a plan about how to save our lives.

"You're supposed to be mister fix-it, right? Victor Harding, the world's greatest trouble-shooter. So how do we get out of this pickle?"

I sat with my back to Adamares, who was standing at the helm in the cockpit, his face and expression shrouded beneath his broadbrimmed sombrero and enormous mirrored aviators.

"Sarcasm won't help things, Alva. This isn't like simply pouring a new foundation under a collapsing building, for Christ's sake. You think I haven't been trying to come up with some way to get the upper hand with these guys, some way to trick them into letting down their guard?

"Well, okay, let me remind you of a couple of things. They're professional killers. They've got guns. They're young and strong and vigilant, They're good sailors. They keep apart and keep us apart. One of 'em is always awake. They don't even eat the same thing, so it would be pretty hard to poison them, even if we had some kind of poison, which we don't. All in all, not a great formula for turning the tables, I'd say."

"I'm sorry, Victor. I didn't mean to dump on you. You know I get pissy when I'm scared."

"You didn't seem scared when you were soft-soaping Eamon yesterday. To me, it looked like you were the one with a plan. I saw you seducing him, saw you working your slow con on him, and I thought, 'God, Alva's actually playing this guy!'"

"I never would have had the idea of teaming up with Armagh, of building his trust and disarming him by playing to his greed. That just sort of spun out of his bragging. My only thought had been to try to get off the boat alive by stealing the life raft and activating the EPIRB.

"Problem was that I couldn't think of any way to distract them both while we unfastened and launched the raft, couldn't imagine how we'd get into it undetected. Couldn't imagine how we'd get far enough away from *High Horse* so that they couldn't just shoot holes in the raft and watch us sink."

I shook my head. "As for me, I confess that I am suffering a major case of analysis paralysis. I honestly can't figure out what we should do."

I reached over and took Alva's hand. "Alva, my distress goes beyond the here-and-now challenge of keeping ourselves alive. My whole life has ceased to make sense to itself. I'm really struggling here."

Alva looked at me sternly. If I was expecting sympathy, evidently I wasn't going to get any.

"Alva, I've been doing a lot of contemplation of death, which is only prudent under our present circumstances, wouldn't you say? And for me, this contemplation is not going well."

Alva took my hand, put it up to her lips, and kissed it softly. Then she put it up to my lips. "Shuuush, Victor. Turn down the volume. Let that racing brain just be still a moment."

Her expression hardened. Now Alva looked determined, and when Alva looked determined, she could look downright scary.

"So, you want to know what I've been thinking? 'Time and tide wait for no man.' That's Chaucer. Meaning that I don't think we should just sit around and wait to see what happens to us. We have to be the ones to make things happen."

"Make things happen, right. What things? Just what're we supposed to make happen?"

She set her jaw. "Things. Use your fucking big brain, Harding. Rescue the damsel in distress."

We lapsed into silence.

"Alva," I finally said. "That magnificent sales pitch you gave Eamon. Do you think he bought it?"

"Nah. I think we were just doin' the dozens on each other. I'm going to keep trying to play him, but the guy's no fool. And why should he believe me? For all he knows, I could be making up everything I said.

"For all his charming brogue, he's still a fucking drug-runner. I think he still intends to kill us. But who knows? Maybe I bought us a little extra time as he chews over the prospect of banking some serious money and getting some wise guidance from someone who isn't part of his drug cartel. Besides, right now he has the luxury of a cook and two extra bodies to stand watch."

Chapter Twenty-Two

Don't Phone Home

Two uneventful days had passed. We had fallen into a relatively stable routine, and Alva was at least speaking to Armagh again. Adamares was at the helm and the rest of us were lounging below when Armagh unpacked the satellite phone.

"I should check in with Mafin. Update him on our plans, give the Louisiana guys an ETA, let him know about the shit the Cubans pulled."

"Probably not a great idea," I said.

"And why is that, Mr. Wizard?"

"*You damn well know why, Eamon.* Because sat phones can be tracked so easily. Tracking phone traffic may not be legal by individuals, but it's a piece of cake for military and security services, and by now I'm assuming the word is out that we've gone missing.

"We didn't have a detailed check-in schedule with our folks, but by now Colin would have expected to hear from us several times. I've registered my sat phone frequency, so any trained technician who has the registration number can track any calls you make.

"In addition, this phone model has a piggy-back GPS carrier signal that will announce our location if you light it up. I thought it was risky of you to talk to the Cubans on my sat phone to set up your rendezvous, and I think if you call Mafin now you're really going to blow our cover, either with everybody's Coast Guard or the Cubans, or both."

"No choice. Got to tell Mafin about our new course. If he doesn't hear from me, he's bound to assume something's gone wrong, and you definitely don't want him getting all steamed up. If he does, one, the shit's going to hit the fan in Louisiana—for all of us—when we finally get there, and two, Delia's definitely in hot water. Victor, Checo Paredes cannot protect Delia's ass from Alberto Mafin."

I shook my head vehemently. "Okay, so maybe Mafin might be beginning to worry that something's gone wrong, but for the moment, that's all he can do—worry.

"There are no steps he can take with respect to us because he doesn't know where we are, and I don't think he's going to hurt Delia as long as he's still in the dark. Could just be a false alarm, right? When we get to Louisiana, you can call Mafin on a regular phone and fill him in, and then everyone can cool their jets. You set us free, Delia's ransom gets delivered to Mafin's people there, Mafin cuts Delia loose, and everyone lives to see another day.

"But, Eamon, if we get tracked on the sat phone, things will likely get very hairy very fast around here, because I think we're within Coast Guard helicopter range of the United States. Ironic as it may seem, *Alva and I don't want you to get caught* because that likely means serious bad news for us. And if things completely blow up here, Delia Chamberlain is dead, ransom deal or no ransom deal."

Armagh wiped his hands across his face, wincing as if in serious pain. Then he slowly put the sat phone back in its yellow case and closed the clasps with a loud snap.

Chapter Twenty-Three

Things Get Interesting

Several hours later, as we sailed into a gentle dusk, Alva stood up from the salon table. "I'm going to go on deck and stand watch with Adamares."

"We told you," I said. "You don't have to stand watches at all, much less watches at night."

"It's okay. I want to admire the moon and stars," smiled Alva. "Besides, Adamares is better company than you two jerks busy yelling at each other."

She turned back to Armagh. "What's the story on Adamares, Eamon? Where's he from? How'd you two end up partners in crime?"

Armagh leaned back, staring up at the salon's varnished ceiling as if recalling distant lore.

"Honduras. A little fishing town called Cardura Real. Adamares had always been a water guy. And solid citizen—widowed, nine-year-old son, no other family. Mass on Sundays. And they needed mass, because this had become a gang town, and a lot of very nasty shit was going down. You know about La Mara Salvatrucha? Your guys call it MS-13. It's mostly immigrants from El Salvador, although the gang actually started in Los Angeles, believe it or not. Now they're everywhere in Central and South America, too. Adamares tried to stay clear, but he was getting a lot of heat to join and pay his dues, so to speak."

"Meaning?"

"Killing people, raping women, extorting protection money from everybody."

I straightened, caught up in the story. "So what happened?"

"*We* happened. My cartel—my *employer*—came to town, you see. They were looking for a transfer depot, a mid-voyage layover place if we needed one occasionally. My...*colleagues* did not waste much time flexing their muscles. They machine-gunned a bunch of MS-13 guys, began troopin' up and down the streets aiming AK-47s at everybody. Tensions rose, you might say."

"I had been tasked with drivin' up from Colombia, deliverin' a Land Rover for my local lads to use. One of our guys had painted 'U.N. Peace-Keeping Force' on the doors, thought it was real amusing. Adamares and his boy were living on a sailboat in the marina."

"And..?" asked Alva.

"And the very day I arrived—the very moment I arrived, actually—some MS-13 goon had Adamares' boy pinned to the sidewalk and had shoved a pistol in his mouth. Said that Adamares had been holding out on them, and now it was time to watch his boy die."

"How did you understand what he was telling Adamares?" Alva asked.

"I speak Spanish," Armagh said simply. "Quite well, actually."

He exhaled loudly, shook his head at the recollection of events. "So anyway, Adamares was completely paralyzed with fear. His boy was tryin' to scream, but he was chokin' and gaggin' on the gun. So I do what any good Samaritan would do: I gun the Land Rover, run it straight into the gang guy, and squash him up against the side of a bodega like a fookin' bug. Another MS-13 guy runs up to my window, getting' ready to blow me away. But I blow him away first. Rest of the MS-13 guys scatter, I yell for Adamares to grab his kid and climb in, and off I drive to our compound. You could say we became pretty good friends after that."

"Where's his boy now?" asked Alva.

"Duluth, Minnesota."

"How'd *that* happen?"

"Not your business, Alva. That's 'need-to-know' information, and you don't need to know. And don't you go askin' Adamares, either. You do, and I'll be very cross with you."

"That's some story," I said, shaking my head. I stood up. "Anyway, that's it for me. I'm turning in. This all should trigger some wonderful dreams."

"Yeah, me too," said Armagh. "No worrying about the bad dreams for me, though. When you been doin' what I do for as long as I been doin' it, you stop having them dreams."

Later, Alva told me exactly what had happened to Adamares Thuna. Or, more accurately, what she did to Adamares Thuna. It seemed that Alva relished telling *a tale,* dwelling on all the sights and sounds and details, adding colorful flourishes to her narration, Very colorful indeed.

"When I came up to stand watch," she said in a dramatic conspiratorial whisper, "I found Adamares reclining at the helmsman's station, letting the autopilot steer. Although the evening was warm and cloudless and we had a nice gibbous moon providing a surprising amount of light, the surface of the ocean was being churned up by a brisk chop, which created a constant roar of white noise. I nodded to Adamares, and then I eased myself down on the settee on the cockpit's high side. We sailed on as it got dark.

"I found myself pressing my fingertips against my temples, clenching my jaw. Quite abruptly, Victor, and quite clearly, I reached a moment of decision: *I'm too young to die. I have to follow the advice I gave you: 'If 'twere done, best 'twere done quickly'. Best 'twere done now.*

"I got up and began walking slowly up the windward side deck toward the bow. When I reached the forestay, I turned around and shuffled back aft, past the cockpit where Adamares was sitting. Then I turned and retraced my steps back up to the bow. Then I turned and paced back to the cockpit again.

"'Basta,'" Adamares said to me. 'Sit.'

"I sat down on the leeward settee, away from the wind, only a few feet from where High *Horse's* toe rail now was almost buried in the water as we heeled. Rather than tucking my legs under me like I usually do, I let them dangle down into the cockpit, with my legs straddling the pocket that holds our heavy double-grip winch handle. I could feel those two hard black handles pressing against the back of my calf.

"We stayed that way for a long time, Adamares steering, or, more precisely, watching the autopilot steer, me just sitting.

Breathing slowly and deeply, pretty jazzed up, trying to settle myself. Finding my center and gathering my courage. Working my way up to it.

"And now I had an 'it,' Victor. I knew what I was going to do.

"Finally, Adamares checked the autopilot and stood up to take a pee, taking hold of the leeward backstay and leaning out over the water. In a single motion he loosed the draw string on his trunks and let them drop to his ankles.

"Well, Victor, I had to draw an appreciative breath. His back was a powerful 'V' shape, his buttocks were lean and powerful. His legs were strong and athletic. And Victor, his cock was *gigantic*. That dude was *hung*. No two ways about it: Adamares Thuna was a *hunk*.

"As he steadied himself with his right hand on the backstay and used his other hand to direct his pee away from the boat, I quietly and gently eased the winch handle out of its pocket.

"I gripped those two smooth, black handles as if I was grasping a baseball bat. I tiptoed several steps toward Adamares, lifted the winch handle over my head and spun it as if I was twirling a lariat. I remember letting it spin freely to gather momentum: *Once, twice I let it spin*. On the third spin, I leaned in toward Adamares and aimed the spinning end of the winch handle into the back of his head, just behind his ear.

"I didn't know what to expect, but I was surprised that there was no scream, or shout, or even much of an audible thud. All I heard was the sound of the water rushing along the side of the hull. I recall the splashing of the bow as it lifted out of the water and then the *bang!* as it pounded down again.

"For a moment, Adamares' right hand still grasped the shroud. Then his knees buckled, and he swung sideways past the toe rail and out over the water, kind of like a garden gate. He just...*rotated* out over the rushing ocean, his trunks still around his ankles.

"Then he was gone. I didn't hear a splash, a cry of distress, or anything. No frantic churning of the surface behind *High Horse*. I looked back over the stern, expecting to see a body, perhaps floating face down, perhaps staring sightlessly up at the heavens. I saw nothing, Victor. Adamares Thuna had simply disappeared.

"At first, I had no emotional reaction to all this. I just sat down behind the helm. I examined the winch handle for signs of blood or flesh, but I didn't find any, so I just inserted it back into its pouch. The autopilot was still set. I remember the knotmeter was reading seven-point-nine. Man, we were leaving the scene of the crime in a big hurry. I don't know how long I just sat there. Finally, I spoke out loud to myself. I said, 'Well, Alva, at least you did *something*. Now you have to figure out what to do next.'"

Two hours later, I stirred, my well-wound circadian clock telling me it was nearly time to assume my watch. As I slid my legs over the side of the bunk, I sensed something unusual, something...amiss. *High Horse* was bobbing and pitching as the swells rolled under her, *but she was not driving forward, not sailing*. Then I heard the impatient slatting of a mainsail luffing head-to-wind and flapping uselessly from side to side.

Shouting to wake Armagh, I dashed up into the cockpit and was horrified to see Alva lying face-down in the cockpit, her legs lifted over her back behind her, her feet tangled in the multiple lines of the mainsheet. Feverishly, I freed her feet from the rat's nest of ropes and turned her over. Her eyes were closed, and her mouth was agape. Her head flopped from side to side as *High Horse* rolled in the waves. I sought a pulse on her neck and found it, slow but strong. Her respiration appeared shallow, but regular.

"Alva! Wake up! What happened?"

Alva did not respond.

"Eamon! Smelling salts! Quick!"

I followed this immediately with another shocked shout.

"Eamon! Adamares is gone!"

The smelling salts brought Alva around instantly. Her face recoiled from the sharp stench, her back arched, and she shook her head like a dog that's been skunked. "*What, what, what!?*" she groaned. She brushed my hand away violently. "*Stoppit, stoppit!*"

Superficial examination revealed no signs of injury or trauma anywhere, no lacerations or swelling, no broken bones. Letting *High Horse* continue to luff, Armagh and I eased Alva down into the salon and parked her in the dinette. I stood behind her, holding her by her shoulders, keeping her from slumping to the side or slamming her head down on the table.

Armagh spoke to her softly, urgently. "Talk to me, Alva. Where's Adamares?"

"Who?" Alva's eyes were blinking rapidly, but I could not tell if they were focusing.

Armagh took her cheeks gently in his hands.

"Where...is...Adamares?"

"On watch," Alva replied drowsily. "*His watch.* S'kay. Autopilot on. Let 'im sleep."

I felt a deep horror well up within me...accompanied by sharp suspicion. *Is best 'twere done quickly...*

"Alva, do you remember when you came on watch?"

Her voice was vague, distant. "Didn't come on watch. You said I didn't have to stand watch anymore."

"Well, what time did you come on deck?"

"I dunno. After we talked, right? After I heard the chime ding for Adam...Adama...*the other guy's* watch."

"Was Adamares there when you came up?"

"'Course. His turn to be on watch."

"Was he at the helm?"

"Sitting behind the leeward wheel. That was strange, Victor. Why wouldn't he sit up on the high side?"

"Was the autopilot on?"

"No idea."

"Did you talk with him?"

"Sorta. Said I wanted to learn Spanish and he laughed."

"What happened then?"

"Dunno. I guess we sailed awhile."

"Do you remember the last thing he said to you?"

"No."

"*C'mon, Alva! Think!*"

"Don't yell at me, Eamon. I think he said, 'Take helm. Gotta pee.'"

"Did you take the wheel?"

Alva's jaw clenched. "Dunno."

"Did you switch off autopilot?"

"Dunno. Probably not. Why would I do that?"

"Did you fall asleep?"

"Dunno. Musta."

"Did you hear any shouts or cries?"

"Dunno. Don't think so."

"How did you get tangled in the mainsheet? Did you trip?"

"Dunno. Dunno. Dunno. Eamon, *I don't know, okay?*"

With Alva tucked into her bunk in the master stateroom, Armagh and I sat in the cockpit, unaware that the hatch over the aft stateroom—the one directly over Alva's head— was partially open—open enough for her to hear our conversation.

"Go back?" I asked.

"No point. He probably went in at least ten or fifteen miles back, autopilot just kept us sailing along for as long as it was set. It would be dark all the way back, still dark when we got there. We don't know if he's hurt, or what. Face it, Adamares is lost at sea."

"Well, what now?"

"What now is that I've got a lot of serious thinkin' to do, boyo. I don't know *what* happened, if Adamares got careless and slipped while pissin,' or if Alva somehow killed him or pushed him over, or what.

"And her? Don't know if she tripped and knocked herself out. Or maybe she's play-actin.' If so, give her a fookin' Oscar. What is clear, Victor, is that the balance of power on this boat has just shifted, and I have to think about how I should handle all this goin' forward. I trust you will not be offended if I am very, very cautious from now on, if I take steps to make sure I don't end up swimmin' with Adamares. Any way you cut it, I sure as hell am in for some serious sleep deprivation, *aina?*"

"Okay," said Armagh as we all sat in the salon, the autopilot guiding us serenely onward. "This is how it's going to happen from now on. Simple split watch system, four hours on, four off, me and Victor. Alva, you will not be standin' any watches, but except when I'm usin' the head, you're going to spend every minute with me, never out of my fookin' sight for a moment. When I'm off watch, I'm going to use the aft stateroom to sleep, and Alva, you're going to be in there with me. Sleep or not, as you choose, but you and me are goin' to be constant companions.

"See this combination lock? Well, I just changed the combination. I'm going to take the hasp off the cockpit lock and move it to the inside of the stateroom door. Alva, I'm going to lock the two of us in whenever I'm sleepin.' Please don't get any ideas about scramblin' out the back hatch, because you can't get out without wakin' me, and Alva, if you try to do that, I'll hurt you.

"And as for you, Victor, don't you be tryin' some rescue stunt by comin' in through the back hatch, because if you do, I'll shoot you without so much as blinkin' an eye. I'm not going to try to stop you two from talkin' together, but understand that you won't be doin' any talkin' unless I'm there. Talk yes, whisper no.

"Look, you two. I know this is an unpleasant arrangement, but you only have to put up with it a few more days, then we'll be reachin' Grand Isle.

"Listen, I don't know what really happened to Adamares, but I'm sure you see that my back is up against the wall, and the best thing for me is to assume the worst about you two. It's a shame, Alva, 'cause I was startin' to trust you, but I'm not sure I can any more, *aina?*"

Chapter Twenty-Four
Fail

I was at the helm. Alva and Armagh were off watch, locked in the master stateroom, as dusk crept up on us. In my mind's eye, Eamon Armagh was probably fast asleep, and Alva was seated by the chart table, legs propped up on the queen-size bed, twiddling her thumbs. Waiting for time to pass before Armagh came back on watch.

Or waiting for something to happen—maybe waiting for *me* to make something happen. To do something to save our lives. After all, she had certainly done her part: boldly and brazenly, she had bashed Adamares Thuna's brains out and sent him over the side.

Entirely on her own initiative, Alva had opted for action, stepped up, made her move, and drastically changed the odds in this whole kidnap drama.

I wondered if I should be upset—or feel upstaged—because Alva acted without first clearing it with me or even conferring with me. I surveyed my emotions, and I found that I was *not* upset, found that instead of annoyance I felt intense admiration for her courage. *God, that woman is so tough.*

Thanks to Alva, we were now in a position where we could outflank Armagh. We could wear him out with long spells on watch (with Alva present, yes, but offering no trustworthy support). I could make sneaky, secret moves while out of his sight, make him wonder over and over whether we are active enemies or just a submissive elderly couple waiting passively to see what their fate will be.

You should do something, Victor, I told myself. *Time's flying. we'll be arriving in Louisiana soon.*

I let the autopilot take over, holding us on a rock-steady course with only an occasional electrical *brr-brr* to let me know it was keeping us on track. I moved back to the aft lazarette to recline on the sun pad and let the evening breezes wash over me. As I lay back, my calf caught on something and gave me a stinger.

I looked down and saw that I had caught my leg on the latch that locks the lazarette lid closed. The latch was open. *Which meant the lazarette was unlocked.* Which meant there was nothing between me and the Ruger carbine clamped to the underside of the lazarette lid except the decision to act.

I slapped my hand against my forehead, astonished at my stupidity. For days I had rambled around the back alleys of my brain seeking solutions to salvation, had inventoried all the tools we might use to stage a rebellion, had imagined various attack scenarios...and come up empty.

I had never *once* thought of the Ruger. The mere thought of it clamped under the lazarette lid gave me a blood rush, and for a moment I felt dizzy with excitement. A simple solution, if ever there was one: a single nine-millimeter shot through Eamon Armagh's chest.

I slipped the carbine quietly out of its clamps, turned it my hands. I'm not a gun guy and I had never fired the Ruger, but how hard could this be? Unfold the stock, make sure the magazine is in the receiver, slide the safety to 'fire,' aim at center mass, and pull the goddamned trigger. As I admired the Ruger's light weight and all-business appearance, I felt an enormous surge of power. *I was going to get us out of trouble. I was going to save the day.*

I decided I would not make the first move, go charging down the companionway and yell, "stick 'em up!" No, I would sit here quietly with the Ruger resting in the crook of my elbow, wait for Armagh to come on watch, and then get the drop on that son of a bitch.

The watch chime on the binnacle rang eight bells, and I heard Alva and Armagh stir in the stateroom below. I heard him retrieve a cold beer from the refrigerator and politely usher Alva up the steps in front of him. When she emerged, I urgently waved her to the side and raised the Ruger to my shoulder. As Armagh stepped into the cockpit, I pointed the gun at his chest and said, as calmly as I could, "raise your hands, Eamon, and sit down. Alva, come here and stand behind me."

Armagh cocked his head, put his beer down carefully on the cabin top, and seated himself about six feet in front of me. I was surprised that he did not seem surprised.

"We're going to take our boat back now, Eamon."

He smiled. "Well, actually you're not, Victor. Go ahead, mister knight in shining armor. Pull the fookin' trigger, put a bullet right in me black heart."

I was not going to play games with this asshole. I slid the safety off, aimed at where I thought his heart would be, and squeezed the trigger.

There was a dry click. No explosion, no gout of blood spurting all over the cockpit. Now Armagh pulled the luger from the waist band behind his back and aimed it at my face.

"If this were a movie, I'd tell you to put the gun down. But if it makes you feel good to hold it, go right ahead. Pull the trigger as often as you want. By now it's probably clear to you that it's not going to fire. That's because although there is a magazine inserted in your carbine, there are no bullets in the magazine. As a prudent precaution, I took all the rounds out after the Cuban ambush. You're running on empty, Victor."

Alva whimpered and put her hands over her mouth. I set the useless firearm on the floor of the cockpit. Armagh stood. He did not appear upset or angry.

"Did you think I wouldn't anticipate something like this? I don't believe you thought I was so stupid as to leave a loaded gun lyin' around, so I'm not insulted, Victor. But obviously you thought that I was *careless*, that as far as the Ruger was concerned, for me it was 'out of sight, out of mind.' And in that you seriously underestimated me. I've been in this whole hijacking game a long time. I sweat the details. I have learned *never* to leave myself open."

Still holding the Luger, he ran the fingers of his other hand through his hair. When he next spoke, his voice had a strange lilt, but no trace of his customary Irish brogue.

"Victor, you remember when we were talking about Alva's criminal exploits and you scoffed at me, told me I had taken a long walk off a short pier?"

"I remember that," I said.

"Well, *you're* about to take a long walk off a short pier. I want you to feel what Adamares felt when he ended up in the ocean. So now I want you to turn around and climb down to the stern boarding platform. Then I want you to step off into the sea. If you refuse, I will shoot Alva in the head, and then I will shoot you in the head."

The brain does funny things when exposed to ultimate stress. At this moment, the thought that crossed my mind was a quote from Samuel Johnson: *Nothing so concentrates a man's mind as the knowledge that he will be hanged in a fortnight.*

In order to keep Alva alive, it was clear what I had to do, but my fear surged over me like a tsunami. I felt Alva's hands tugging at my jacket sleeve, but, unable to look her in the face, I pulled away from her and stepped down onto the stern platform. I unclipped the safety gate and took a deep breath. I looked out over the deep green ocean. I was urinating copiously in my shorts and down my leg.

"Okay, now stop!" barked Armagh. "Turn around and look at me! And pull yourself together, man! The fact is that I am not going to insist that you jump in the ocean, but I want to impress on you who's really in charge here. Can we agree that I am really in charge here?"

Alva and I stood mute, both trembling violently.

"Do you remember when I told you two that I would not kill you unless I had to? *Well, I don't have to.* Not right now, anyway. Because I've got the Luger, and the Ruger has no bullets in it."

I could not believe what I was hearing. Alva began a low, keening wail. Armagh's expression was absolutely neutral, not friendly, not angry. Not warm, not cold.

"Look, Victor, I can't blame you two for wanting to save yourselves. I know that everything that's been going on since Aruba is very scary, a lot to handle for a couple of aging midwestern squares. In your position, Victor, I probably would have tried the same stunt. Only if I had tried it, *I would have made sure the fookin' gun was loaded.* Because I am a professional mercenary, and you are a smug old has-been who is totally out of his depth."

Now he brightened. "Alva, on the other hand, has convinced me that in terms of her financial skills, she is not in over her head. Her pitch was very convincing, and believe it or not, I intend to talk to her more about that. And I figure she probably would not want to talk to me, Victor, if I have shot you dead."

At that, Armagh laughed. I didn't.

"We are not far from Grand Isle. Can I get your promise—both of you—that you will not try this kind of stupid shit again? That we can finish our sea cruise in peace without me having to hold a gun on you every inch of the way?"

Chapter Twenty-Five

STILL PITCHING EAMON

I was back standing my watch in the cockpit, with Alva and Eamon off watch and closeted in High Horse's aft stateroom. The porthole facing into the cockpit was open, and once again I could both see into the stateroom and hear most of their conversation.

After several minutes of spinning in circles in the revolving chair at the chart table, Alva propped her heels on the bed and stretched her arms behind her head.

Eamon Armagh sat at the head of the bed, legs crossed comfortably, his back propped up against the upholstered headboard. He held a small red ledger open in front of him. Next to him on the bed rested a larger dark blue folio. His head bobbed left to right as he ran a sum on his hand-held calculator and then entered the number in the red ledger. Back and forth, forth and back. They sat in silence as the rush of ocean reverberated through *High Horse's* hull.

The boat suddenly pitched up, lifted by a rogue wave, and crashed back down into the wave trough, sending a powerful shudder through the boat. Armagh laughed and lifted his pen from his ledger.

"Stout boat, this," he said.

"I think it's an incredible boat," said Alva. "The attention to detail just floors me. I mean, look at this coverlet."

Alva's feet rested on a deep blue quilted bedspread, ornamented with a large gold compass rose embroidered in its center and edged with gold piping.

"Well," said Armagh, "a lot of this fancy stuff, all the extras and special plates and custom upholstery was ordered by the guy who had Oyster build this boat. Very rich guy. Bolivian. Wanted to make a floatin' honeymoon suite for his new bride. Not much of a sailor, but a proud owner, if you catch me drift."

"Where is he now?"

"He's dead. I killed him."

Alva's shock at Armagh's matter-of-fact tone was evident.

"*Killed him*! Why? When? Where?"

"The when and where are not important for you to know, Alva. The why is because he pulled some underhanded moves that made him needing to be killed. He tried playing both sides, and our side didn't like it. I got my orders from the higher ups."

Armagh raised his head and gave Alva a friendly smile. "But don't be gettin' your knickers all in a twist, Alva. I was ordered to kill Ottavio because he needed killin,' not because we intended to take possession of his boat. That was an…incidental benefit.

"Alva, I still don't know what happened to Adamares, but my opinion is that you and Victor don't need killin' at the present moment. But surely you'll understand if my senses are on high alert. Still, at least if you don't try any funny stuff, you should be okay, and I mean that.

"You might not believe this, but my people really are not into silly killin'. Like I said a couple of times already, no point in killin' people who don't need killin'. Besides, you were suggesting before that you and I might be doing some business together. We should focus on task at hand."

The utter calmness with which Eamon Armagh uttered these words shot a shiver up my spine. *This man is not to be trusted, is not honest, is not safe. He acts sane, but I think he is a sociopath.*

Armagh waved his hand in a shooing motion, signaling a change of subject. "But back on a jollier note, we were talkin' about this fine boat, *aina?* From the moment I first stepped on board, I coveted this boat. Oyster builds a very special boat, 'specially in the bigger sizes. Everything is hand-crafted, all the furnishings and curtains 'n' stuff is bespoke. When the owner takes delivery, they give him a binder that records which carpenter or engineer or whoever made what, installed what, tested what. Lot of peace of mind with an Oyster 62, let me say. It's a pleasure to be back on her again."

"So what happens to her after you drop the load in Grand Isle?"

"Had no time to discuss that with Mafin before I visited you folks at the marina in Aruba. I know that Mafin and Paredes don't give a shite about this boat. They've come to think that sailboats are a bad way to run cocaine. Once they manage to assemble a reliable fleet of narco-subs that won't fall apart in the middle of the ocean, they'll probably abandon this boat or just sink it."

"No!" exclaimed Alva sitting up abruptly. "They can't do that!"

Armagh shook his head, as though talking down to a small child. "But they can, darlin.' It's their boat, they'll do what they want."

"No, it's Victor's and my boat!"

"Listen, missy, don't be countin' on getting' this boat back. Odds are the boys will strip it in Grand Isle, take all that lovely expensive gear off—me, I want that Oscar unit—then tow it out to sea and scuttle it. Eliminate the evidence, you might say. But who knows? Maybe they'll listen to me if I say I want to buy it, let me keep it down at the marina at Isla Gazela for personal use. But I'm thinkin' that's a long shot."

"Why so?"

"Well, Paredes, he's a reasonable enough lot, understands the value in keeping his contractors happy. But Mafin, he's crazy suspicious, always worryin' that his cartel bosses or his own people will turn on him.

"I'm sure he thinks I would jump ship—just skip town and sail away, that is—if things get dodgy or I just get tired of makin' trip after trip up to the U.S. and back. And he's right, by the way. I've got nearly enough put away to think about enterin' another line of work."

Armagh tapped the cover of the red ledger with his index finger.

"This trip alone makes me more tired of temptin' fate than ever. Such troubles! This was supposed to be a straight up six-ton run in our brand new narco-sub. Noisy, smelly, but pretty fast. Instead it's a sailboat run, elegant, with delightful company to be sure, but way too damned slow, and with just a half cargo. Too risky. God, think of what those thievin' Cubans were goin' to do to us! Enough is about enough, I'd say."

Eamon Armagh is opening a door, I thought as I listened. Now I heard Alva tiptoe in and explore the territory.

"How old are you, Eamon?"

He seemed surprised at the question, unsure why she was asking.

"I'm forty-five. Just last week, in fact."

"How long have you been running drugs?"

"Since, like, forever. But from a tender age, I wasn't just a pusher, or dealer, or a mule. By eighteen, I was a *broker,* Alva. I put the parties together, like. The buyers, the sellers, the product.

"That got me into travelin' the world. Made the acquaintance of Mr. Pablo Escobar and sucked up to the Medellin crew as they were growing global and warring with the Cali Cartel.

"Understand, Alva, that I wasn't into *making* product. I was purely a distribution and logistics expert. I tended to my affairs, let Pablo Escobar and Carlos Lehder tend to theirs. When their shite hit the fan, I slid back to Ireland for a while, laid low, took back up with Irish Moira, then…"

"What do you mean, '*Irish* Moira'?"

"Well, there's another Moira, y' see. That's her actual name, believe it or don't. She's living in San Jose, Costa Rica. And then a third lass, she's not really a Moira, she's Marian, only sometimes I'm calling her Moira, and she laughs. She's in Louisiana, I won't tell you where."

"Well, that's all very domestic!" laughed Alva. "Do they know about each other?"

"Yuh, they do. They've never met, of course, but they all know the score. Know all about me, who I am, what I've done, what I do."

Alva voice dripped with scorn. "Why would any woman put up with such an arrangement?"

"Well, there's me great natural charm, of course, but one powerful incentive is probably the money."

"Money."

"Yeah, Alva. These ladies all do right by me, I do right by them. Each gets a hundred grand a year walking around money. Each is holding a paper to give to the bankers that says if I'm sent to prison for more than a year, there's a quarter mil payment, lump sum. If I'm killed, each gets two million. And they've got instructions on how to collect it, right and proper. There's lawyers."

"Wow," laughed Alva again. "And I thought I was the champion of situation ethics. Wouldn't it be cheaper just to buy your companionship a la carte?"

"Don't be a patronizing wise-ass, Alva. My ladies are not whores. Not women I rent for sex. I'm not looking for 'cheaper,' I'm looking for full-strength trusting relationships. It just so happens I have three of them. Each relationship is over a decade old, so how bad an arrangement can it be? All my Moiras live full, rich lives in their own location, pretty much on their own terms. And each seems to care quite sincerely for me, each understands that I come and I go. So be it."

I heard Alva shift gears. "And just how much money do you have put away, Eamon?"

Armagh closed the red ledger. "And that wouldn't be none o' your damned business, would it?"

"Well, it would be, if you engaged me as your laundress and financial advisor. Look, Eamon, if I can't bring anything to the party, I'll give you a round of applause and back off, leave you to your little red ledger. But I've been laundering millions of dollars for over thirty years, my friend, and I know about ropes where you didn't know there were ropes."

"I have to admit that you're probably right, darlin'. Fact is, I wrestle with numbers, when it comes to finances. But this here book says I'm doing okay."

He tapped the red ledger.

"What's the blue ledger?"

"Ah, that! That's the cartel's numbers for whatever I do for them. The shipments, the weights, the...'*consignees*,' the payments, the bankers they use, where the cash is at any given moment. Lord, and wouldn't the Drug Enforcement Administration love to lay their hands on that book!"

Alva waved her hand dismissively. "To hell with them. Back to you. What's your current net worth, and what vehicles do you have it invested in?"

Eamon laughed loudly. "Now ain't that a right squeeze of a question to ask a proud Irish man! On one hand, I'm keen to brag on myself, show you I'm playing A-level cricket. On the other hand, I always play my cards with my hands close to the vest. So…part of me answers 'about nine million dollars stashed here 'n' there.' And another part says, 'none of your fookin' business.'"

He laughed brightly.

"That's serious money, Eamon," said Alva. "Worthy of respectful first-class attention and active account management, I'd say."

"And that's what you claim you bring to the party?"

"Not claim, *deliver*. And here's what I can deliver: First, *confidentiality*. You'd just have to accept my say-so on that, Eamon. Second, *security*. My bases of operation—and I have several—are both invisible and impenetrable. All legitimate to the naked eye, all in plain sight."

Alva paused, to see if any of this was sinking in. It seemed to be. Armagh sat with his head cocked, listening attentively.

"Third, *liquidity*. When needed, no one can unlock your locked up assets as quickly and smoothly as I can. My systems are very complex, but I can really make them hum when there's a need. Need cash? I can always get you what you need, where you need it.

"Finally, and most important, *growth performance*. Your funds won't be sitting as cash in a locked room somewhere, safe but stupid. If I can't get you at least twenty per cent annual rate of return, you should fire me. But you won't. Because I can. Have for years, regardless of the global economic climate."

Alva paused for a moment, and I saw her reach out toward Armagh.

"How 'bout we do this, Eamon? Lend me your precious red ledger for an hour, let me do a preliminary review, get a sense of your big picture. I will give you, free of charge, an advisory opinion—strategy, tactics, allocation of assets, allocation of responsibilities, action items. And then I will hand your red ledger back to you. What happens next is entirely up to you. Think of this as an opportunity, not a sales pitch."

"And what does Victor get to know about my...*situation*. Do you two work as a team?"

"Victor is my husband, and he's also a valued client. But he's not my business partner. He's a baby when it comes to offshore financial management. Sure, I'd tell him in general terms how well you're doing, but the details are none of his business. And he would like it that way, Eamon. That way, if he's ever squeezed by the law, he can say, 'I don't know a damned thing' with the absolute ring of truth."

"Interesting."

"Are you just play-acting with me, Eamon, or are you really interested?"

"You are a very convincing woman, Alva. But I can't let myself lose sight of the fact that you're a crook. Maybe there's honor among thieves, maybe not. Let's see what plays out when we get to Grand Isle."

Chapter Twenty-Six

PHONE HOME

"Colin Harding speaking."

"Colin, don't speak, just listen."

"Delia! What is this…"

"*Just listen!* We have a major emergency. Actually, two emergencies. First, I have been abducted, and I am being held for ransom."

"Who, what…"

"My kidnappers are standing right here, listening to everything we say, so please just listen and then do what I ask, okay?"

A gasp. A pause. Then, "'Kay."

"In addition to grabbing me, a cocaine trafficking cartel—the same people who have grabbed me—hijacked *High Horse* in Aruba, along with Victor and Alva, right after you left. They are going to use the boat to deliver a big load of coke to someplace on the Louisiana coast.

"They've taken me to their base on an island somewhere along the coast—I don't know if it's Colombia or Venezuela or what. I have agreed to pay them ransom, and after the payment is made, they say they'll return me to Aruba and let me go. They also say they will release Victor and Alva once they make their coke delivery to the U.S. We have no choice but to believe them.

"*But that's only if everything goes smoothly, Colin.* If anything goes wrong, they'll probably kill all three of us. Our only hope is to follow their orders. So, do not contact the authorities—*any authorities anywhere*, understand? I assume that the ransom guys are able to contact the sailboat hijackers by sat phone, but they're certainly not going to let me talk to Victor or the other people on *High Horse* in order to coordinate everyone's activity. For that matter, they are likely to maintain radio silence so their phone calls can't be traced or tracked. So basically, what we've got is everybody flying blind right now."

"So how are we supposed to…"

"*Just listen!* That means we all have no way to coordinate what's going on, either them on the boat or us down here. We just have to hope the hijackers manage to land their load without problems, and it means all we can do at our end is to get the ransom payment to go off without a hitch. That's where you come in, Colin. Now tell me you understand everything I've told you."

"I understand everything you've told me."

"Good. I have agreed to a ransom payment of one gold ingot."

"An ingot! Holy Christ, Delia. That's worth over…"

"Colin! *I said I have agreed to pay a ransom of one ingot.* No cash necessary, no wire transfers, just a simple hunk of metal. I need you to hand-deliver that ingot. You can find one in my safe in my atelier. Please grab it, pack suitcases for you and Casper, and…"

"Casper? Who…?"

"Colin...*you know all about Casper*. You and *Casper* are going to drive straight through to New Orleans. I trust Casper as much as I do you, so you can let her in on what's going on. But don't tell anybody else, okay? Do not tell Christine about this whole situation, she'll go ape shit. Don't even tell her where you're going. Just grab the gold, get in the car and go. When you get to New Orleans, check into the Bourbon Orleans Hotel in the French Quarter and wait to hear from somebody. It probably will not be me. I'm not sure when we'll talk again, Colin, but you will hear from someone to arrange a meeting to give them the gold.

"Insist that the delivery be made in the lobby of your hotel. We definitely want it made in a public space. Do not let them take you off premises or drive you anywhere. Wrap the ingot in velvet and place it in a metal lock box. You can buy one on the way down at Wal-Mart or Target. Put the key to the lock box in a separate envelope. You keep the key and have Casper hold the lock box, okay? Give the kidnappers the key only when it's clear you're safe and the deal is done.

"Now here's the catch, Colin. I don't know how long all this is going to take or when the ingot delivery will go down. I'm assuming they won't do the ingot deal until the coke delivery has been made, but I don't know, maybe they'll want to wrap the ransom end up first. Their call. So you need to get down to New Orleans fast. Still, there's a good chance you may be sitting on your hands for a while.

"Victor's kidnappers were supposed to sail directly to Louisiana, and I bet that's over fifteen hundred miles from Aruba, maybe more. Victor told me *High Horse* can average seven knots, get up over eight if the conditions are right. That means we should figure about a hundred and seventy-five miles a day, maybe more if they power up the diesel. So, allowing for variable winds, their trip is probably going to take no less than ten days, and that's if all goes smoothly and there are no storms or anything. And all you can do is wait. I have no number for you to call or person to contact to find out where things stand. I'm sorry to put you and Casper through this, but we gotta do what we gotta do.

"One last thing, Colin. Please have Casper pack a suitcase for Alva with some of her land clothes in it, like sun dresses or dress-up stuff, plus some fresh underwear. She's going to be tired of sailing clothes, for sure.

"So that's it, Colin. For the moment, I'm fine. I'm being treated courteously, and I'm just going to sit tight. I'm sure everything's going to be all right if you guys handle your end. I'm counting on you, Colin. Can you two handle this? Keep your heads down and just get it done?"

"We will handle this," said Colin.

"When all this is over and I get up to New Orleans from Aruba, we'll have a bunch of stiff drinks at the hotel, right?" said Delia.

Delia ended the call and handed the phone back to Checo Paredes. "You satisfied?"

"Nice work, Delia," said Checo. "You sure do keep your cool under pressure. Are you sure you never been held for ransom before?"

———

Collie later told me that Cara remained calm when told that her respectable midwestern family was in the middle a crisis that combined kidnapping, ransom, hijacking and cocaine trafficking.

"You guys sure tick all the boxes, don't you? And here I thought you'd all put your lives of crime behind you."

"We thought we had! Or at least we were trying to, Cara. Who could have foreseen that buying a sailboat for a sea cruise would have led to this kind of bind? It's not Catch-22. It's more like Catch-five million. First the Cape Verde intruders, and now all this."

"What's all this about Casper? Why did Delia keep calling me Casper?"

"Casper the friendly ghost gun is what we named the ghost gun made by the intruder who intended to kill Alva. When it's closed, it looks like a bar of soap, so it's pretty easy to conceal. Delia was telling us that she has it and that she is armed."

"Then why did she say she was going to sit tight?"

"That was Delia's way of telling me she intends to escape."

Chapter Twenty-Seven

Catastrophe

I had to strain to make out Alva and Armagh's words, and I became drowsy, glad I would go off-watch in an hour. Between eavesdropping on them and tending *High Horse,* I was beat. I was finding it progressively harder to stay alert, harder to focus on what I was seeing.

The horizon had become a soft blur. The sea wore a strange short chop this morning. The wave height wasn't all that high, and the crests were manageable, but the waves had steep vertical faces, and the space between waves was short, making *High Horse* feel as if the boat was bouncing down a rutted country road. Rather than let the boat continue to slam directly into the swells, I bore off a bit to let *High Horse* quarter the oncoming sea. This resulted in a rhythmic rolling which I found faintly nauseating, rather like I'd had too much to drink and the room was spinning around me.

Now, in the near distance—perhaps only ten wave sets away—I thought I saw a flash of red buried in the body of a wave. But when I looked closer all I saw was a bluff dark green wall of water as the wave crested and broke in a sheet of foam. To clear my vision, I turned my head to the horizon for a moment. With my focus reset, I turned my gaze back to the sea in front me.

And cried out in horror.

Looming directly in front of *High Horse* was an enormous square shape, shiny and slimy with marine growth, sinking and rising as it bobbed from wave crest to trough. A shipping container, dark maroon with the numbers 33963K emblazoned on the top in white paint, was bearing down on the Oyster, and although I spun the helm to avoid a head-on crash, a collision was inevitable.

Behind the first container, I now saw another, this one a deep blue, and behind that a third, a mottled yellow, being jerked along on a length of hefty chain, like a dog on a leash.

High Horse was about to run aground on a steel island in the middle of the ocean.

I barely had time to scream "Hold on!" when the Oyster rammed into the first container and climbed up the container's side as it plunged into the wave trough beneath *High Horse*. Holding on to the windward helm with all my strength, I was whipped through the air in a vicious arc until my left knee smashed into the rim of the other helm. An excruciating pain, like an enormous jolt of electricity, shot up my leg and spasmed up the length of my back. My fingers opened involuntarily, and I dropped to the cockpit sole and began to slide backward toward the base of the helmsman's seat.

For a long moment the Oyster remained perched atop the container with its bow thrust high into the air until the cresting wave had passed under us. With an agonizing shriek of metal against metal—this had to be the sound of the Oyster's keel grinding against the giant red steel box—*High Horse* then slid backward down the face of the container, which now was jerked away by the thick chain connecting it to the other two containers.

As *High Horse* dropped free of the container, it flopped onto its port side, momentarily spilling the wind from its sails. As the Oyster began to right itself, the jib continued to flap wildly, but the main, still tightly sheeted, caught the breeze and refilled with a resounding bang. The effect was like stepping on the gas pedal of a spinning car. *High Horse* accelerated dramatically as the stern pivoted around, turning the boat to face the containers head on.

The next impact was thunderous, and my ears were filled with the sounds of destruction, an awful mixture of metal being bent and rent, cables snapping, fiberglass shattering, wood splintering and bolts being torn out of their bedding. The boat shuddered from bow to stern, staggering like a boxer caught full-face by a dreadful uppercut. Shards of fiberglass and teak—white pieces of hull and beige chunks of decking—flew through the air, were caught by the wind, and flung out over the sea.

Now the raft of shipping containers seemed to draw back, as if preparing for yet another attack. I later would have no idea where I had found the presence of mind to spring to action, but now, in one continuous motion, I twisted the key to fire the diesel, gave the diesel full throttle, and thrust the gear lever backward into reverse. The engine roared to life, revving wildly until the transmission slammed from neutral into reverse with a painful grinding protest. *High Horse's* stern squatted as the propeller found purchase, and the boat shot backward, pulling away from the heaving mountain of steel.

With a rush of relief, I saw the red and blue containers slide past the bow, but, like the wagging tail of a dog, the yellow container swung to the side, crashing into the Oyster and grinding down the length of the boat's entire starboard side. At last, the dreadful stack of writhing steel receded into the distance, leaving *High Horse* wallowing in its wake.

I stood shaking violently in the cockpit, my mind overwhelmed by conflicting commands and priorities: *What do I do first? How bad are we hurt? What about Alva? Will we lose the mast? Check the bilges! Send a mayday! Damage control! Am I all right? What now? What now? What now? What now?*

After agonizing seconds of paralysis, I slowly reached forward to the binnacle, pulled the throttle back, and eased the gear lever into neutral. The din of the roaring engine abruptly subsided, and *High Horse* settled with her beam to the oncoming waves. I looked up at the boat's rigging and saw the Oscar assembly mounted on the masthead swinging like a tetherball in an arc through the sky above the madly flapping mainsail as wave after wave pounded the boat.

I pressed the 'main furl' button on the console and felt a surge of relief as the mainsail slowly began to wind itself up inside the mast.

I wonder if it will ever come out again, I thought. *I wonder if this boat will ever sail again.*

I peered forward over the front deck and was shocked to see that the bow pulpit had been demolished, wrenched completely out of the deck, bent back over itself and twisted into a bizarre tubular sculpture. The chrome jib furling drum was visible in the pulpit's wreckage, slamming loose against a lifeline stanchion that had been bent double. The base of *High Horse's* forestay was now attached to nothing, and the forestay itself sagged in an untethered loop, swinging in the wind like a child's jump rope.

I pressed the 'jib furl' button and heard the click of the solenoid, but the furling drum did not rotate. The jib continued to slat violently against the inner forestay, now opening an ugly tear all along the sail's base. *Well, that sail is toast,* I thought with a curious detachment. *Wonder how much that repair will cost?*

I now realized that the only thing now holding the mast up was the inner forestay—and if that pulled loose, the entire mast would topple over backward like a drunken sailor cold-cocked in a bar brawl. I touched the 'Inner FS furl' button and was relieved to see the inner forestay's furling drum spin a quarter turn. *Good! That meant it was intact and the electric furler was still powered.*

I plopped down on the helmsman's settee and gasped in agony as a searing bolt of pain shot up from my knee as I flexed it. *That can't be good. Definitely serious damage there. I'm in for a world of hurt, for sure.* I sat for over a minute, panting deeply, waiting for the waves of pain to subside. When they didn't, I braced himself with my arms, forced myself to my feet and limped over to the open companionway.

"Alva! Alva!"

My shout was met with a tortured wail. I stepped down into the main salon on my good leg and was so shocked by what I saw that I sat down heavily on the companionway steps. The salon looked like a bomb had gone off. Packets of white-wrapped cocaine were strewn everywhere, the maple-decked floor was invisible beneath a sea of white, and mounds of cocaine packets had been thrown across the dining area and down the passageway to the galley. Several had ruptured, throwing a mist of white powder into the air. Plates and cups had been ejected from the overhead cupboards in the galley, and a pile of cooking pots and pans had spilled out of the lower cupboards. The pantry door had swung open, and jars and packages of dry goods lay intermixed with the cocaine packets.

I slid through the soggy white mess to the door to the aft stateroom.

"Alva!"

"Victor! Victor, help me!"

"Alva, are you okay? Let me in!"

"I can't! I can't! Eamon has it padlocked!"

Ignoring the terrible pain in my left knee, I took several steps back and charged at the door with all my strength. The impact tore the door from its hinges, and it crashed down on top of a prostrate Eamon Armagh, who lay crumpled and inert at the base of the bulkhead across from the bed. Alva sat stiffly on the edge of the bed. Her face was a mask of blood.

I pushed her gently onto her back and reached into the head to grab a bath towel. My first attempt to wipe away the copious blood merely smeared it, leaving Alva's face still covered in red. I reached into the sink, spun the spigot to soak the towel, and then again tried to wipe Alva's face clean. When I could finally see her skin, I carefully checked her face for lacerations, probed her cheeks and jaws for fractures. I found none and straightened up.

"Victor, what happened?" Alva whimpered.

"We hit a floating shipping container at full speed. Then we rammed it again. Actually, there were three shipping containers, all chained together."

"Am I hurt?"

"I think maybe you broke your nose, but that may be it—for your head, anyway. Alva, move your fingers and hands for me. *They seem okay.* Now lift your arms...Now bend your knees...Can you feel your toes? Now slowly, *slowly, Alva,* lift your head and turn it side to side. How does all that feel?"

"It feels...okay, I guess," whispered Alva. "I don't think I've broken my neck. I'm surprised I didn't. I got tossed into the side of the desk like a sack of bricks. What about you? *Are you hurt, Victor?"*

"Something's seriously wrong with my left knee or kneecap or something. I am in awful pain."

"What about Eamon?"

"Where is Eamon!?"

"He's pinned under the door you're standing on."

I jumped aside as if scalded, then flipped the stateroom door aside. Armagh lay rammed against the bulkhead, curled like a snail, with his chin pressed down to his chest. I noticed he wasn't wearing any shoes. A ballpoint pen was protruding from his chest at the base of his neck, spurting little gouts of blood in time with his pulse.

I jerked the pen out of Armagh's neck, relieved when a stream of blood ran from the hole, but not the gusher of bright red blood that would signal a ruptured artery. I checked for a pulse under Armagh's chin. I found one easily, firm and fast. I rolled Armagh onto his back and saw that his face was turning blue. I pried his jaw open, reached in, looped my fingers around the base of his tongue, and jerked sharply upward. Now he gasped and sucked in a huge draught of air.

"My God, Victor!" Alva bleated. "How'd you know to do that? Did you just save his life?"

"If I did, I regret it. If that bastard hadn't turned Oscar off, we wouldn't be in this mess."

An hour had passed since the impact. Alva had scrubbed her face clean, and, except for her peculiar matte complexion, she looked more or less normal. If her nose was broken, it wasn't a serious injury. She reported that she was able to breathe through her nose. Armagh, still unconscious, now lay on his back on the master suite berth. The spurts of blood from his neck had stopped of their own accord, and I decided the wound did not need tending. Alva had wrapped a bath towel into a tight cylinder and slid it behind the back of his neck, forcing his neck to arch.

"That should keep his airway open," she said.

"You should smother him now and just be done with it," I spat. "That son of a bitch isn't going to be of any help to us."

"Can we get going now?"

"Probably not a good idea, not until we know how badly we're damaged. Certainly, we're not going to sail anywhere. That would put huge stresses on the whole boat. But if the hull isn't too seriously compromised, I vote we fire up the diesel and try to get ourselves closer to land."

"*Where are we, Victor?*"

"The chart plotter says we are exactly forty-four miles due south of Port Fourchon, right off Louisiana's south coast. How's this for irony? Port Fourchon is a big oil depot just down the coast from Grand Isle, where the cartel was going to offload their coke. A bunch of good guys are only about ten miles away from our bunch of bad guys. Christ almighty, we were just about there, Alva. And now we *are* just about there. It sure would be nice if we could get to land before we sink."

Alva gestured for me to sit down at the dinette, forgetting that every flex of my knee shot a bolt of lightning through my leg. After my pained panting subsided, she spoke softly, as if deep in thought.

"I've been trying to think. Strategizing. I'm not so sure we shouldn't sink. Yeah, I think maybe it would be best if we did sink."

"What!?"

"Victor, my thought processes are still a little fuzzy, but let's think things through. Suppose Eamon calls his buddies at Grand Isle for help, and suppose they zoom right out. Either to offload *High Horse* here out on the ocean, or to try to nursemaid her into port. Once they get involved, what happens to us?"

The hard truth dawned on me as if I'd been slapped in the face.

"They kill us," I said.

"Well, that's my bet, and I'm not sure any pleas for mercy from Eamon Armagh would carry much weight with them, given all that's happened on this trip, what with the Cubans and all."

I knew Alva was right. "And Plan B is just about as bad," I mused, trying to put ideas together. "Suppose we call out a mayday, and the U.S. Coast Guard comes to our...*rescue*. What happens then, and what happens to *us?*"

Alva spread her hands in an 'ain't-it-obvious?' gesture. "They find a sailboat loaded with cocaine. And, they think, *a bunch of smugglers*. So they arrest all of us. We claim we were hijacked. *Think they just let us walk away*? No way, Victor! They slam us in the brig while they take their sweet time investigating just who the hell we are.

Even supposing I come away clean as Mrs. Elva Harding, innocent elderly newlywed, what do they find when they look *you* up? Check *your* criminal record? *Hmm, this Victor Harding's been a busy boy.* Feds let a Louisiana jury, who are likely to just *love* Yankees, decide our guilt or innocence. We run up huge legal fees, get convicted anyway. Bottom line? Some heavy time in the slammer. If I'm lucky, I get to share a cell with Eamon Armagh."

We lapsed into silence. "I'm not sure we have to decide what to do right now," said Alva. "I think first we have to figure out what shape this boat is in, whether we can possibly make shore on our own."

"Amen to that."

"But one thing you absolutely have to do first."

I arched my eyebrows.

"I want you to take one of our mooring lines and tie up Eamon Armagh good and tight. Lash him to the bunk. I do not want to be dealing with him—even talking to him—until we get our thinking straight."

Now she made a eureka, the-lightbulb-just-lit-up face "Oh…hey! That gives me an idea. What's our first aid kit like?"

"It's not a *kit*. It's a suitcase. The full nine yards, just like the kind of medical kits the round-the-world ocean racers carry. It's got everything, including Ace bandages to wrap this crippled knee of mine."

"Before we do your knee, does your marvelous suitcase have any chloroform?"

I blinked in surprise. "Why…yes, I guess it does. In case they ever had to do emergency surgery and needed to put someone out quick."

"Well, I want you to chloroform Eamon Armagh. Put that bastard out."

"What? Why? He's already out. Isn't having him tied up enough?"

"Well, I want to *keep* him out. I don't want him coming to and thrashing around. I don't want to hear him, I don't want to talk to him. Or worse still, sneaking on to the radio, sending rescue calls to his buddies, or trying to gas-light us, or trying *anything*. I want him *out.*"

"God, Alva, I'm no medic! I don't know how to use chloroform! This isn't some James Bond movie! I could end up killing the guy."

"What's wrong with that?" said Alva.

As the sun rose higher in the morning sky, the chop abruptly subsided, leaving *High Horse* bobbing gently on a shiny sea as smooth as a mirror. Using Alva as a crutch, I hobbled up to the bow, wended my way past the demolished pulpit. The entire front of the boat—both deck and hull— had been smashed in, its once-elegant nose and chin pushed back all the way to the anchor windlass.

Our sleek ocean cruiser looked like a bulldog, or like a prizefighter who has walked into a sharp jab straight to the nose. On the side of the hull about two feet aft of the first impact point, a deep gash penetrated through the gelcoat and hull layup, an ugly laceration that traveled all the way down to the waterline. As *High Horse* bobbed quietly, most of this dark slash remained above water, but I was sure the damage extended below the water line.

"How bad is it?" whispered Alva hoarsely.

"Looks scary, but might not be too bad," I said. "It's ugly, but the boat has a large anchor locker up front, with a stout bulkhead between the locker and the front stateroom inside. If that bulkhead isn't compromised, the boat may not take on water through this gash, except into the locker itself."

"Can we use our fancy inflatable collision mats on this?"

"Excellent question, Alva! Clearly you were listening during our orientation. But I'm not sure how well the mats would work on this irregular pushed-in shape. The mats work best when you wrap 'em around a smooth round surface, like if the boat ever got holed directly through the bottom. They like a nice continuous surface to hug."

"Shit," muttered Alva. "So what do we do?"

I began to tremble again. I did not want to unravel. Not here, not now. I was operating on autopilot, and I wasn't sure how long the plane would keep flying before I lost control. "I assume you brought your underwater camera along on this trip?"

"Yeah," said Alva. "I bought a very spiffy Sea Life Micro a couple of months ago. For scuba diving. It has a spotlight on it. Produces great shots, razor sharp."

"Digital?"

"You bet."

"Well, get ready to shoot. We're going to need underwater shots of the damage. I need to see what's what down there, and I'm also going to need to document the damage for insurance purposes."

Before Alva went over the side for photo recon, we stopped long enough for a light meal—some cheese and cold chicken and hot tea. And for me, four fingers of rye whiskey, gulped from a tumbler.

As we sat at the table in the salon, I felt myself relax a little. "I'm pleased, Alva. I think the bow damage may look worse that it really is. Structurally, that is."

Alva looked down at her feet. "Then why are my shoes wet?"

I stared at the salon floor where piles of cocaine packages lay strewn randomly over the cabin sole. Now the packages over the panel in the cabin sole that covered the keel sump began to slide back and forth in time with *High Horse's* soft rolling motion.

"Oh, no," I whispered. "I should have thought of that. What an idiot I am."

"What? *What!?*"

I hobbled over to the electrical panel, began flipping circuit breakers on and off savagely. "Shit, shit, shit!" I cried out.

"What, what, what?" Alva echoed me.

"We should have been hearing the bilge pumps all along. I don't hear any."

"How many are there?"

"Four. A big Rule pump to pump the bilge down in the keel sump, one smaller unit in each of the shower stalls. They're supposed to switch on automatically the moment they sense moisture. Now I can't get 'em to turn on at all, even with manual override. Something's wrong with all our pumps."

Fighting panic, I forced myself to slow my breathing, ran my brain through a checklist of options.

"Alva, while I'm dicking around here, I want you to crawl up to the forepeak and reach through the little door into the anchor locker and see if we're taking on water up there. As you do that, I'm going to switch out and replace the circuit breaker for the main bilge pump. Our first order of business is to pump out the bilge pronto—the sump is deep, and it holds a lot of water. A lot of water means a lot of extra weight."

"What about the Kifco pump? You told me that thing could pump the ocean dry."

"Next order of business. But it will take a while to drag it out of the aft lazarette, set it up on deck, rig hoses and crank it up. We're still doing first things first."

Alva hopped up from the table, and after much thrashing and cursing in the forepeak, she called back, "I can't get to the anchor locker! It's completely blocked with all those bundles of cocaine. I can't even reach the locker door, much less open it!"

"Okay, okay," I called back. "Actually, that's probably a good thing. All those packages leaning against the bulkhead are probably reinforcing it. Try doing this instead—move back from the bulkhead about five feet and try to dig a tunnel down through all the cocaine packages. Just throw 'em out of the way and see if you can reach all the way down to the cabin sole. Again, what we need to know is if they're wet or not."

Once I had snapped a new circuit breaker into place, I flicked the switch and felt a wash of relief as I heard the big Rule pump prime itself and begin loudly sucking up water from the bilge. Now the water no longer covered the cabin sole, and I could hear the pumped-out water splashing into the ocean outside *High Horse*. The main bilge pump was working.

Now I stood to retrieve our huge rechargeable marine spotlight from the chart table and accidentally stepped on a package of cocaine. The package ruptured, spilling its contents across the sole, and the coke immediately turned into a slippery gooey paste. I lost my footing, crashing down on my back and slamming my bad knee against the table leg. For a moment I lay in speechless agony, trying to find the voice to scream.

I was still lying there, feeling the water soak into my clothes, when Alva cried out. "Victor? Victor! I'm down to the bottom row of packages...*and they're soaked!* I don't know where the water's coming from, but there's got to be a lot of water up here."

Panting with pain, I crawled to the chart table and pulled the flashlight from its rack. When I shone the dazzling beam down into the sump, at first all I could see was a slowly receding oily black surface. Then, after what seemed like an eternity, the powerful pump sucked enough water out of the bilge to allow me to see the tops of the eight huge bolts that held *High Horse's* 20,000-pound lead keel to the bottom of the boat.

I froze, then heard myself whimper in dismay. The impact of the keel with the shipping container had torn the front four keel bolts right through the bottom of the boat. Every time *High Horse* bobbed in a swell, I could see the tops of the keel bolts and the huge nuts that secured them moving from side to side. And every time they swung left and right, a jet of water shot up from each bolt.

"Alva," I called out as calmly as I could. "Would you come back into the cabin? We have a major emergency on our hands. We just ran out of options."

I should not have been surprised at how willingly Alva, always a responder-in-the-moment, agreed to go over the side.

"Hell, piece of cake," she said with a forced smile. "Water's warm and calm, visibility's good. No sign of sharks. Let me grab my mask and fins. My trusty camera is charged and ready to shoot."

This was pure bravado. I was betting that Alva was scared to death.

It was not more than five minutes before Alva climbed back up the stern boarding ladder. She shook the water out of her hair, wrapped a bright turquoise towel over her head, and flopped back dramatically on the large white sun pad. She scrunched up her eyes, shook her head in dismay, handed her camera to me.

"You're not going to like what you see," she said flatly "The pictures are clear, even when I was looking at the screen underwater. The news is bad."

I looked over Alva's shoulder as she scrolled through her photos. She had started her photography at the bow, shooting head-on and then begun taking shots from both sides. The collision damage we had seen above the surface continued downward past the water line and curved around the hull's curved forefoot. Most of the white gelcoat was missing, and the dull brown layup of the fiberglass hull underneath was smashed and ripped clear through. In short, there was a large hole in the front of the boat. The anchor well bulkhead was the only thing preventing massive flooding.

As it dragged along the side of the hull, the yellow steel shipping container had carved huge gouges out of the boat's gelcoat and created three particularly large gashes. Alva had held the camera close to these wounds, and the focus was good. I saw that none of these awful-looking abrasions had penetrated all the way through the hull, but repairs—if any were ever attempted—would basically require removing the entire side of the boat and remolding it from scratch. In such cases, I knew insurance companies usually just totaled the boat.

Next, Alva had carefully photographed the leading edge of the keel and had taken numerous shots of the keel-to-hull joint. The pictures were grotesque, and I gasped with dismay at *High Horse's* death sentence. The impact with the container had carved a large chunk of lead out of the front of the keel, leaving a pie-shaped gap. Worse still, the keel had been sprung from the bottom of the keel sump and wrenched sideways.

The tops of the front four keel bolts still projected into the hull—just where I had seen them in the beam of my spotlight from inside—but they clearly had no purchase. They were not supporting or being supported by anything, and every lateral movement of the hull rocked the entire front of the keel from side to side.

I drew my hands over my face and exhaled deeply. "Looks like we're cooked," I said. "The whole keel has had a major structural failure. That's not just a leak, Alva. The remaining hardware that's holding the keel to the hull is on its last legs, and although shooting the gap full of Aqua Flex caulk might slow the keel leak for a short while, Aqua Flex is a just rubberized sealant. It doesn't add any structural strength. It's soon just going to be torn away."

I paused, letting a vivid picture of the ultimate catastrophe paint itself in my imagination. "As the keel continues to work back and forth, it's going to exert more stress on the remaining keel bolts than they can handle. One by one, they'll fail. When the last one fails, the keel will fall off. When the keel falls off, *High Horse* will fall over on its side like a pole-axed ox. If we dog down all the hatches and ports to keep water out, the boat will continue to float on its side for little while. But the pumps would be sucking dry air, and eventually the boat will fill with water…and just sink."

When Alva Batek turns ashen, she *really* turns ashen. Not only did her dark skin pale and turn chalky gray, but the shine vanished from her complexion. She looked dreadful, terrified. "My God, that's awful!" Alva squeaked in a strange mewling cry that I had never heard before.

"You have no idea how helpless you feel when a boat turtles on you, Alva. And I've been there. Twenty-five years ago, I was on a Maxi—a big seventy-foot ocean racer—when we hit something at full speed. We never found out what. Our boat had a long, thin vertical keel with a big torpedo-shaped lead bulb at the bottom. It was like a huge lever, and *bang!* the impact instantly tore the whole keel right off the boat. Left a big hole in the bottom—we shot pictures through it later as the boat was floating on its side. Fortunately, this boat had been built with a foam core to give it strength while keeping it light. The foam was buoyant. So we just floated happily on our side, waiting for rescue. Until a squall came up."

I shook my head at the horrible memory. "*Finito!* Life rafts. Life jackets! Survival suits! Fortunately, we were within helicopter range of Johannesburg. Only one guy died. I said at the time it was an experience I never wanted to have again. And...here we are."

I moved over to sit down next to Alva on the sun pad, put my arm gently across her shoulders as she began to cry. Now I took her hand, kissed it lightly.

"Alva, let me say this calmly, so I don't panic the crew. After you've gone back down and squeezed some Aqua Flex all around those jiggly keel bolts to try to seal them a bit, come up here, dry yourself off...and prepare to abandon ship."

Alva's eyes grew wide. "*Now? Already?*"

"No time like the present. The water's calm. The day is warm. We've got about ten hours of sunlight left. We're within fifty miles of shore, and radio reception is likely to be good. We've got all the equipment we need to save ourselves, but we have to get that equipment ready. Half an hour should do to pack up, another half hour to scuttle the boat."

Alva's shoulders shook. "Oh, no. Oh, no, no, no."

"Alva, choices come easy when there is no choice. We're sitting here in a fatally crippled boat filled with thousands of pounds of cocaine. If the coke runners find us, they'll sure as hell kill us. If the Coast Guard finds us, they'll arrest us. Our only chance to get away clean is to be floating around in our nice new bright orange life raft, elderly victims of a freak accident. We'll be a dandy human-interest story for a couple of days: *'A Dream Turned to Tragedy.'* Or *'Midwestern Seniors Cheat Death.'* Or…"

"Okay, okay, I get the picture," Alva snapped. "So okay, here are *my* ground rules once they fish us out of the drink. No newspaper interviews, no TV interviews, no YouTube, no video that shows our faces. Remember why we left Cape Verde, Victor. *I do not want to make news.*"

"I hear you," I said. "Let's just get our asses back to Green Lake and go into seclusion for a while. Take a hot shower. Get soused. Eat my wonderful cook's buttermilk pancakes and Maine lobster salad. All that."

"You're totally forgetting something. Highest priority."

I drew a blank.

"How do we save my daughter?"

I felt like I had been punched hard in the stomach, and for a moment I could not draw breath.

"Holy Christ," I whispered. "We are really screwed. Remember what Armagh said? In order for the whole ransom deal to go down, everything had to go smoothly with the cocaine drop. 'No hitches,' that's what he said."

Alva began to sob, and I pulled her face tight against my shoulder. "The answer, Alva, is that *we* are not going to save your daughter. Delia is going to have to save herself. The only good news is that she's a lot smarter than they are and that she's an incredible survivor, has been all her life. That and the fact that she is armed with Casper."

Alva looked at me, confused.

"Don't you remember Casper the friendly ghost gun?" I asked. "It's going to give Delia the element of surprise," I said, "providing they didn't find it on her."

"What can she do with that against all those animals with Glocks and AR-15s?"

"A lot more than she can do without it."

Alva seemed to like hearing that, and she gathered herself even as tears continued to roll down her cheeks. "So, first thing, let's save ourselves. Just one detail," she said, now fixing me in an intense stare.

"What do we do with Eamon?"

For me, anyway, a life-and-death decision was easy and instant.

"Simple. We have to take him out. At this point, it's a matter of self-preservation. No different from Cape Verde."

"But at Cape Verde, people were pointing guns at us. Here the guy is out cold. What's more, Eamon specifically said he wasn't going to kill us. And he let you off the hook when you tried to shoot him."

"Are you actually suggesting that we save this scumbag just because he postponed murdering us? Do you think we owe Armagh a fair shake now just because we're sinking? As I see it, the moment Eamon Armagh hijacked our boat, he was okay with imposing a death sentence on us. And when he turned Oscar off, he put all our lives at risk."

I noticed that Alva's tears had dried, that her expression had hardened. She sighed, cast her eyes up to the heavens. "Yeah, okay. You're right. I'm sorry you saved his life when he swallowed his tongue. I must say that at this point I would gladly take revenge on that son of a bitch for ruining our life."

"So now you're comfortable with vengeance?"

"I'm not hard-hearted, Victor. Sure, I'm tough, but I'm not mean. If I took justice into my own hands, I wouldn't be acting for pleasure. I'd be doing what is necessary *to survive.* And I think that's where we are now. Survival mode."

"I'm glad you see it my way. My opinion is that if we let him live, our own chances of survival, whether right now or in the long term, basically drop to zero. If Eamon survives, he'll just lead the cartel to us, and they sure as hell aren't going to let us live."

Alva washed her hands over her face, shook her head as if clearing cobwebs. "Well, there's a remedy to that problem," she said. "Okay, before we discuss details, would you excuse me for a minute? I've got to hit the head. I'll be right back."

She rose and shook the kinks out of her legs, eased herself down the companionway. I heard her move into the master stateroom and assumed she was just going into the head for a pee.

"Shit!"

"You okay?" I called.

"I'm okay," Alva called back.

Now I heard the desk drawer being jerked out in the navigation station.

"Shit!"

"Alva, what's going on?"

"It's okay, Victor. Stay cool. I'll be right up."

Now I heard Alva banging around in the galley. More drawer pulling.

"Alva, I'm coming down!"

"No, Victor. Just stay there. I'm on my way."

Perhaps two minutes later, Alva climbed out of the companionway carrying a bottle of Irish whiskey and two crystal tumblers.

"Buy you a drink, cowboy?"

"What the hell was going on down there?"

"Well, Eamon Armagh seems to have died, and I thought we might mourn his passing with a tot of Irish Whiskey."

For a moment, I was completely confused. "Did he…did you…what…?"

"I checked Eamon's waistband for his pistol. It was there, but the magazine wasn't. I had no idea where it was. That was 'shit' one. Then I checked under the nav station drawer for the hidden Luger. It was there, but that magazine was gone, too. That was 'shit' two. I was running out of options."

A horrific picture came to mind. "Did you *smother* him, Alva?"

"No, sir, I did not. I thought that might take too long. Thought I might lose my nerve as I stood there leaning on his face."

"So what…?"

"I went into the galley and grabbed our boning knife. Then I slit Eamon Armagh's throat. Simple as that."

As I recoiled in shock, Alva placed the tumblers on the cockpit coaming and poured three fingers of Irish into each. Now Alva looked at me, smiled triumphantly, and lifted her tumbler. "Cheers, Victor. Here's to a brighter day."

Chapter Twenty-Eight

FLIGHT RISK

Provided the sentry was present, which he invariably was, Paredes allowed Delia to recline on the bright green lounge chair positioned in the shade outside the door of the apartment and enjoy the cool tropical breezes blowing across the boatyard. From here she had a panoramic view of all the comings and goings in the marina.

After several days of feverish activity down at the dock, she saw the relaunching of the failed narco-sub, now with a patched bottom, the diesel engine, propellor and rudder removed, and two enormous outboard motors hung on a new bracket fastened to the stern. It looked absurdly tail-heavy, but when the crane lowered it into the slip, it floated evenly, its deck just barely above water, its cabin looking like a duck blind sticking up out of the mossy green water. They fired the engines up and everything appeared to work. There were cheers from the boatyard workers.

On this eventful day, Delia also observed the arrivals of two distinctly different sets of visitors. First was a parade of three black GMC Suburbans, all polished to a high luster and shining brightly in the sun. When the SUVs stopped in front of Mafin's office, the occupants of the front and rear vehicles leapt out and formed a security cordon around the middle one, from which alighted an extraordinarily tall and extraordinarily dark-complected man.

His suit was impeccably tailored, his polished black oxfords reflected the morning sun, his black hair, matching his black shirt and black tie, was pomaded and slicked back, his eyes were hidden behind dark aviators. *"He's a total cliché,"* Delia thought, *"but man, I would not want to get crosswise with that cliché."*

The visitor's gait was a smooth, confident glide as he eased into Mafin's office, the door to which opened before him, as if he had been expected. After he disappeared inside, Checo Paredes came sprinting across the parking lot from the slip where they'd launched the patched-up narco-sub, his face a mask of alarm. He hurried into Mafin's office, and the door slammed. To Delia's great interest, what followed was a half hour of screaming voices, one clearly Mafin's tinny bark, the other a deep, full rumble. She couldn't make out the words, but it was clear that everyone was deeply unhappy.

When the door to the office popped open, the visitor, fists clenched and his stride urgent, hurried to his Suburban, climbed in and slammed the door as his security detail sprinted to their cars. The shiny black parade tore out of the parking lot in a hail a gravel. Through the office door the visitor had left ajar, Delia could hear Mafin continue to yell at the top of his lungs, evidently at Paredes.

Moments later, a caravan of four utility vehicles drove in—battered, mud-splattered trucks that looked like the trucks used on African safaris: flat sides, olive drab paint, giant tires, canvas tops, tall antennas sticking up from their rear bumpers. No markings, no license plates, no items unnecessary for jungle travel.

The caravan's eight olive-skinned occupants, dressed in dusty fatigues—jaws set, scowls deep and menacing, brows shaded with soft floppy olive drab hats—jumped out of their rides and strode forcefully across the parking lot into Mafin's office. Now there was more yelling, but this time there was only one voice,

Mafin's, and he spoke with uncontrolled fury. Delia jumped as she heard the crash of breaking glass, as if a mug or tumbler had been thrown against a wall.

The tirade went on for several more minutes, Mafin's screaming now alternating with someone's calmer, deeper responses. Delia did not hear Paredes' voice. When this second set of visitors emerged into the bright sun, their leader wore a broad smile and the others seemed energized, expectant. Delia thought the leader looked like a general leading his troops off to war.

Now Paredes stepped out of Mafin's office, closing the door carefully behind him. He stood for a moment, his head first looking up at the sky, his chin then dropping as he stared at the ground. Ordinarily, Checo Paredes was a cool customer, and Delia thought the change in his posture and demeanor both striking and alarming. *This guy has just been reamed out,* she thought.

Checo was trembling—from fear or anger Delia could not tell—and he was taking deep, heaving breaths. Now, in slow, measured steps he crossed to Delia, his brow furrowed and looking as if he was trying to organize his thoughts. He stood in front of Delia, his hands clasped behind his back, the cords in his neck taut and strained. He *phooshed* a deep sigh. His speech was strained, almost whispered.

"Delia, a great many things have gone wrong, all of them involving Armagh and the sailboat. First, we hear from the Cubans that after they loaded half the cocaine shipment into the sailboat at their shore base and headed out to transfer Victor and Alva back on to the sailboat, their boat—and their people—simply disappeared. They waited several hours, tried to raise their crew on the sportfisherman by radio, and then motored out in their launch.

"All they found was a slick, a lot of debris, and some flames still burning on the surface of the water. Their conclusion was that they'd been double-crossed and that their crew had been ambushed. They tried to contact Armagh on the radio and got no response.

"This was a few days ago, and now they are telling us, basically, that they plan to go to war with us. They say our cartel's boats and our people are open game. This group had never been warm friends with us, but on several occasions they had been *useful* friends, you know, and everyone had worked to mutual advantage. Now they are our enemies, and there does not seem to be any way to calm things down or even negotiate with them.

"Mafin was blind-sided by this, and as you would expect, he went crazy. Of course, he does not know what really happened, but he's assuming that Armagh stole the boat and the shipment. Forgetting all about whether his transmissions can be tracked by authorities, Mafin has been trying to raise Armagh by sat phone and radio over and over again, and he is getting no response.

"He also has contacted our base up in Grand Isle, and that's all bad news, too. Even allowing for bad weather or lack of wind, Armagh should have been there by now, but they have not seen him or heard from him. They have called him repeatedly—on VHF radio, cell phone, sat phone, everything—and they get no answer. They have several big speedboats they could use to go look for him, but they have no idea where to look.

"To top things off, the U.S. customer for Armagh's shipment, our biggest customer, says he's had it with *Cartel de los Soles*, and will not do any more business with us, ever. He was already bent out of shape by all the delays in delivery of this shipment, and he says he can't rely on us. I cannot tell you what a huge blow this is to Mafin. This route has been our life blood, and you can't just put another network of customers and logistics together overnight. Mafin is in a very, very bad place.

"That brings us to you, Delia, and what to do about the ransom. Before all this bad stuff happened, all the arrangements seemed to be in place with your courier in New Orleans. We were going to send our people to pick up the ingot this weekend. Mafin still intends to send them, hoping that your courier has not heard about the Cuban disaster or the fact that Armagh and your people have gone missing. Our people are going to show up at the hotel, and if your guy is in the dark and still ready to deal, they'll just grab the ingot and vamoose.

"But Mafin suspects that all these events are part of a coordinated and carefully staged conspiracy, and that your courier is probably in on Armagh's disappearance. If that's really the case, all bets are off, and our guys will not try to complete the ransom deal, they'll just bolt. If that happens, there is no way Mafin is going to let you go. He says he won't kill you right away, because if he does finally track down Armagh somewhere, you're still a valuable bargaining chip.

"But the longer things go without Mafin finding out what happened to that sailboat, the more you're just a nuisance. And as you've seen, Mafin's patience is as short as his temper. In any event, you're going to be staying with us for a while. I will continue to act honorably and try to protect you, Delia, but you must understand that compared with the stakes of the missing cocaine shipment, the ransom deal is lower priority right now.

You should pray we locate Armagh and that there is some good explanation for all of this."

Delia cocked her head politely and rose to go into her room.

"Thank you, Checo. Thank you for being honest with me. I have been in frightening situations before, but I confess none has ever been as scary as this. If I could trust Mafin, it might be different, but…"

She trailed off as she closed the door behind her.

Once in her room, Delia checked her leather cross-body pack to make sure her passport and American Express card were still in the zippered bottom compartment, and slung the bag over her chest, commando style. Then she dug into her carpet boat bag, removed the plastic toiletries pouch, and took the loaded ghost gun from the Tampax box. She also pulled out three additional rounds of ammunition. There were more bullets left in the box, but Delia, knowing the gun had already been fired three times to kill the Cape Verde intruder, thought it probably was only good for a total of six more shots before warping and jamming.

Delia looked out the window across the parking lot to the helipad to where Leon appeared to be finishing some maintenance in the engine compartment of the helicopter. Apparently done, he lifted two access panels from the ground and carefully refitted them to the rear of the fuselage. He then wiped the whole side of the helicopter down with shop towels, climbed into the cockpit, and began attending to some paperwork on a clipboard in his lap.

Now Delia heard footsteps on the patio outside her apartment door. She cracked the door and saw Aldo, the burly sentry, walking toward the men's room on the other side of the marina store. Checo was nowhere in sight. Mafin's door was closed. Leon was still sitting over in the helicopter. For the moment, the sentry guarding her was absent.

It had to be now.

Delia opened the apartment door and walked, slowly and nonchalantly, across the parking lot to the helipad. She moved around behind the helicopter's tail and eased down the passenger side, quite sure she could not be seen from across the parking lot. She slid the ghost gun out of the cross-chest pack, unfolded the grip and snapped it into place. She racked the slide and could feel the round slide into the chamber. She rested her finger lightly on the trigger.

Leon looked up, startled, when she opened the passenger door. "Delia, what are you…"

Delia put her finger to her lips. "Shush, Leon. No time to talk." She pointed the ghost gun at his face. "We are going for a trip, right now."

Leon gaped in disbelief. "This some kind of joke? That looks like a toy gun. You must be…"

Delia moved the ghost gun a foot to the right and pulled the trigger. The sharp report reverberated throughout the cockpit, and a neat circular hole appeared in the helicopter's plexiglass windshield in front of Leon's shocked face. He recoiled in terror and started to open his door.

"Don't Leon, or I will kill you!" Delia hissed. She clambered up into the passenger's seat and again aimed the gun at Leon's face. "Start us up and get us out of here! Now!"

"I can't!" Leon yelled back. "You have to warm up the engine to get the oil to…"

Delia again interrupted him. "Fuck the engine oil! Start the engine *right now,* and get us out of here, or I will shoot you! I will, Leon, believe me, I will!"

Leon frantically tripped three switches on the dash board, and the large main rotor slowly began to revolve overhead.

"Speed it up, Leon!" Delia shrieked.

"I am, I am! That's as fast as it will start!"

As the rotor gained speed, Delia saw the door to Mafin's office fly open, and Checo Paredes sprinted out into the sunlight, waving his arms frantically. When he saw Delia in the helicopter, he raced across the parking lot. Delia was relieved to see that he was unarmed.

"Lift us off, Leon!"

"We don't have enough lift!"

Now Delia shrieked at the top of her lungs. "LIFT US OFF!"

Leon jerked up sharply on the collective pitch control in his left hand and twisted the throttle. The helicopter lifted slightly, and its nose drooped down, now bouncing along the ground in short weak hops. Checo Paredes reached the helicopter and grabbed on to the landing skid beneath the door to the cockpit.

"Let go, Checo!" Delia screamed. "I've got a gun!"

Checo did not let go, but rather threw his leg up over the skid, trying to hoist himself aboard.

"Lean back, Leon!" Delia cried, and the pilot flattened himself against his seat.

Checo Paredes and Delia Chamberlain were looking directly into each other's eyes when Delia pulled the trigger. The shot punched a hole in the pilot's window and then punched a hole in Checo's shoulder. He screamed and tumbled to the ground, clawing at his chest.

Delia fought to catch her breath and finally was able to lower her voice. *"Get us out of here, Leon.* Take us out over the ocean. Keep us pointed directly away from the marina, understand? Don't you give those fuckers a broadside shot!"

Leon, also panting hard, nodded frantically. He pulled the black helicopter into a steep climb and banked away from the shoreline. When they'd flown for several minutes and were out over open water, Delia exhaled loudly and leaned back in her seat.

"Stop, Leon. Hover."

Leon's inputs to the collective and cyclic controls were jerky and spastic, and the helicopter was bouncing all over the sky. Finally, he was able to steady himself and get the helicopter to settle. Once they were in a stable hover, Delia reached over, put her hand gently on Leon's shoulder, and smiled.

"Let's talk, Leon. I don't know how much you know about what's been going on here, but let me explain what just happened and what's going to happen. Okay?"

Leon nodded warily.

"I was not a visitor, Leon. Checo and Mafin were holding me captive. They were demanding ransom. I was all set to pay it, but then a lot of things suddenly started to go wrong, and I could see they were going to kill me. So right now, you are going to fly me back to exactly the same place you picked me up, the Varadero Aruba Marina. You are going to fly as fast as you can make this helicopter go. I remember it took us two hours to get from Aruba to Isla Gazela. You are going to make it back to Aruba a lot faster than that, because I know this is a very fast helicopter. Do you have enough fuel to get to Aruba?"

"Half tank. It'll get us there, but we'll be running low."

"All it has to do is get us there. When we arrive, you are going to land in the parking lot of the marina, just like you did the first time you flew there, and I am going to get out. You are going to leave me there and fly away. I don't care where. Whatever happens after that is up to you. I don't think you'll get in trouble with Mafin just because I hijacked you at gunpoint."

Leon looked at Delia, looked at the gun. His expression hardened. "What if I say no?" he said.

"What!?" snapped Delia.

"What if I decide to fly someplace else or just fly us right back to Isla Gazela?"

"Then you die," said Delia.

"You forget that I am flying this helicopter and we're two thousand feet up. You kill me, and you die."

"You're right that if I shoot while we're you up *here*, we'll both die. So I won't shoot you now. But if you don't fly me to Aruba and decide to just keep flying instead, at some point this helicopter is going to run out of fuel, and unless you want to crash and die that way, you're going to land. The moment you touch down, wherever it is, I will shoot you in the head and take my chances from there. C'mon, Leon, use some fucking common sense."

There was a long pause, during which all Delia could hear was the *thwop-thwop-thwop* of the rotor blade overhead.

"Aruba it is," said Leon.

———

Ourelia Sanchez looked up from the concierge desk at the Ritz Carlton Aruba, surprised to see Delia Chamberlain striding across the lobby toward her. "Ms. Chamberlain! I thought your party had checked out."

Delia sat down across from her and leaned in conspiratorially, in response to which Ourelia Sanchez also leaned in, as if they were about to share a secret. "We did, Ourelia, but an urgent emergency has come up and I need some immediate assistance. Very serious assistance, Ourelia. I am in very grave danger."

Ourelia's eyes opened wide.

"First, book me into a room for one night. Make it on the lowest floor you can so I can get out of the hotel without using the elevator and escape if I have to. I won't actually be here overnight, but charge me for a full night's stay anyway. Here's my American Express card.

"Second, I want you to get me an armed security guard immediately. I don't care if he's part of the hotel security staff or a rent-a-cop, but I want him with me in my room as soon as possible, and I want him to have a gun. I will need him until I leave, which I would like to be today, if we can manage it. I don't care what it costs, just get him. Put it on the Amex.

"Third, tell the hotel switchboard not to respond to any inquiries about me *from anyone*. Everything we do here now has to be confidential until I am out of Aruba. If anyone comes to the front desk and asks about me, you must blow them off and then personally come to my room and warn me. Five knocks—tap-tap-tap, then pause, then tap-tap.

"The next step may require you to exert some urgent pressure, Ourelia, so put on your tough face and call in some favors if you have to. Contact ExecuJet or some other executive jet charter out at the airport and get me a flight out of here to the U.S. *absolutely as soon as possible.* I don't care what kind of plane it is as long as it's a jet, and I don't care where we go, Miami, New Orleans, Dallas, even Puerto Rico, just *out of here*. Cost is no object. If the price is too steep to get approval on my Amex card, I can give you the number of the Swiss Consul in Cape Verde, who can vouch for me with the charter people and will guarantee payment, if necessary.

"Finally, buy and activate a burner phone for me, one that has an international calling plan. All of this has to be kept absolutely confidential. Ourelia, if you can get all this arranged within a half an hour, I will pay you a tip of five thousand dollars, and I will comp you a handmade emerald necklace. *Can you do all this?*"

With all the poise and unflustered calm of a seasoned professional concierge, Ourelia Sanchez smiled warmly. "Absolutely. Consider it done, Ms. Chamberlain."

Chapter Twenty-Nine

Raft and Rescue

Our Seago life raft proved surprisingly easy to deploy. With me looking on, Alva had unlocked the straps on the fiberglass storage valise, jerked on the inflation lanyard, and stood back while the raft popped out of the valise, merrily inflated itself, and came to rest sitting on the deck, waiting obediently for duty. Alva slid it easily over the side and down into the water and then used the lanyard to pull the raft around to the stern boarding platform. I clambered aboard and spent a few minutes erecting the sun canopy, which looked a lot like an oversized orange boy scout pup tent with a square entry hole cut in the side.

Because it was a six-person raft that had to accommodate only two people, there was plenty of room for me to stretch out my smashed-up leg, now immobilized by fiberglass mainsail battens Alva had lashed tightly to my calf and thigh with Ace bandages. The floor of the raft was comprised of several inflated tubes which were surprisingly comfortable to sit on as Alva began to pass in our supplies and possessions and I arranged them neatly around the interior of the raft.

Alva was bent over the raft's edge, loading a couple of lightweight life jackets, *High Horse's* main EPIRB, our mega spotlight and three other flashlights, four gallons of water, two containers of ready-to-eat rations, her puffy coat and my pea jacket, rubber-soled aqua socks, sunblock and sun hats. Already aboard were Alva's camera, the satellite phone, two handheld VHF radios with fresh batteries.

We also had Alva's and my cell phones, but they were discharged and would be useless until we could freshen them up. Two large floating waterproof dry bags held underwear, socks, several changes of clothes of various weights—*after all, Victor, we will soon be putting in an appearance back home*—and assorted toilet articles in zip-loc bags.

"I got your passport and wallet," Alva called out, pointing to a heavy plastic bag with a slide fastener. "Of course, mine are in there, too."

"What's that other stuff in there?"

"All the ship's papers—our documentation papers, Netherlands registration, bill of sale, insurance documents, equipment warranties, list of email addresses and phone numbers, like that."

"No, those things," I said, pointing to the red and blue ledgers.

"Oh, *those*," said Alva. "Let's just keep those a surprise for the moment. Quite a happy surprise, you'll see."

"Oh, for God's sake, Alva. This is no time to be dicking around with a lot of extra crap. Next you'll be packing steamer trunks."

"Look, Victor, this is a six-man life raft. There's only two of us. Don't worry, I am not overloading us. But we do want to be completely prepared, wouldn't you agree?"

She rose, her brow furrowed, a look of determination on her face. "Okay, let's go below together and do a final check around, see if we forgot anything important before we put in a call to the cavalry."

Water was now four inches deep in the main salon, and packages of cocaine were floating randomly around. I had to shoo them away with my feet as I made my way to the tool locker. Every step meant searing agony in my damaged leg.

"Let me explain how this is going to go, Alva. We absolutely have to make sure *High Horse* has sunk before any help arrives. Just as important, we have to close it up tight so no cocaine packets escape. They find even one, and we're in jail for years. Please close all hatches and ports and dog 'em tight."

"Roger," said Alva matter-of-factly.

I held up a yellow hacksaw. "I am now going to cut through the hoses on all the sea cocks—the engine and air conditioner cooling water intakes, the galley and bathroom sinks, the head discharge valves, the cockpit drains. But I am going to leave the seacocks closed until we're ready to push off. With me?" Alva nodded.

"I want you here when I call out the Mayday. If anything should happen to me, I want you to know who responded, what they said, what kind of help they can offer, even the name of the guy or woman I talked to. I want you to hear any information about our rescue time frame and what we can expect to happen when we get picked up. That make sense?"

"Makes sense."

Cutting through all the hoses took longer than I expected, and by the time I finished the water level in the salon was up to six inches. Now we retreated to the cockpit. I lifted the hatch over the rear storage lazarette and looked sadly down at the big Kifco diesel pump. "God, I'm sad we never got a chance to use this thing. It has the capacity to suck this boat dry in a hurry."

"Yeah, right until the moment the keel fell off and we turned turtle. Then it probably wouldn't be much good."

Now Alva laughed. "Besides, Victor, we're trying to sink the boat, not float the boat."

As I sat down on the sun pad on *High Horse's* aft deck, a sudden wave of giddiness washed over me. I was wracked by a spasm of laughter, which started with an involuntary snort and then grew into a gagging guffaw. Alva's eyes widened in alarm.

"What is up with *you?*" Alva snapped.

"Just a stress reaction. An old joke just popped into my head. Probably haven't thought about it in forty years."

"Yeah?"

"It goes, the definition of mixed emotions is watching your mother-in-law drive your Mercedes over a cliff."

"Just get down to business, Victor."

I picked up our little hand-held VHF radio.

"Why are you going to use that one?" Alva asked. "Isn't the radio at the nav station a lot more powerful?"

"It is, and if we can't raise anyone on the handheld, I'll switch to that. But once the boat goes down, we won't have the big radio any more, and I want to be sure we can stay in touch with whoever is rescuing us when we're out there floating in our raft."

I clicked on the handheld VHF and fingered the 'send' key. "Mayday, mayday, mayday. This is an emergency. Sailing yacht *High Horse* in imminent danger of sinking. We have struck a submerged container and are holed. Our pumps are not keeping up. Repeat, Mayday, mayday, mayday, sailing yacht *High Horse* declaring extreme emergency. Any station or vessel please respond."

The response to my hail was immediate, loud and clear, and I felt an almost unbearably intense rush of relief that brought tears to my eyes.

"I have you, *High Horse*, and I read you five-by-five. This is LOOP at Port Fourchon, Louisiana. By the way, this conversation is being recorded for training and quality assurance purposes. Just kidding, folks. Trying to keep it light. How can I help you?"

"I'm sorry, what is LOOP?"

"Louisiana Offshore Oil Port. Our main platform is eighteen miles offshore from the city of Port Fourchon. We service all the offshore oil rigs in the area, but mainly we're just a giant pumping station. You are talking with Roscoe Bradley, first shift chief safety officer. And look, Captain, I ain't the Coast Guard, so if you want to skip the formal radio speak and talk more casual, that's fine with me. So, what are you, where are you, and what's cookin? How do you come to be sinkin' on my radio? Remember, we're recordin' yuh."

Elated, I tried to put my thoughts in useful order.

"Okay, okay, here's what. My name is Victor Harding. I'm the master of an Oyster 62, documented vessel, Netherlands registration AR 2746 HF. My first mate is my wife, Elva Harding. No other souls aboard. I am now in my seventies, Roscoe. Elva—I pronounced Alva's new name clearly and carefully— is in her late sixties. We're fit and in good health, but I have a serious knee injury. My wife is not injured. I am experienced in sea rescue procedures."

"That'll sure make things easier. Do you know where you're at?"

"We are exactly forty-four miles due south of Port Fourchon."

"Got some coordinates for me?"

Alva took the mic, stepped over to the chart plotter, and read off *High Horse's* navigational coordinates.

"Why, thanks, Miss Elva," Roscoe said. "How you doin', darlin'? You holdin' up okay? Yer voice sounds strong."

"Thank you. Other than the fact we're sinking, Roscoe, I'm doing pretty good."

"No panic, then."

"No sir."

"Okay, please put Captain Harding back on. First, can I call you Victor? I'm not a real formal kind of guy."

"Roger."

"How bad's your boat hurt? How fast you sinkin'?"

By now I'd gotten my voice under control and was able to muster a more calm, businesslike tone. "Collision with three connected shipping containers three hours ago. Big hit. Massive bow damage, but so far the anchor well bulkhead is holding. Bigger problem is the keel. My boat climbed right up the side of the container, tore half the keel bolts out. Keel's hanging by just a couple of bolts at the back, wobbling from side to side. We threw some caulk on the joint, but Aqua Seal's not going to hold it on, Roscoe. When it drops, we turtle."

"Well, all right, then! We better get crackin'! Hey, you want some good news? I got you guys on radar, 'least I think I do. Blip's the right size and it ain't movin'."

"That's likely us," I said. "Thank the good Lord."

"Yeah, well, him too, but on your own time. Right now, you got to deal with me. You got options, Victor. You want me to patch you through to the Coast Guard and let them mount up, or are you okay lettin' us guys ride out to getcha?"

"Who's faster?"

"Well, they'll use a Sikorsky helicopter, fly out lickety-split, and hoist y'all up on a sling, just like on TV. If it matters, maybe they'll come back and pick up your life raft later, maybe they won't. You're in international waters, and they are not obligated to preserve personal property. Some folks don't care, they just want to be saved, you know? Us, we'll shoot out to you in our 35-foot hardbottom inflatable, two Suzuki three-hundreds. Damned rocket ship. We can be at your location in under two hours. And we can take your raft aboard. 'Course, we'll have to deflate the thing."

"Fine with me, Roscoe. Frankly, I'd much rather deal with you guys than with the Coast Guard. They can get pretty…*stuffy*."

"I follow you. But you know I'll have to at least report this to the Coast Guard. Still, I figure first things first, right?"

"By all means, first things first, Roscoe."

"Coupla questions."

"Shoot."

"You already in your raft?"

"Not yet."

"You packed and loaded and ready to step off?"

"You bet."

"You legal? You aren't crooks or smugglers or illegals or anything like that, right? We'd rescue you anyway, but I gotta ask."

"We are solid, law-abiding American senior citizens who just had their retirement dream cruise shot all to hell."

"Man, ain't that a bitch! Well, Victor, y'all get in your raft and just sit tight. Keep your VHF on, and try not to dunk it in the salt water, 'kay? We should be able to fire our chase boat up in about fifteen minutes, soon as I scribble some paperwork and gather a crew."

"God bless you, Roscoe."

"That would be nice. Need all the help I can get. LOOP out, but our radio will stay on."

Now Alva pushed me away from the nav station, faced me to her, and wrapped me in a breath-sapping bear hug. It felt grand.

"I'm through teasing the gods," she whispered in my ear. "When the feds came after Lloyd, I adopted a breezy little slogan I kept trotting out over and over: *If it weren't for bad luck, I'd have no luck at all.* Man, I'll *never* say that again!"

She gave me a long, very intense kiss.

Once I opened the seacocks, it took *High Horse* forty-three minutes to sink. For its long, elegant white hull to disappear beneath the surface, for the sea to close over the cabin top, for the rising water to rip the bimini top covering the cockpit from its frame, for the Oyster's towering mast to slide foot-by-foot into the sea, for Oscar's round globe at the masthead to vanish with a surprising final pop. For Eamon Armagh to be lost at sea.

At first, we had kept the raft tethered to the stern rail and sat quietly in the raft, Alva in a neon green jumpsuit, me in sailing shorts and a white long-sleeved sun shirt. But as *High Horse's* rate of descent increased, I got antsy. "We'd better cast off. I don't think the Oyster will generate enough suction to pull us down, but I'd rather not get bounced around in a raft. I've had enough of that to last me a lifetime."

"You're talking about the Johannesburg thing?"

"I still have nightmares about it all the time. Here, on a glassy sea with plenty of room to stretch out, everything is all hunky-dory. There, in a storm, being hammered by huge waves, we had nine men in a six-person raft, one of them with a broken neck. A fourteen-hour horror show. I have to say, this is considerably less stressful."

Alva documented the entire sinking in detail with her camera, showing the Oyster settling steadily and evenly on her lines, disappearing steadily from the waterline up, as if being wiped out of existence by some giant eraser. To our relief, except for a single cockpit cushion, no flotsam popped to the surface. All the cocaine went down with the ship, and Mrs. Elva Harding and I went back to being an elderly couple whose dream voyage had been destroyed by a freak collision.

"So sad," whispered Alva as Oscar disappeared. "So, so sad."

"Well, I think you're wrong," I answered, perhaps too brusquely. "So, so *lucky*. We lucked out big time. It's a lot better sitting in a top-of-the-line life raft on a smooth sea and eating sea biscuit, knowing rescue's on the way, than to be dead."

"Well, I have to give you that," said Alva.

Thirty minutes later, the VHF buzzed. "Captain Harding, Captain Harding. Go to sixteen."

I switched to VHF channel 16, the standard paging channel. "Got you loud and clear."

"This is Roscoe. Go to twenty-three, please."

I switched to channel twenty-three in order to free up sixteen for other users.

"I got good news and bad news. Good news is that the weatherman says we're going to have light winds and smooth seas for the next coupla days, so you aren't going to be banged around any."

"Well, that's good to hear. What's the bad news, Roscoe?"

"As we were liftin' our inflatable out of its cradle to launch it, the rear sling slipped forward along the bottom. Bow lifted up and the ass end crashed down hard on the cement quay."

"Shit! Is the boat okay?"

"The boat's okay, but it landed hard on our outboards. The lower units and the propellers of both Suzukis are completely trashed. I'm sorry, Victor. I know you guys don't need this."

"So what happens now?"

"We do not have spare lower units or props here at the depot. Someone's going to have to run up to the LOOP warehouse in Port Fourchon, pick up the lower units and props, drive 'em back down. Then we got to get a mechanic over from New Orleans to come all the way down here to install 'em. We still gonna rescue you, but there's gonna be a delay."

My heart sank. Once again I was going to be left floating in a life raft in open ocean.

"Got an ETA?"

"We'll work all night and be pickin' you up about 8:30 tomorrow morning, best case."

Alva made a choked gargling sound. "Oh, noo…" She buried her head in her hands.

Roscoe suddenly was all business. "Best we can do, Miss Elva. But the fact is you going to have to spend the night in your raft. You guys got water? Food? Blankets?"

"Yes," sobbed Alva. "Plenty of water. Dry rations, too. Space blankets."

"Okay, darlin', for God's sake, stay hydrated. That's the most important thing. Maybe you want to lay off the chow unless you want to be shittin' over the side. Nature doesn't stop just 'cause you're on the ocean. And shittin' over the side is not a good idea."

"Thanks for that," I said drily.

"You gonna make it fine, guys, but there is one very important thing. Once it starts getting dark, *do not go into the water for any reason*. Don't even dangle your hand over the side. For that matter, don't dangle your ass over the side. Miss Elva, I don't mean to be crude, but you should pee in the raft if you have to go. There are plenty of sharks around, and they begin feeding at dusk."

"I know my sharks," I said. "What're we going to get?"

"The good, the bad and the ugly, Victor. You're likely to see spinners, all three kinds of hammerheads, some black tips. Spinners are sweet little guys, so don't sweat them, and the hammerheads are curious but not very aggressive. So no problems there. I think whatever danger you got is from bull sharks. Big fat, mean, potbellied sons of bitches. They're aggressive as hell, and they're drawn to bright colors. Orange still shows bright at dusk. Unlikely a bull will attack the raft outright, but don't be surprised if one bumps the raft now 'n' again. Sides and bottom. You'll probably see some dorsal fins meandering around, but don't overreact. Just keep your cool, you'll be all right."

"Will I be able to tell the dorsal fins apart?" asked Alva.

"Blacktip and spinner look a lot alike. Both have a black tip and a concave rear edge. Blacktip is a little bigger. Hammerhead is tall and narrow. The bull is big and triangular. Bulls stick the fin up high, like, 'lookamee, the neighborhood bully is here.'"

We settled in, stretched out. Grew quiet for a while. At one point, I twisted the wrong way and gave out an involuntary yelp of pain.

"If this injury is what I suspect it is, I've got some surgery in my future. Still, like I said, better than being dead."

Alva took my face in her hands. I was relieved to feel her touch.

"Well, Captain Bligh, what next?"

"Simple. We wait."

"No, I mean after we're rescued."

"Well, then everything pivots to getting Delia home safe. But Christ! Talk about feeling helpless! For a while, despite the horror of our situation, I thought we might dodge all the bullets—pun very much intended. Armagh would land his cocaine, they'd dump us somewhere, and our biggest challenge would be getting to New Orleans. Who knows? Maybe Armagh's people would even have driven us there. At her end, Delia would negotiate her ransom, arrange to get it delivered—I'm sure she's capable of doing that—get set free, and fly the fastest jet home. As a certain recently deceased Cape Verde home intruder would say, Bob's your uncle."

"Well, what happens to us doesn't really have anything to do with Delia, does it?"

"Only if you run a drug cartel that's got a million dollars of coke profits at risk. Here you are holding a hostage, the daughter of someone you're holding captive on your drug delivery boat. *That's* quite some leverage! Then suddenly the boat simply vanishes, suddenly stops responding.

"Did it get hijacked, like, let's say, by renegade Cubans? Did your own man simply sail away to early retirement with your cocaine? Did the family members overpower your crew and reclaim their boat? Did the Coast Guard grab it? Did it hit some floating shipping containers and sink? With all those possibilities up in the air, do you think your drug lord is going to set his hostage free just to collect some ransom?"

"I can't process all this," Alva said.

"Nothing to process, Alva. At this point, we're just spectators. Scared shitless, and just spectators."

"Well, the moment we're rescued, I'm going to call Hannes. I bet he knows some angles, can twist a few dials."

"Best idea I've heard since we rammed the shipping containers."

"Speaking of which, what are we going to tell the LOOP people?"

"Simplest possible story. What we tell them, they'll tell the Coast Guard, so let's spare everyone unnecessary details. Left from Aruba, got word of some heavy weather brewing in the Caribbean, detoured west, hit shipping containers, sank."

"Tell me, does the Coast Guard have to get into this at all?"

"I'm hoping not. Particularly if there's a private rescue and they don't have to send a helicopter or cutter out to save us in international waters. With any luck, they just say 'good job' to the LOOP guys, and Roscoe Bradley puts us on a bus to New Orleans. Maybe the Coasties interview us about the location of the drifting containers, but that's out in international waters and not really their remit."

"Wait a minute. I thought international waters extended two hundred miles out."

"No, the Coast Guard only observes a twelve-mile limit. Yes, there is this thing called an 'exclusive economic zone'—EEZ—that's two hundred miles out, but that deals with a country's right to exploit resources found in the water. The Coast Guard operates closer in. Twelve miles is it."

"So would the Coast Guard come and get us this far out?"

"Sure they would, but then they have the right to charge for the service. Who wants that? Let's just rely on LOOP's kind offer. I'm in favor of anything that keeps us under the radar. Our sinking is a big deal to us, but it's not really a big-time maritime event, especially if we choose to play it down. Like I said before, we don't want to read any *'senior couple's hair's breadth sea rescue'* stories.'"

Alva smiled and squeezed my hand. Even this gentle squeeze made my knee shout in pain. "Okay, I get it. No worries, mate."

"Well, actually, Alva, beyond being frightened to death about Delia's safety, I have another very serious worry. *Our safety.* When Eamon doesn't arrive in Grand Isle, Mafin and Paredes are going to go apeshit. Their first guess is going to be that Eamon and Adamares killed us and absconded with their cocaine. Their second guess is going to be that Eamon *didn't* kill us, and that we all absconded with their cocaine.

"Easy for them to track who bought *Lucifer*, pretty easy to track me down. A hundred million bucks street value is a pretty big incentive to find out what happened to their coke. Pretty good chance it's *'Well, hello, Green Lake, Wisconsin. Who do we have here?'* I think we're going to have to be super-vigilant for a long time, Alva, maybe buy ourselves some professional security.

"Now, some good news is that we're probably going to make out like bandits on our insurance claim. Believe me, I've kept copies of all the equipment receipts and service invoices. If they pay replacement value, or even fair market value, we're going to come out a couple hundred thousand ahead. All your pictures should cement the claim."

"Well, I've got even better news than that." Alva reached behind herself and pulled out the large waterproof float bag she'd been using to support her back. She withdrew the clear plastic bag with Armagh's two ledgers.

"Time for show and tell, Victor. Eamon and I had been bantering about the possibility of my signing on to launder his money and manage his finances. This red ledger documents Eamon's personal finances. Everything is in there, all the account information —Colombian banks, Venezuelan banks, offshore banks in Bermuda and Saudi Arabia, all the dates, amounts, and investments. And, most importantly, account numbers and passwords."

I couldn't help but break into a broad grin. "Well, my, isn't *that* interesting! What was our man Eamon good for?"

"Well, his bookkeeping was sketchy, and I haven't had time to go over the ledger in detail, but Eamon was bragging about nine million bucks worth. Think we could find something to do with nine million bucks, Victor?"

I reached across and picked up the larger blue ledger. "What's this?"

"*That*...is an atomic bomb. I'm not sure we should mess around with that."

I raised my eyebrows, shrugged an inquiry.

"That is Eamon's record of all his dealings with the cartel. With Paredes and Mafin and *Cartel des los Soles* and Medellin. I've glanced at it. Goes back years. The boats they had built, their supply sources, shipments shipped, all the trips they made, their landing locations, dollars received, dollars laundered, bankers, coke producers' locations, names, addresses. *The works.*"

"*Ho-oh-ly* cow," I whistled. "Tens of millions, I bet. Even *hundreds* of millions."

"Yeah, well I'm not going to go there. Certainly not going to try to raid their accounts. There are plenty of bad movies about naïve idiots who try to embezzle from some mob or another. They always end colorfully, with plenty of gruesome special effects involving machine guns. Well, not me. I'm going to let sleeping cartels lie."

"Well then, you should just heave the damned ledger into the drink. It's not something you want to get caught with."

"No, no, bad idea. I'm going to risk holding onto it. If we ever get nailed—*for anything*—this could be our get out of jail free card."

I took a deep breath, a signal that I was changing the subject. "Alva, why did you kill Eamon Armagh without talking to me about it first?"

"We did talk about it. We agreed he had to die."

"You know that's not what I'm asking. Why did you jump into action before we could plan our course of action?"

"Two reasons. One, your knee. Cripples make bad killers. Two, I was afraid you would try to stop me. At that point, Victor, *no one was going to stop me.*"

———

Dusk turned to darkness, and we thought we were home free. We hadn't seen a single fin, hadn't had to look a hungry shark in his implacable flat, black eyes. I ate a sea biscuit—I actually *like* sea biscuits—Alva ate nothing. We settled in, feigned sleep in the hope we could lure forty winks into our tiny orange shelter.

You don't know fear until your raft has been bumped by a shark in the middle of the night. Actually, not bumped, but rammed. Earlier, we had felt a couple of gentle tickles through the bottom of the raft, but when I looked out and shone my flashlight on the glassy ocean surface, all I saw was the little sickle fin of a spinner shark swimming away. Then several hours later, we took a blow that lifted the raft out of the water and threw it sideways. This was followed by being firmly goosed by pressure from underneath the raft. Our flashlight actually illuminated the track of a large dorsal fin across the three inflated tubes of our raft's bottom.

Alva screamed, then clapped her hand over her mouth, as if silence would convince the shark there was nobody home. She screamed again, louder, panicky, when the bull shark made a second charge at us. I flicked the torch on, grabbed Alva's diving knife, and peered out the raft's entry opening.

And there he was, big, brown, ugly, perhaps seven feet long, looking up at me from three feet away as if we were in a staring contest. His dorsal fin stood tall and intimidating, summoning up every shark attack story and myth I'd ever heard, sending the message, *I mean business.* They say sharks are dumb and mindless; this guy looked deliberate, purposeful, malevolent. His mouth was closed, his eyes wide open, reflecting an opal-colored pearlescence back at me. Believe me, this was a whole new kind of fear.

I shone my bright LED torch directly into his left eye. *Nothing.* He didn't react, didn't blink, didn't turn his head or writhe. He just stared at me. I felt the urge to vomit. Alva was keening behind me, *"No, no, no, no, oh, no, no."* Then the shark opened his mouth halfway, far enough for me to see his teeth, and pulled it firmly shut again, making a *pop!* like a snapping turtle's jaw. I felt myself sliding into panic. I was trying to remember all the bullshit advice I'd been given over the years for fending off shark attacks: *Hit 'em on the snout with your fist! Stab 'em in the eye! Scream at the top of your lungs until his jaws clamp across your chest and crush the life out of you...*

I sat kneeling in the raft's opening, looking down at Alva's dive knife. The shark was too far away for me to reach his eye. I was sure his skin was too tough for me to penetrate with a blade designed to pry oysters off the ocean floor. I was utterly defenseless against nature.

The bull shark blinked once...and then sank vertically out of sight, his fin disappearing like the conning tower of a submerging submarine, leaving only a circular eddy to mark where he had visited the surface. He did not return. My pulse racing, I lay back in the raft. Alva curled into a fetal position next to me. We said nothing, trying only to control our ragged breathing.

It was still dark when I heard a faint buzzing in the distance. I looked out of the life raft's open hatch, and I saw a faint speck barely discernible against the northern horizon. As I watched, the speck grew larger, the buzzing louder. The cavalry had arrived.

Thirty-five feet hadn't sounded that big when Roscoe had described the LOOP boat on the radio, but it made for a *big* inflatable, a black fiberglass half-hull surrounded on three sides by large, bright white inflatable tubes with LOOP written on them in blue letters. Two huge Suzuki outboards coughed and sputtered as they were throttled back and then lapsed into silence as the inflatable coasted up to the raft.

"Hi, folks!" sang out an athletic-looking young man with dreadlocks dressed in white overalls. "Everybody okay?"

"Right as rain," lied Alva, who looked like death warmed over. "You Roscoe?"

"Naw, Roscoe's a desk jockey. We're the real seamen. We're the guys who bring tanker crews to shore, ferry oil rig crews out and back, transport supplies, like that. This here rescue is sort of an interesting change in routine, you could say. You be the Hardings?"

"The incredibly relieved Hardings," I smiled.

"Well, I'm Norbert Woyak. This here's Robert Chen."

The inflatable had six rows of bench seats, arranged like church pews. The driver sat in back under a bright blue bimini top, directly in front of the massive engines. There was a padded platform in the bow.

"Well, not much for us to rescue!" grinned Woyak. "I'm assumin' you want to keep yer raft. Let's jes' get all yer belongings out and we'll pop the raft's valves and collapse 'er down." "Norbert, I've wrecked my knee and couldn't possibly bend it enough to sit on one of those benches for a fifty-mile ride. When you've deflated the raft, can you just set me down on top of it, please?"

"Sure thang," Woyak chirped, with Chen nodding vigorously behind him. "You the guest. You git the luxury 'commodations, Captain."

Even with a smooth sea and the inflatable throttled back to only twenty-five knots, the ride in to LOOP was hellish. The slightest swell generated a bounce through the inflatable's hull, and therefore through me, that made me want to cry out. I tugged a vinyl-covered life vest out of the deflated raft and bit down hard on the corner all the way in. Alva sat silently by my side, squeezing my hand.

Finally, we roared past a strange yellow spidery platform with LOOP painted on a derrick extending out over the water.

"Isn't that us?" I called out to Robert, who sat perched in the bow looking like a proud Asian hood ornament.

"Yes and no," shouted Robert over the rush of the waves. "LOOP is the only U.S. deepwater port. We provide some logistical support to the offshore oil platforms 'round here, but mostly our job is to offload crude from biggest tankers—here he spread his arms wide and grinned broadly—*in the whole world!* No way they could ever get into inland ports, so we milk 'em out here. You're looking at the marine terminal platform. It's basically a pumping platform to get the crude to our onshore facilities. Still, it's got a control room, some living quarters, a helo pad, communications center.

"Roscoe Bradley usually works there, but he's going to meet us at the Fourchon Booster Station onshore. Right now, we're still eighteen miles out from there. We've called forward to have a doc waiting. Got a gurney, too. If it turns out you need an ambulance to take you into Galliano or even New Orleans, we can call one from Fourchon. Sorry, but you'll have to pay for your own ambulance 'cause we're not a public facility. We're strictly restricted access, so we're sort of stretchin' the rules for you."

"God, Robert, you guys are the best!" I shouted over the roar of the Suzukis.

Roscoe Bradley was a very strange-looking man. His face was almost a cartoon caricature—so Elmer Fudd round that it looked like his cheeks were about to burst. His smile was simply enormous, with giant white teeth reflecting the sunlight. Roscoe's eyes, a startling blue, were large and slightly protuberant. From the neck down, Roscoe was a stick-man, a tall gaunt creature with a sunken chest, a small spherical pot belly, and no apparent butt at all. His hands and feet were huge, and he moved in jerky fits and starts, as if his motor neurons took a while to process messages from his brain.

His voice was a reedy, excited rasp. "Mr. Victor Harding! And Mrs. Harding! Welcome to LOOP! We don't get a whole lotta rescue survivors out here, so you two are a bit out of the ordinary for us oil dogs."

Pretty much spent by the trip to shore, I waved weakly as Alva said, "Thank you, Roscoe. Thank you for coming to our rescue."

Roscoe squatted at the end of the pier, a posture that made him look even more discombobulated. "Victor, this squad is going to lift you out—*you be gentle, boys, this here's an injured man*—and get you right to the infirmary. Dr. Darhan is waiting for you. Good man, fine doc."

"Does he have morphine?"

"You want morphine, you get morphine. At LOOP, we specialize in service."

Chapter Thirty

UNDER THE KNIFE

At the tidy little infirmary, LOOP's medical director, Dr. Mahmoud Darhan, promptly rescued me from a world of hurt, courtesy of a giant syringe loaded with morphine. Dr. Mahmoud seemed a strange choice to be the resident doc—a role that basically called for a trauma physician on what was basically a giant roughneck oil rig.

A slim young Indian gentleman with slicked back black hair so shiny it reflected the ceiling lights, Mahmoud was very formal, impeccably dressed in a starched white lab coat, neatly pressed wool slacks and spit-shined lace-up oxfords. His speech was precise and measured, although his tone was artificially bright, as if he'd been taught his bedside manner at charm school. He avoided eye contact. Hell, I didn't care—it wouldn't have mattered to me if Bozo the Clown was shooting the juice. I just needed my agony to end.

Morphine works more or less instantly, at least it did on me, mercifully totally blocking my agony and sending a delicious warmth throughout my body. Pain *gone*. Damaged area fully anesthetized. Movement possible, breathing possible, conversation possible.

I wept, the relief was so intense. And I laughed obligingly when the youthful Dr. Darhan straightened up after the shot of morphine and said brightly, "Well, that should carry you until we can get you to a proper hospital. Please do not operate heavy machinery or make important life decisions for the next twelve hours. And be sure to have Robert Chen take you to University

Medical Center in New Orleans, not Larry's Fine Infirmary and Abortion Clinic down in Port Fourchon. This injury requires serious attention. To use medical terminology, your knee has been well and truly trashed, Mr. Harding. I also fear possible damage to your leg bones as well."

He actually bowed to me. Obviously relieved at my relief, Dr. Darhan touched me lightly on the shoulder. "After your exciting rescue—Mr. Bradley has told me all about it—I have no doubt that nothing sounds better right now than a trip to the spirits cabinet, but I must caution you most strongly against that. Because alcohol and morphine are both depressants, combining them is dangerous. At best, a combination of these two drugs can result in extreme drowsiness, lack of coordination, motor skill impairment, and delayed responsiveness. And terrible judgment, as well. Either drug alone will impair thinking and cause problems completing tasks. A combination has exponential impact. Too much of both alcohol and morphine in combination can cause a coma or death. Am I being suitably serious?"

I nodded. Now Dr. Darhan extinguished his smile and put on his serious face.

"Mr. Harding, let's be clear. Regardless of the precise diagnosis of your knee injury, you will shortly be undergoing some form of surgery and a subsequent period of rehabilitation and physical therapy, during which period you will be administered various different painkillers. None responds well to alcohol. Please reconcile yourself to the prospect of complete abstinence for the next several months.

"I emphasize this because I've been told that Roscoe Bradley intends to treat you to a fancy dinner tonight, and he would like nothing better than to get you intoxicated and tell very many funny jokes. No offense, sir, but please do not rise to the bait."

"None taken," interjected Alva, visibly relaxed now that I was more visibly relaxed.

I asked Doctor Darhan for his first impression of my injury.

"Please understand that I am a general practitioner and not an orthopedic specialist. Still, I see a lot of leg injuries from the oil rigs. My preliminary guess? Best case, start with subluxated patella. In layman's terms, dislocated kneecap. Probably fractured kneecap too, which is not self-healing. Also, Mr. Harding, the wobbly lateral movement in the knee signals to me big damage or a tear in the medial lateral ligament. X-rays will also tell you if you have fractured the head of tibia—that's your bigger leg bone. You might even need a knee replacement. All serious, but all reparable.

"For your transport to a hospital, I'm going to encase your knee in a full leg air splint. It looks insubstantial, but it will immobilize your knee until a genuine orthopedic surgeon can look you over. Speaking of qualified orthopedic surgeons, my cousin Dahlin Bhat is on staff at University Medical in New Orleans. He's even younger than me, but he's very, very good. Just say the word, and with a quick phone call I can assure that you will get in to see him immediately, a benefit of having family in the trade.

"Also, while it is not my province to tell you what to do, Mr. Harding, if you do not already have an expert in orthopedic reconstruction back wherever you live, I might suggest that any needed surgery be done down here, by Dahlin. Why not get going on repair and recuperation straightaway? A fine prescription would be two days post-surgery in a private room at University Medical, perhaps three days at the rather luxurious Intercontinental Hotel in the French Quarter as you learn to navigate with a walker, and then a flight home for follow-up care.

"Or even, and forgive me if I overstep, why not think about taking a leisurely riverboat cruise up the Mississippi? They can be very luxurious, and you will surely get served hand-and-foot during the first week or so of your recovery. Or perhaps I should say, 'served hand and knee,' if I may presume to jest. Keep your leg elevated on a deck chair, eat marvelous food, and anesthetize your discomfort with various pain medications."

He slid out of his white coat and started toward the door, then turned. "Oh, and this part is very, very important. After your surgery, you must take physical therapy very, very seriously. Your knee will not regain mobility and flexibility by itself. You must make every effort to break down the scar tissue, or else you will spend the rest of your life walking like a pirate."

———

I was still pretty loopy when I called Collie from LOOP's landline, and, after the follow-up morphine shot Dr. Darhan administered, I suspect I was something less than entirely lucid. In fact, I probably sounded like I was plastered.

"Colin? This is your brother. Me. Victor."

"Victor! *Where are you?* Are you guys all right?"

"We are alive and mostly all right because we are alive. Although I am injured."

At this point, Alva took the phone and tried to talk sense to my poor confused brother.

"Collie, where are you?"

"Cara and I are in New Orleans at the Bourbon Hotel, waiting to deliver the ingot."

"What ingot?"

"The ransom. Haven't you talked to Delia?"

"We haven't talked to her—or anybody—since we were hijacked. Because we thought the Cubans would be chasing us, Armagh refused to use the radio because he was afraid we could be tracked."

"What Cubans?"

"You don't know about the Cubans?"

"I don't know what you're talking about. All I know is that I got a call from Delia saying that she had negotiated a ransom deal with the people who kidnapped her and that I was to drive a gold ingot to New Orleans and wait to hear from the kidnappers and give the gold to the kidnappers' people when they called. No one's called, so we're still sitting at the hotel."

"And you haven't heard anything further from Delia."

"I told you, no. And we didn't hear anything from you, either, so we were afraid something had gone wrong, and now we don't know what to do."

"Oh, it has, believe me. Gone wrong, I mean. Terribly, terribly wrong."

"What's this about *Cubans*?"

Alva sighed loudly, clearly exasperated. "Collie, I'll give you the briefest summary just to pull all the moving parts together, but the moment we end this call, *get out of that hotel.* You are in danger. Do *not* meet with Delia's kidnappers, do not give them the ingot. Just get the hell out of there. Find another hotel and keep your cell phone charged. My cell phone is operative again, so you should use me as your contact point."

"Okay, but what's all this about Cubans?"

"We will fill you in fully when we can get together, and since we will all be in New Orleans, that will be soon, okay?"

"Look, here is all you need to know until we can meet up. One, the boat sank. Two, our kidnappers are dead. Three, Victor and I are alive and in New Orleans. Four, the ransom deal is blown, and you've got to get out of your hotel *now,* or *you're* going to get killed. Last, once the cartel finds all this out, there's no reason they won't kill Delia. Now wrap your head around all that and get your ass moving!"

She ended the call. I was sobbing like a baby.

Roscoe Bradley did indeed press us to stay for dinner after we'd had a chance to calm down and shower and get into fresh clothes. Pale green jumpsuits, very stylish. As we dressed, Alva and I tried to talk strategy, and we decided on the K.I.S.S. principle: *keep it simple, stupid.* We agreed that we would say nothing except that we were on a honeymoon cruise and had hit shipping containers and the boat had sunk.

As Dr. Darhan had predicted, the food was marvelous. Still buzzed from the painkillers, I proclaimed it "the greatest meal I've ever had in my life." Alva immediately got herself seriously buzzed on vodka. Roscoe was marvelous company, and it seemed as if everything he said was uproariously funny. If I expected fatigue and stress to overcome Alva, I was wrong. Perhaps her adrenaline was still flowing like a river, but after knocking back a few neat shots of Stoli, she matched Roscoe and me joke for joke and anecdote for anecdote.

As the steward cleared the dessert plates, my senses and balance still impaired, and temporarily oblivious to my non-functioning knee, I fell flat on my ass when rising from the table and sat on the floor giggling as I again sang the praises of morphine. Supported by Alva under one arm and Roscoe under the other, I was basically towed back to the guest room, supposedly "just to pick up our things." Alva and I both promptly passed out on the bed and were awakened to a hearty oil rig worker's breakfast at seven the next morning.

I donated our life raft to Robert Chen as a token of gratitude, and Robert told me that LOOP would leave it inflated in the corner of the mess hall as a reminder of The Great Rescue. To my surprise, Roscoe Bradley, slightly slobbery with emotion, gave me a parting hug— "I am delighted you two are alive, for sure" — before Robert and Alva shoehorned me crosswise into the back bench seat of the LOOP minivan. Robert drove us carefully through verdant bayou country to New Orleans, where he checked us into the Intercontinental.

Talk about bedside manner. When Dr. Dahlin Baht met us in our hotel room, he instantly charmed Alva nigh on to giddiness. I couldn't blame her. Later Alva and I agreed that he was unquestionably the most handsome human being we had ever laid eyes on. In fact, she said, if thirty-five years younger, she, a brown-skinned vixen, would throw the aging pasty white cripple Victor Harding over in an instant and go in hot pursuit of this gorgeous young, brown-skinned man, consequences be damned.

Dr. Baht—*"Please, call me Dahlin"*—arranged for expedited admission to the New Orleans University Medical Center, and by late the next morning we were going over a thick folder fully documenting a battery of ex-rays, MRI scans, blood work and other diagnostic work. Dr. Mahmoud Darhan's diagnostic 'guess' at LOOP had been spot-on: *Total train wreck.* Worst case scenario.

"Victor," said Dahlin sympathetically, "sorry man, but you're in for a total knee replacement, plus a lot of other reconstruction work. Excuse my French, but it's just a war zone in there—spiral fracture of the tibia, cartilage all torn up, torn ligaments, fractured kneecap. I can't imagine how much impact momentum it took to create a mess like that. This situation represents a major physical insult to a man your age. Whether I do it or someone else does it, you need a major rebuild and this shouldn't wait. Injuries like this don't age well."

"What does age have to do with it?"

"Well, the fact is that people your age heal slower than younger patients, so you should be prepared for some 'rough innings.' You've heard about 'rough innings?' It's a cricket term."

Dahlin pushed on. "So here are our options: if you've got a lot of money, I can splint you up and stick you into a jet air ambulance to get you back up pronto to, what is it, Milwaukee, Wisconsin? That keeps you supine, doesn't put bending pressure on the knee like sitting in an airplane seat. Or we could put you on a commercial air flight, let's say first-class ticket. But first class or not, Victor, that would be a painful journey. You do not want to be in a sitting position for any length of time. Stiffness and swelling would both go through the roof."

"Final option, the one I recommend, is join me in our OR here at University Medical at 2:00 AM tonight and just get this thing done. As Shakespeare said, 'if 'twere done, best 'twere done quickly.'"

Alva and I looked at each other and burst into laughter, undoubtedly confusing Dr. Baht. "In joke," Alva explained, "having to do with an old friend of ours, Mr. Thuna."

When I finally was able to choke back the giggles, I turned to the good doctor. *"2:00 AM? Really?"*

"Yeah, well, they keep the lights on around here. High volume pays the bills. Victor, my surgery calendar is fully booked for the next ten months. I've got six full knee replacement procedures in line ahead of you. The only non-emergency openings would be if someone had to cancel a scheduled procedure. Or, as an accommodation to my cousin and an appreciative nod to your gorgeous East Asian wife, as well as recognition of your present highly-stressed circumstances…*2:00 AM tonight.* All I have to do is tell the hospital it's an emergency case. I'm game if you are."

Chapter Thirty-One

THE ELEMENT OF SURPRISE

Alva kept Colin in the loop by phone, post-surgery, but for two days we decided it was best not to see him in person. This made him very angry, but I was still coming out from under the effects of anesthesia, and the moment I did so, I was bathed in various flavors of excruciating pain. Astonishing, blow-torch-in-the-bones pain. Oxycodone could knock the worst edge off the pain for four hours, but I was only allowed to take it every six hours. That left two hours of unmitigated agony before they could dose me again.

Tramadol and Ibuprofen did not work well for me. Nothing except Oxy, an addictive narcotic, worked for me. I was bad company, for sure, but Alva was superb with the cool compresses and tasteless comedy routines.

After I'd been released from University Medical on an expedited discharge, we took up residence at the Intercontinental, where Collie and Cara joined us for a muted but much relieved reunion. We booked a string of rooms on the top floor, Alva and I settling into the most luxurious suite they had.

Collie called the Bourbon Hotel and asked for the manager, who turned out to be a fellow named Marvin Simmons. Collie asked Marvin if there had been any inquiries about him. Marvin's voice dropped to a terrified whisper. "Two gang types, Latin American, very mean, very ugly, came in, and they got very… hostile when I said you'd checked out. They demanded your home address and your forwarding address and when I said I could not disclose that, this little Hispanic thug stuck a gun under my chin and choked my throat. *But I did not tell him, Mr. Harding, I did not tell him.*"

Collie whistled. "Marvin, I'm terribly sorry you had to go through this. You can report it to the police, but it won't do any good. These heavies work for a Venezuelan drug cartel, and they're undoubtedly dug in far back in the bayous. But let me tell you this: look for an envelope in the mail addressed to you at the hotel. It will have five C-notes in it, to compensate for your trouble. It's for you, Marvin, just for you. Just continue to keep my contact information confidential, please."

———

A loud knock on the door of our hotel suite. "Room service!" I was propped up in the living room with several pillows under my knee and several ice packs on top of it. Alva, Collie and Cara were standing in the doorway to the balcony, where a fresh breeze riffled the curtains. They talked in hushed tones, as if afraid normal conversation would cause me pain.

"We didn't order anything," Alva called back. "Must be a mistake."

"Champagne and caviar, Mrs. Harding. Compliments of the Intercontinental Hotel."

Alva pulled the door open, and rather than wheeling the service cart into the room, the diminutive server backed in, pulling the cart after her. Then she spun around.

"*Ta-Da!*"

And there stood Delia Chamberlain.

"Shall I pour, Mr. and Mrs. Harding?"

Delia looked as if she was ready for a photo shoot. She was dressed in a high-fashion dark blue silk pants suit with flared bellbottom legs and dramatic white lapels, contrasting with acres of dark brown cleavage, a heavy emerald choker around her neck. Her scarlet wedge sandals had emerald-colored jeweled straps across her ankles. Her hair had been coiffed into a tight French Twist, and she had been expertly made up. Her smile was luminous, rapturous.

"Do I look like an escaped prisoner of war?"

Alva gasped, dropped to her knees and hugged Delia tightly around the waist. *"No, no, no, no, no! This cannot be!"*

Delia lifted Alva gently to her feet and kissed her ardently on the forehead.

"I love you, Mom. I love you, so much." Then, "I love you, Victor. I love all you guys. I love being alive and free. I love it that we're all alive, and free, and *safe*."

Delia sat down on the sofa next to me, causing me to cry out in pain. She leapt up, and I pulled her back down. I took her hands in mine. "C'mere, you." I was crying like a baby.

Cara was waving her arms wildly. "How did you get here? How did you get away?"

"Swiss special diplomatic charter, Aruba to San Juan, Puerto Rico, Bombardier Challenger 60, compliments of Mr. Hannes Schlossberg. Seats twelve. On this flight, it seated two, me and a polite young man holding a submachine gun. ExecuJet could not accommodate me quickly enough in Aruba, so I gave Hannes a call. *Man, can that guy ever make things happen!*

"From San Juan, it was American Airlines to New Orleans. First class. Diplomatic mission. Extra security, a U.S. air marshal. Kind of security overkill, actually, but it sure made me feel good. Picked up at the airport in one of those black bullet-proof SUVs, driven here, escorted to my suite, which is right next to yours, Mother. This fine new suit—the correct size—was laid out on the bed, and the hairdresser and makeup person were waiting for me. That was two hours ago. Room service was pleased to play along. Gave 'em a huge tip."

"But how did you get away?" Colin asked.

"I'll fill you in on all the exciting details, but first, Colin, let me present you with a special gift, something you once said you wanted, something I now want you to have, something we can pull out for a show-and-tell on special occasions."

Delia reached into her suit jacket pocket as if searching for something, then slowly withdrew her hand. When she opened it, there in her palm was Casper the friendly ghost gun.

"It's now been fired a total of five times, Colin, so I don't think it should ever be fired again, because it might blow up. But I think it makes a wonderful trophy to hang on the wall, and I really want you to have it."

Chapter Thirty-Two

Lost and Found

Checo Paredes knocked softly on Mafin's office door with his good arm and stuck his head in. Alberto Mafin looked up, annoyed, as usual.

"Got news."

Mafin waved him away dismissively.

"About the boat."

Mafin's eyes opened wide. "Yeah? Talk to me."

"Sunk."

"You're shitting me."

"Donnie, who works for us at Grand Isle, has a cousin at the Coast Guard station in New Orleans. Paid the guy a hundred bucks to read through all the incident reports for the last month. There it was. Not anything the Coast Guard did, but there was a summary report of a call they got from an offshore oil loading platform called LOOP."

"And…"

"LOOP heard an SOS from a sinking sailboat. Said they'd hit a floating shipping container about fifty miles offshore of Port Fourchon and were abandoning ship. LOOP sent out their big RHB and picked 'em up."

Mafin cocked his head inquisitively.

Checo looked away. "Two people in the raft. Man and a woman. Old guy, Caucasian. Badly injured leg. Black woman, Indian or East Asian. Identified as husband and wife, U.S. citizens. No other survivors or casualties mentioned. Except for the raft, nothing else found or recovered. LOOP contact named Roscoe Bradley. Coast Guard summary ends 'NFA,' meaning 'no further action.'"

Mafin began to pant, his chest heaving in ragged gasps. "We are totally fucked," he wheezed.

"Well, not entirely," Paredes said. "That ingot Delia Chamberlain was going to deliver as ransom was worth five hundred grand. The pickup in New Orleans fell through, but the value of that one ingot alone is worth paying her a visit up in the U.S., no?"

Mafin actually smiled. "*For sure.* And if she's got one, it's a safe bet she has more, no?"

Chapter Thirty-Three

Rollin' on the River

"Mint julep, sir?"

From my plushly-upholstered deck chair, I looked up at the waiter—starched white slacks, light blue shirt with epaulets, dark blue officer's cap—and told him that because of the meds I was on I'd have to forego the julep, but a virgin Mary would be mighty fine, thank you very much. Told him a virgin Mary also would be fine for the other man in our party, who was a non-drinker, but to take drink orders from the rest of the family out on the sundeck. "Tell your bartender to pour 'em with a heavy hand."

I rested my head back on the bright lemon-yellow pillow and found myself savoring the present—basking in the warmth of the noonday Louisiana sun, soaking in the sweet earthy organic smell of the Mississippi River, and listening to the rhythmic chop-chop-chop of the *America Queen's* gigantic red paddle wheel.

Alva and I were presently ensconced comfortably in the *America Queen's* King Cotton suite, with Delia, Collie and Cara in the adjacent Pride of Dixie suite. We were headed toward St. Louis, where Christine, flying in from Milwaukee, would join us. The plan was to disembark in St. Louis to drive a rental the rest of the way to Green Lake, or maybe to stay aboard all the way to Minneapolis, depending on how my bad knee felt.

We, meaning Alva, had a medications checklist, actually a spreadsheet with all my assemblage of meds listed on the left and little boxes—6:00 AM, 2:00 PM, 10:00 PM, and so on—to be checked off when each dose had been administered. Normally I, a cynical lifelong scofflaw, would have laughed at such oppressive anal-retentive rigor, preferring to adjust medication to the symptoms I was experiencing in the moment. But this wasn't normal, it was crazy painful, which resulted in us following my medication regime to the letter. Alva was perfect, never missing a beat.

The post-operative fun was compounded by the fact that I was not only expected to bear the pain, *I was expected to exacerbate the pain.* Dr. Bhat had told Alva that in addition to icing the knee and keeping my leg elevated above my heart, during the day I was to climb out of bed at least once an hour *and "take a short walk. You can use a walker or a cane as you choose, but I want you to put load on that knee—not for too long, but absolutely regularly during the day. Also, here's a list of leg exercises for you to do regularly to promote flexibility and combat the muscle atrophy that goes with this kind of surgery."

At this, Dr. Bhat's expression had grown stern. "You *must* do this! Ignore this initial post-op exercise, and you will be very, very sorry. Your leg will stiffen, scar tissue will form, and the physical therapy you're going to start in a month will be very much more difficult—and maybe not completely successful. I assume you do not want a limp for the rest of your life."

Well, he certainly had *my* attention.

I reckoned that before long it would be too hot to remain out on the open top-level sundeck and decided that after my booze-free midday mocktail it would be time to retreat to the shade of the private mini-veranda outside our suite on the 420-foot riverboat's Deck Five. Alva slid the veranda door open, eased herself out into the humid morning air, sat down on the edge of the lounge chair, and ran her fingers through her hair.

"You look as bad as I feel," I said.

"Well, thanks for that, mister kind-and-considerate." Alva's head dropped forward, her shoulders sagged, and she began to weep.

"*I'm not okay*, Victor. I've tried to keep a brave face on because you were going through such hell, but—if you'll pardon a truly horrible pun—I'm really at sea. Really feeling kind of lost. This is new territory for me. I just don't know how to process things *now*.

Until recently," Alva sobbed, "I thought I had put the crimes of my past life behind me. Here I was, living in a sanctuary of peace and quiet in Cape Verde...a nice, serene life of leisure in a nice diverse culture. Nice place where people don't get demeaned for having brown skin. I was enjoying every day in my fabulous house and handling my advancing years pretty philosophically.

"And then, within a couple months, suddenly my entire life is all about death. And...*killing. I'm a person capable of killing people...who's been forced to kill people.* And my fantasy of sailing away on a dream voyage with my new romantic interest is a nightmare—this after being attacked in my dream house, being forced to abandon my sanctuary.

"*Oh, but wait! There's more!* When we started our sea cruise, we were supposed to be safe in our wonderful big sailboat out on the ocean, at peace, eluding any pursuers' bullets and enjoying each other's company, right? Creating new bonds with our family members, right?"

Alva's words were coming faster now, tumbling over each other, punctuated by labored gasps for breath. "Who could have foreseen a mid-ocean hijacking? I mean, *really!* And the Cubans! Tell me, Victor, who thought *that* part up?. This was a *bad script*, Victor. Too improbable even for a cheesy Clint Eastwood action thriller."

Alva was rolling. I let her roll.

"And now we get Act III! If this was that Clint Eastwood thriller, the screen would be fading to black as Clint and Meryl Streep stand holding each other on the back deck of a Mississippi stern-wheeler as it vanishes into the distance. *End of story.*

"Except it's *not,* because now we have to figure out the rest of our lives—where to live, what to do with ourselves to keep our minds alive, what to do with our money, how to evade Venezuelans and Colombians and Cubans and defrauded investors, perhaps how to avoid people who may pursue us and try to kill us.

"*I'm scared, Victor.* Really scared. I'm used to being in control, and I don't know how to behave when things keep spinning out of control. I need to feel safe, and I don't feel safe. And to top it off, now I'm tied to an older man who may have a permanent limp. Our next exciting action thriller should be titled *The Adventures of Alva and Her Aging Cripple.*"

I guess she had dulled the edge of her distress, because now Alva smiled and moved into me, wrapping her arms around my waist.

"Okay, now that I've blown off some steam, I'm ready for that reassuring hug now."

When we docked for a tourist stop at Cape Girardeau, I told Alva I was going to take a nap. She said she had some shopping to do and was headed ashore. I dropped off fast and slept well. Two hours later I awoke to find Alva punching figures into a laptop. The packaging from a new sixteen-inch Apple laptop and a bunch of software programs lay strewn across the top of the desk.

"What's up?"

"This is my Eamon Armagh memorial laptop. Purchased with the proceeds from trauma, you could say. I've got this baby loaded with *everything,* thanks to our late, lamented Irish shitheel. I've already started transferring the financial data from Eamon's ledger. Then I'm going to get in touch with Hannes Schlossberg and wire him all of Eamon's numbers. Tell him to get all of Eamon's assets behind walls ASAP."

"You really have to do this now?"

"Sooner the better. I made a quick run through Eamon's ledger, and there's some hefty coin we have to begin to put to work."

"How much?"

"Eamon was not nearly as flush as he told me he was, that lying son of a bitch. Still, looks like about five and half million."

"You just going to dump it in our accounts?"

"I think not. I think the better idea is to diversify our accounts even more. Have Hannes create a new Cape Verde-based LLC, make himself the Managing Principal. Compensate him adequately, and he'll be happy to do it. Frankly, I'd like to spend Eamon's money as fast as possible, make this new company the source of our most liquid funds, our walking-around money.

"My plan is to have fewer firewalls on Armagh's repurposed accounts than our other holdings, and just trust Hannes to stand guard and sort of throw an invisibility cloak over things in case anyone tries some hacking and sniffing."

Now Alva had Armagh's red ledger spread open on her lap, and her head was bobbing like a chicken's as she typed entry after entry into the shiny new MacBook Pro.

"What do you propose to call this…*entity?*"

She laughed brightly. "I was thinking about Aftermath, LLC."

I shook my head. "Clever, but I can't go for that. I don't need to be reminded of our pain and agony every time I cash a check."

"Irish Rose?"

"Screw that."

"You got a better idea?"

"Maybe I do. How about N.Q.A. Holdings?"

"Meaning…?"

"No Questions Asked."

"Make it 'No Questions Answered,' and I could go with that."

We both slept well and awoke feeling better, calmer. The first thing the next morning, Alva, the bit in her teeth, insisted we call Hannes Schlossberg immediately. We gathered the troops, and using the satellite phone, I dialed Hannes in Cape Verde and plugged in an auxiliary speaker so we all could speak and hear.

We were in for an awful surprise.

It took a while for Hannes to answer. "He's probably trying to figure out what this strange phone number is," said Alva. "Or else it's taking a while for our signal to bounce up to the satellite and back down to Cape Verde."

Finally, after some beeps and some buzzing static, there was a loud click. "*Grüss Gott.* Schlossberg."

"Hannes!" Alva cried brightly. "It's me, Alva!" An animal-like howl issued from the speaker.

"Hannes! Is that you? It's me, Victor."

There was a frantic edge to Hannes Schlossberg's voice. "*Sind sie am Leben? Was machst du gerade! Wo sind sie?*"

"Hannes!" I barked. "Calm down! Get a grip! English, please! We're fine, we're fine. Yes, we had a catastrophe, but Alva and I are fine and safe."

"How did you know?" wailed Hannes. "How did you find out?"

"Know about what?" asked Alva, obviously confused.

"About the attack!"

"*Don't know what you're talking about.* We called to tell you that after we got hijacked, our boat sank in the Gulf of Mexico, but we got rescued. And as you know, Delia managed to escape from cartel kidnappers who were holding her for ransom. Now the whole family is on a river boat on the Mississippi River, and we're on our way to Wisconsin."

Hannes was gasping for breath. "*Lieber Gott!* This is too much."

"Okay," I said trying to control my voice. "We're obviously talking about two different things here. So I am going to go first, and then I will shut up and you can tell us what's going on at your end."

"*Ja. Bestimmt.*"

Although Hannes obviously knew Delia's end of the ransom story, he had no way of knowing what had happened to Alva and me, so slowly, carefully, I filled in the blanks for him—*Cartel de los Soles,* Armagh, the live Cubans, the ambush, the dead Cubans, Alva's role in Adamares' demise, the shipping containers, the knee surgery. I finished by saying, "So at our end, we're all a little shaky, but things are getting better."

A kind of strange whine, a keening, issued from the speaker.

"Things are about to get much, much worse. Alva, if you are not sitting down, *sit down.*"

Hannes exhaled loudly. "About ten days ago, someone—probably several people—attacked your house, Alva. They set it on fire with petrol, and the whole house was destroyed. Everything in it was destroyed. Everybody…was destroyed."

"What do you mean?" Alva squealed. "Are Artur and Gracia okay?"

Now we could hear Hannes sobbing. "Alva, Artur and Gracia are both dead. Murdered."

Alva gaped at the speaker, as if daring it to issue such shocking garbage again. As for me, I learned what it means to truly have your blood run cold.

"Murdered," I repeated dully.

"*Ja*. In a very ugly way. I'm not sure you want to know."

"God damn it, Hannes. Talk to me."

"Victor, did Alva have samurai swords in the house for some reason?

"Yes. They were museum pieces, three hundred years old. On display in the guest room."

"The attackers tied Gracia and Artur to chairs and chopped their heads off. They left the swords behind."

I felt like I had been punched, hard, at the base of my throat. I gagged and could not make a sound.

"If there are any small mercies," Hannes said, "the medical examiner believes they were already dead when they were beheaded. They both had been shot in the back of the head."

We decided to stay on the *America Queen* all the way to Minneapolis so we could keep Alva under sedation. She was in and out of consciousness for two days. When she was conscious, she usually was not lucid. As she tossed, turned and writhed—*slept* would be too tame a term for what she appeared to be experiencing—I had a long satellite phone conversation with Hannes.

He started off with magic words: "Victor, I will take care of *everything* at this end. I am going to fax you a power of attorney form to you on your riverboat, and you will authorize me to conduct all affairs, financial and personal, for Victor and Elva Harding here in Cape Verde. Dealing with the police—to whom I will explain that you are on the open ocean and cannot be reached—getting police reports and forwarding them to you, arranging the funerals, creating modest pensions for Artur and Gracia's families, dealing with the insurance company, hiring a contractor to gut the house, engaging an architect to discuss rebuilding, removing all legal references to one Alva Batek in Cape Verde, and anything else that comes up. Don't worry about fees; we can talk about that later."

I was awash with gratitude and felt myself tearing up. "What a godsend you are, Hannes. I can't tell you how lucky we feel to have you as our shield and protector."

"Don't mention it," Hannes said modestly. "You know I would do anything for Alva."

"Well, let's talk about something I *should* mention. I think we're in a major bind, Hannes, maybe several major binds, and some of our problems may have serious implications for your personal safety."

"*Mine? Ja?*"

"When it comes to strategizing our next steps, Hannes, I'm torn between asking for your *participation* or wrapping you in ignorance and providing you with *deniability*."

"Oh, that's easy. *You must tell me.* I will take care of myself." *Big breath. Dive in.*

"It may not be so easy. Hannes, there are a variety of people who, for quite different reasons, want to take revenge on Alva. And me."

"You, too, Victor?"

"Yes, me too. And I'm quite sure the form of revenge they want is to kill us. I will be pleased to provide you with every last detail, but for the moment, let me just sketch bare bones."

"You have my attention."

I tried to sound matter-of-fact. "I believe we have three categories of possible revenge-seekers, Hannes. First, members of a burglary ring in Wisconsin who are upset because, as a former coconspirator of theirs, I was responsible for a sting operation that put them in jail last year.

"Second, victims of Alva and Lloyd's various Ponzi schemes over the years, and—hold on to your hat—third, the drug cartel that hijacked the sailboat and kidnapped Delia. They probably think that we owe them reparations of about a hundred million dollars. That's the street value of the cocaine that sank with the sailboat.

"And then there's the value of the ransom they'd negotiated for Delia's release. That was to be one of our gold ingots, worth about five hundred grand, and of course that deal didn't go through. So the cartel is bound to be royally pissed off."

"*Was!? Unglaublich!* This is dreadful, Victor. You need protection, security."

"Man, I'll say! Like maybe all the 'made men' who guarded the Corleones' house in *The Godfather* movie. Actually, three houses—mine, Christine and Delia's, and Colin's house on Green Lake."

"I will see to it. I have…*friends* in the U.S. I can arrange to get some good local people there fast."

"Maybe it's just like in Cape Verde, maybe our family should just get the hell out of Dodge."

"What does that mean?"

"It's an old line from American cowboy movies. Dodge City, Kansas was very dangerous around the turn of the century, lots of gun fights, and smart crooks always knew when it was time to 'get out of Dodge.'"

"'Get out from Dodge.' Hah, I like that. Is a Swiss guy allowed to say that?"

I blew past his attempt to lighten things up.

"Hannes, Alva did not expect that first scam victim to show up in Cape Verde, because he was sort of a wimp. But now she's worried about someone who might be even worse."

There was a pause. Then Hannes said, "I bet you are talking about Ashi Fukashi."

"You know who he is?"

"Unfortunately, yes. All the way back from when he was partnering with Lloyd. I met him several times in Zurich. A very charming fellow, actually. Just rather ruthless."

"Alva's scared of him. Should she be?"

"Scared of a Yakuza gang leader? *Oh, yes.* But it's been some years since Fukashi was fleeced by Lloyd and Alva, and I thought—hoped, really—that he'd gotten too old to care about revenge. I guess I may have been wrong."

"You think Ashi torched Alva's house?"

"Well, perhaps. Well, actually *probably* if we consider the use of the samurai sword as a Yakuza calling card."

"Do you think he's satisfied? Regards the score as settled?"

"*Oh, heavens no!* Alva escaped him. He's old-school *bushido*, samurai moral code and all, so now Ashi has lost even more face. This has become a very, *very* dangerous situation, Victor. Obviously, you cannot take this fellow lightly. He will not go away by himself, I'm afraid. This calls for a whole new level of security."

Hannes now exhaled loudly, thinking this conversation was over.

"We're not done, Hannes. Not done with our revenge stories."

"Oh, *stop*."

"No, we also probably have to worry about the cartel. They won't have any trouble finding us. My purchase of our boat is public record. And here's an irony for you: the boat we bought for our sea cruise? The cartel used to own it and use it to smuggle cocaine."

Hannes whooshed. "No Hollywood scriptwriter could come up with this."

"No, but we did. And now we don't know how to get the movie to end."

"*Mein Gott,* I cannot imagine the Alva Batek I know going through all these things…or doing all those things to people, for that matter."

"Hannes, *she is not the Alva Batek you know any more.* She's been both toughened and softened by all this crap. She's been through the meat grinder, just like I have. We're both pretty rocky, mental health-wise. That's why I have her sedated."

Silence. Nothing but the crackling of static from the satellite phone. Finally, Hannes spoke.

"This all really rocks me back on my heels, Victor. A lot to take in."

I could picture Hannes rubbing his hands down his face, once again staring at the elaborate ceiling of his richly-furnished Cape Verde Swiss Consul's office.

"Listen, Victor, I need some time to think—both about you and your whole family in Green Lake—and to start making a few phone calls. I will have some ideas and information when we next speak."

I was flooded with another rush of emotion, a combination of relief and gratitude. "Once again, thank you, Hannes. Who could have guessed that we would drop a bomb like this in your lap?"

"No one. No one could have guessed all this, predicted all this. But Victor?"

"Yes, Hannes."

"This is serious, but it is not fatal. Have faith."

ACKNOWLEDGEMENTS

A long time ago, I heard a wonderful one-liner: *If you want to make a realistic sculpture of a wild bull elephant charging out of the jungle, just find yourself a huge hunk of granite and carve off everything that doesn't look like an elephant.*

Sea Cruise proved to be a *big* piece of rock, and by the time we had finished eight revisions, there was a lot of unused elephant lying around. The chiseling and polishing benefited from a huge amount of wonderful help, and the astute suggestions of my diverse beta readers smoothed and sharpened the eventual artwork considerably. I deeply respect all the folks who were not afraid to tell it like it was (and what it was often was overlong and overwritten, meaning my helpers often had to wield scissors as well as an artist's chisel).

My patient co-conspirators included Glen Loev, George and Gabby Pellinger, V.J. Pappas, Pam Bridwell Cain, Tobey Chier, Holly Richardson, Bill Antheil, Steve Becker, David Richter and Cynthia Shelton.

Unique among contributors was Dr. Nick Scharff, who brought his gentle voice and impeccable ear to bear time and again through the seemingly endless iterations. Nick's patience and perseverance were extraordinary and miles beyond the call of duty or friendship. My astonishing wife Pam Woldow is not only the greatest copyeditor in the world, but also the skilled champion of female readers' sensibilities and yardstick of their tolerance for techno-jargon. Pam and I duked it out often, and when I lost, it was because I deserved it.

My heartfelt thanks to you all.

WHAT'S NEXT

Before digging into *Sea Cruise,* perhaps some of you had already met Victor Harding and his family in the first of the Victor Harding Adventures, *Old Dogs, New Tricks.* A Thrillers Mystery Suspense Book Club selection, it can be found on Kindle, Torchflame Books, and whereever offbeat thrillers are sold.

If you've read this far, you know that Victor and his kin survived *Sea Cruise,* and we are not done with them yet. The next book in the Victor Harding Adventures, *The Best Revenge,* is complete and now undergoing the whole elephant-chiseling process. Watch for it on Kindle and in bookstores later in coming months.

Thanks for reading *Sea Cruise* and, when the time comes, for delving into the next Victor Harding Adventure. For a preview of what to expect in *The Best Revenge,* turn the page.

A SNEAK PREVIEW OF

THE BEST REVENGE

Chapter One

TARGET PRACTICE

The first shot was supposed to be a head shot, punching a neat hole right between the crude pair of eyes drawn on the target silhouette mounted on poles a hundred and thirty yards away. Easy shot for a war-tested sniper. Which Mutter was, with seventy-four confirmed kills in Iraq, seventy-four of Saddam Hussein's Palace Guard down for the count.

But now this: *A clean miss.* Not off-center, not just a bit too high or a tad too low. *A complete zero.* Mutter squatted down to look through his battered war-surplus spotter scope and was astonished to see that the target was completely unmarked. No hole in the target's head, no center-mass damage, *no nothing.* Then he panned the scope down and saw that his round had dug a brown furrow through the green grass in front of the target. *Two yards* in front of the target. *Which was fucking impossible.*

"'Splain *that* one to me," he murmured.

As much as he detested the nickname the guys in his motorcycle club had hung on him, Mutter couldn't deny that it fit. He went through life in constant breathy monologue with himself, whispering an incessant running commentary on all the things, people and events that so constantly frustrated him and shaped his angry world.

Today Mutter wandered back and forth across Marvin Dohler's forty-acre spread south of Green Lake for over an hour before finding the right site to set up shop and calibrate the sights of his assassin's weapon. He was looking for a sloping uphill run that closely matched the pitch of Victor Harding's back yard—the span from the low row of bushes along the lakefront to the sliding door of Victor's veranda. Elevation and windage were going to matter on this shot, so in sighting his rifle, Mutter wanted to have his settings absolutely spot-on.

His target was a fresh paper torso-and-head outline, the kind cops use for snap-draw-and-fire practice. Mutter had taken it from the shooting range and mounted it on a piece of foam board. Now it was erected on a couple of two-by-two poles driven into the ground well over a football field's length away. His jury-rigged arrangement was stable enough to be an acceptable facsimile for a human form. Victor Harding's form.

"Head shot or center body mass?" Mutter had said aloud *as* he paced off the right distance to his firing point. Head shot would be a more rewarding score, once again proving that his military shooting medals had been well earned. But a center mass body shot was a safer bet if his father's ancient Remington didn't fire straight and true. *Center body,* he decided. *It's the result that matters. I ain't going for style points here. Just want to kill the son-of-a-bitch.*

Lying prone on a black four-by-six-foot tarp, Mutter had shot the bolt of the ancient deer rifle he'd liberated from his father's gun locker after the old man's brain went south. As he chambered the round, Mutter had kept up a soft breathy narrative. "Lordy, Lordy, I wish I still had my Iraqi kit," he whispered. "But at this range, Daddy's piece be plenty good enough. This ain't such a tough shot. The slope's a little challenge, but not too much, no sir."

By Iraqi 'kit,' Mutter meant the M24 sniper system he'd used to such good effect on the outskirts of Al-Fallujah and at Um Qasr—the bolt-action M2010 enhanced sniper rifle with its adjustable stock, the collapsible titanium stabilizing bipod poking out from the sides of the barrel, the powerful telescopic sight with its terrific optics, the separate tripod-mounted infrared scope his spotter Skippy used to get a precise fix on his human targets and call out sighting adjustments.

Still, his dad's old gun felt familiar and comfortable because both his military-grade sniper rifle and the gun he now held were based on the classic Remington model long favored by hunters and soldiers alike. The civilian-grade telescopic sight Mutter had mounted couldn't hold a candle to the mil-spec U.S. Army issue, but if he sighted his daddy's rifle in carefully, computed the windage and drop correctly, he figured the rifle's accuracy would be good enough to turn Victor Harding into one very dead duck.

The bipod he'd fashioned to cradle the barrel appeared crude, just a couple of short two-by-twos bolted together in the middle in an X pattern, but it seemed solid and probably would prove adequate. The barrel of the deer rifle now nestled firmly in the crotch at the X's center, secure, stable and ready for action.

"Okay! Mind's made up! Head shot!" Mutter had yelled out across Dohler's empty field, as if yelling a 'betcha' to competitors at the firing range. He had inhaled slowly, caught his breath, pressed the eyepiece of the telescopic sight lightly against his eyelid. His finger had caressed the Remington's worn trigger as gently as a fleck of goose down blown by the wind.

Mutter loved the feel of recoil, loved feeling all that firepower. He expected to hear a sharp *ka-thock!* as the round punched through his human-shaped target.

But *nothing*. He had heard nothing. And now that he saw what a dreadful shot he'd just made, he cursed his father. "What'd ya do, you old bastard! Use your deer gun to pound fence posts? This thing is junk!"

Then Mutter examined the gun carefully, sight-to-stock, and found that the knurled front mounting knob on the telescopic sight was slightly loose. Mutter realized that he had carefully calibrated a sight that wasn't firmly mounted to his rifle.

"You are such a dipshit, Mutter! You horse's ass!" he screamed at himself. "*You* mounted that scope! *You the one what screwed up!*"

He knew that after tightening down the mounting knob, he'd have to start calibrating all over again. After an hour of fiddling, adjusting, firing, and adjusting again, Mutter finally put five shots into the target's chest, dead center mass. Then he had placed three shots within a five-inch radius in the middle of the target's head.

"Now, *that's* better," he said softly. "That clinches it: I'm gonna go for the head shot. I got this. Sorry, Daddy, I shouldn't have cursed you out like that."

AUTHOR BIOGRAPHY

Douglas Richardson became an award-winning novelist after retiring from his earlier careers as a federal prosecutor, award winning Dow Jones columnist and global legal consultant.

Doug's debut action thriller, *Down Wind and Out of Sight*—which is not a Victor Harding Adventure—published when Doug was seventy-five, has won six literary awards, including a Literary Titan Award, three American Fiction Awards (General Thriller, Cross-genre Fiction and Multicultural/Diverse Mystery and Suspense), a Reviewer's Choice Thriller/Suspense Bronze Medal on Reader Views, and two National Indie Excellence Awards.

The first of the Victor Harding Adventures, *Old Dogs, New Tricks,* is available online and wherever heart-stopping thrillers are sold.

A Certified Master Coach, Doug is graduate of Harvard Law School, the University of Pennsylvania's Annenberg School of Communications and the University of Michigan. He lives outside Philadelphia in Narberth, Pennsylvania with his wife Pam, also a recovering lawyer, and their three delightfully gonzo dogs.

Made in the USA
Middletown, DE
27 March 2025